Samurai Bluegrass

Craig Terlson

Literary Wanderlust | Denver, Colorado

Samurai Bluegrass is a work of fiction. Names, characters, places, and incidents are the products of the author's imagination and have been used fictitiously. Any resemblance to actual events, locales, or persons, living or dead, is entirely coincidental.

Published in the United States by Literary Wanderlust LLC Denver, Colorado.

www.LiteraryWanderlust.com

ISBN Print: 978-1-956615-22-7
ISBN Digital: 978-1-956615-23-4

Cover design by Craig Terlson

Printed in the United States of America

For Kerry, who believed.

Now

Chapter One

Every day I remained in the City, I thought of my death.

I rose with the sun on this bright May morning, drank my green tea, and left my apartment. Yet, all the while, my death walked with me. Walking over the cracks and lines of the sidewalk, I passed faded buildings that had long since lost their sheen, and then into the small park I visited every day. Death was always with me. The trees and lush grass were a comfort, and I breathed in their scent. A young boy kicked a red ball and then stopped to look at me, searching my pale face for the shortest of moments. Perhaps he knew that this was not the skin I was born with.

My death happened far away from the City I had now inhabited for three years. Thoughts of that true home were woven together with a deep longing that traveled with me as ever-present as death. So much made little sense. Yet, I tried to understand my new surroundings. Why did I remain here? The desire to return home burned in me with the hottest of flames.

Still, this world cared not for my aching soul. No one did.

I began all my mornings in the City by walking through the park, which led me to Queen Street, and then to The Pearl. This eating establishment was owned by Mr. Stan, who served people in the long narrow room with tall-backed benches and tables made out of something that looked like wood, but was not. People from all classes came in search of a hot drink and for the sun that poured in the large window by the entrance. Mr. Stan allowed all people to stay as long as they wanted.

The heat wafted from my steeping tea and moistened my face. Small beads of sweat broke across my forehead. Even in this new life, surrounded by the citizens of a strange city, my death lingered at the edges of every hour. I was told by my teacher to respect this awareness of death, that it would bring vibrance to my daily life. The death I had experienced was not the kind my teacher spoke of—but there was no way to ask him now.

"Gordo, you gonna drink that?"

"Just taking my time, Mr. Stan."

"You're never in a hurry to go anywhere, are ya, Gordo?"

"What will I do when I arrive?"

"Good point. And you don't need to keep calling me Mister."

"I used to call you Master," I said, which made Mr. Stan laugh. This was a conversation we'd had many times.

He turned his back to me and cracked eggs over his hot metal plate. The eating establishment, what the patrons called a diner, smelled of fried meat, sweat, and smoke. Since arriving in the City, I had visited The Pearl for two of the last three years. Though, to say "arrive" meant that I understood how I came to be here. I did not.

I could count the exact days, and even hours I had spent in the City. I was taught to be ever-aware of the passing of time, how it moved in the smallest of moments, as well as in sweeping waves. My awareness of time was not a regret. I understood that time was a river we swam in, its water forever spilling into unknown territory. It had no end.

Stan didn't know who I was or where I once lived. No one did. I tried to tell Harry, but he was not capable of understanding. When Harry warned me of a place he called "the crazy house," I decided it would not be wise to inform people of my true home. There were authorities in the City who could be called upon at any time to take a person to such a place.

The part of the river I now swam in was unfathomably far away from where my life began, where I grew as a child, and where I was trained until my banishment.

"Hey, Gordo, you gonna want some toast with your English?"

"I'm fine. Thank you, Stan."

Stan flipped eggs onto a dish, then placed strips of meat on either side, ending with a scoop of potatoes the color of sand and a circle of pink tomato. I observed Stan often, marveling at his skill and the discipline he had mastered. Once a week, I allowed myself the indulgence of a Stan breakfast. It was all my funds allowed.

"Suit yerself. But I can cook you an egg if you need something this morning."

"Thanks, Mr. Stan—sorry, Stan. I'm really fine."

Stan believed I had no money, or very little. He was somewhat correct—although, I was much better off than when I arrived. With the help of my guides—Harry, and then Joshua—I had learned to survive in a place that required currency. I worked as a painter now, not on canvases or paper, but in rooms and sometimes entire buildings. The money I earned helped pay for my rent, my food, and my morning tea at The Pearl. My needs were simple.

Gordo was the name given to me by a man called Harry, who became my first guide. The name I gave to officials, Gordon, was no more my name than this shortened version. I preferred the sound of Gordo, as it felt closer to my true identity. Joshua, the guide who came after Harry, told me that Stan had named his diner after his wife, who was dead. I understood this kind of honor.

The tea from The Pearl tasted better than where I was before. Not in the time before, but at the shelter where I first met Harry. The tea in the City tasted nothing like what I was used to, and it was empty of all ceremony. Some put a sweet white powder in it, which made it worse. Joshua put the powder in his coffee, a beverage I'd not heard of until my arrival. Everyone here drank coffee much more than tea. Joshua told me the City ran on it.

Stan took me in as he did anyone who came off the street. For him, this was simply an exchange of funds for food and beverage. There was no offer of a bed, or shelter of any kind, beyond the time I spent sipping tea and eating bread—but Stan welcomed me, as if to his home, even if he didn't know my real name or my true home.

—

Heather knew it was all about the spring of the brush, the way it responded to the paper, filling the depressions of the cold press, the paint flowing across the surface at the exact rate she wanted. It was control, but more than that, it was finding the confidence to let the brush be an extension of her hand.

The Cure blasted from the small stereo in her studio. She'd packed it in the car with all her worldly belongings when she drove to Toronto, a place she always knew she'd end up. Saying goodbye to her father was the hardest part. He had done so much for her these last few years. Not since her mother died had she seen such tears on his face.

Her studio was the open space between the kitchen and the living room in her apartment. The plan was to make enough money as an illustrator to be able to rent some studio space in a warehouse. She thought she could afford something in the fashion district, especially if she shared it with another artist. After she booted Michael out, she had moved from Etobicoke and into the two-bedroom on the third floor of a duplex. Her new neighborhood, a few blocks down from College and west of Bathurst, made her feel like she was actually living in the city now.

From the beginning, moving to Toronto was a huge risk, but she was ready for it. Michael had found a small house in Etobicoke with two bedrooms, so Zach could have his own room, and it had the bonus of a cubby room that fit her drawing table perfectly. Michael was great with Zach, and was supportive of her goal of becoming an illustrator, even if he didn't fully understand it. Her father never understood it either.

"How do you expect to make money?" her father had said, sitting across from her in his smoky kitchen.

"Magazines pay artists to illustrate articles—so do book companies and advertising agencies, newspapers even," she said.

"Why not just have someone working for the magazine draw the pictures?"

"It doesn't work that way. They're looking for freelancers. That's how they put the magazine together."

"And you'll get enough for rent out of this? Toronto rent? It's a lot more there, you know. I wish I could help you, but now that I'm being forced to retire because the garage shut down . . . And who is—"

"I'll make it work, Dad."

She stopped him from continuing with the story she'd heard from him daily since she'd finished art school in Calgary. He crossed the room and gave her a hug.

"What about Zach? Can you make enough for him, too? Why don't you stay a few more months here? Or even a year."

She sucked in a long breath. She hugged her father back, and whispered in his ear.

"Trust me, okay? I'm strong. Just like you."

Her father stepped back, then looked away at something he pretended to see out the window.

"Is he going with you?"

"Michael? Yes, you know he is." She leaned back in her chair.

"He's going to work construction and see if he can work his way into the film industry there. He knows a guy who builds sets for the lawyer show they film in Toronto. Michael said it was good money. We can share the rent, and he can help look after Zach."

"How is he with Zach?"

"He knows we're a package deal, Dad. And Zach really likes him."

"Assuming he can hold down a job."

She didn't answer her father. She knew what he thought of Michael—she had similar thoughts. But he was willing to travel with a single mom and her ten-year-old son to an unknown city, and an unknown career. She planned on going to Toronto whether Michael came or not.

"You ever think of contacting you-know-who?"

"Tired of answering that, Dad."

Her father had become the dad that Zach needed when Markus left the province after she got pregnant. She and Markus were both kids themselves, so part of her didn't blame him—he would have been a lousy dad. Last she heard, he'd driven a VW van down to Mexico. She didn't even know if he was still alive. She gave a version of the story to Zach, but he didn't ask her much.

Heather's mother died when she was thirteen. As if that wasn't enough, she'd had to deal with puberty and with a distant father drowning in his own grief. But what was he supposed to do with a wild daughter who'd discovered alcohol, pot, and sex at the same time? When she had a son at seventeen, it ended the ridiculous ride she'd been on. Her father changed when Zach was born. She wouldn't have made it through those tough early years without his love and support. He even helped her pay for that first year of art school when her student loan didn't come through.

As it turned out, Michael did find work in Toronto, but after six months of living together, she saw something in him she didn't like. They only fought after Zach was in bed, but she knew it was falling apart. She told him it was time to go. Zach was sad, as he'd started to grow close to Michael—but if anything, the kid had developed resilience over the last couple of years. Between her job at Grafite and a couple of illustration jobs a month, she could swing the apartment rent. Every month was a financial tightrope walk, but she had pulled it off so far. If things got tough, she'd just get tougher. It was a mantra she repeated to herself daily.

"Shit."

Heather reached for the paper towel to blot up the dark wash before it stained the paper. *Preserve the white, you always need to preserve the white, the paper is the only white you have in watercolor.* Her instructor's words droned in her head, right along with XTC's lyrics. She loaded the brush with fresh water, did a brief scrub on the surface, and sopped up more of the gray-blue wash, letting the crimson shapes sparkle through.

"Dammit, dammit."

She stared at the spot she'd lost control of, trying to decide if it was worth saving or if she should start over—there were no redos in watercolor. *You'll watch a lot of paintings die in front of your eyes.*

The illustration was due tomorrow. Did she have enough time to start again? She glanced at the clock. Zach would be home from school in an hour, and then there was supper and taking him to T-ball, before getting him to bed at maybe 9:00. She could start the piece again, and finish painting it later.

This was the first assignment she'd gotten from *Toronto Life*—only a spot illustration, but it paid well. The three hundred and fifty was almost half her rent. Heather had dropped off her portfolio at the magazine three times since she'd arrived, and *Toronto Life* was a part of her promotional mailouts every second month. When she finally got a call from them, and said yes to the deadline, she gave a huge whoop as soon as she hung up the phone.

She'd overthought the concept and put way too much

pressure on herself, especially for a small piece. She needed to do a good job if she hoped to get another piece in a future issue. The junior art director liked her rough drawings, but said to crop it in a bit and make the expressions stronger. Her second drawing got approval. Now she just had to paint the damn thing.

She stared at the gray stain. Dammit. It was unfixable. She had to start again. She cut off a fresh square of watercolor paper, and taped it on the window against the rough drawing still in position on the glass. Once she started making some actual money, she'd buy a real light table. But for now, it was all about rent, groceries, and buying Zach a pair of decent shoes to replace the ones that were falling off his feet. He was finally fitting in at school; she didn't want him to become the kid with the ratty shoes.

When the drawing was inked for the second time, she taped it to her board, knowing she didn't have time to properly stretch and dry the paper. She dipped her new brush in the water and flicked it, staring at the beautiful point. Her father had sent her a birthday card with thirty bucks, telling her to treat herself. She did, by heading down to Grafite and picking out a Winsor Newton, Series 7, kolinsky sable brush—the Porsche of watercolor brushes. The long black handle ending in a perfect point was like an extension of her finger. When she painted, she marveled at the control the brush gave her. When things were going well, she lost herself in the strokes of wet paint catching light.

The phone rang, interrupting the meditative state she'd only just entered.

"What? Yeah, I'm just finishing it. It's due tomorrow. No, I can't go, I need to hit the deadline."

Heather watched the line of paint drying. She caught the wet edge of the wash with the brush and moved it across the paper.

"Hang on."

She pulled the wash, smoothing it out to a gradual fade.

"He's home in . . . shit, any minute now. I gotta go. Hmm?

Who's playing? Really? There, at that club? How in the hell did they manage that? That would be fascinating, or weird, or something."

The door opened downstairs, and she heard her son coming up.

"Look, if by some miracle I get this done, and Alice can be with Zach, then I'll come out for one drink. But I also have to take him to T-ball. What, tickets? No, I don't want to . . . all right. If you have an extra one already, I'll see what I can do."

She put down the phone and dunked her brush again.

"Nice," Zach said over her shoulder. "I like how you did the sky—the clouds just come out of the paper and you didn't even outline them."

"Thanks. Say, can you just make yourself a sandwich? There's bologna in the fridge. I'm going to see how much of this I can finish."

"Bologna's gross. Don't we have any salami or something?"

"It was on sale. And I got another package of cheese slices."

"Okay."

"I might go out after T-ball tonight, but Alice would come over. Would that be all right?"

"'K."

She half-listened to Zach rustle around in the fridge, as the other half of her mind returned to the painting. She told herself that there was no sadness or disappointment in Zach's okays, and he liked Alice. If she could get work in some of the bigger magazines like *Toronto Life,* it would be the start of her breaking in. She made a slow pivot with the brush, creating a gorgeous cobalt blue wash that bled perfectly into the alizarin crimson, producing a purple that made her shiver.

Everything was going to be fine. If things got tough, she'd just get tougher.

Chapter Two

This morning at The Pearl, I observed a man shifting in his seat by the sun-filled front window. He wore clothing the color of moss. He peered outside, studying the flow of people on the street, and then at Stan. I'd watched the man since he entered the diner. He was unaware of my observing. After ordering a coffee, he drank it without looking at the cup. His movements, swaying from side to side and craning his neck, told me his motives.

Another man entered The Pearl, someone I knew well, and came to sit with me, obscuring my view of the moss-man.

"Yo, here's the man himself."

"Hello, Joshua."

"Why always so formal, Gordo? I keep telling you only my mother ever calls me that, and she's four provinces away."

"Josh doesn't sound right to me."

My friend smiled.

"Gordo, you're looking burnt. I told you before, you gingers need to put on some suntan lotion when the Toronto furnace gets going. May has been one hot sucker. At least wear a lid."

Though I was familiar with Joshua's use of language, at times I felt confused.

"Gingers?"

"The hair. That's what they call you folk." Joshua smiled again. "Anyway, I'll bring you some white stuff a guy at work uses. It's got zinc in it."

"What is a lid?"

"Here, listen to this."

He took the orange circles of foam off his ears and placed them on mine. I flinched until he reached and turned a dial.

"Sorry, too loud. Hang on."

Joshua had done this with me before, so I knew what to expect. A room of drummers filled my head, and strings that were not strings produced a melody. The music pulsed like a heart does after a run in the woods. I didn't hate it.

"Lazerhawk."

I nodded and listened. Another song started, much like the first, but now a wind sound joined the drums. While the music played, I kept my gaze on the moss-man who had grown agitated. He drank from his empty cup. I slowed my breathing. I would be ready when he moved. Strangely, Joshua's music helped me focus.

Joshua took the orange circles from my ears and used the metal strip to hang them from his neck.

"Is this your music?" I asked.

"God, no. I mean thanks, but that is a full kick-ass band. It gets ya pumping, right? Different than my stuff. I'm more three chords and the truth like Van said."

"Is he a friend of yours?"

"Van the Man, Gordo. Seriously, do you listen to anyone?"

"I listen to everyone."

"Right." Joshua raised his hand. "Stan, could I get a black coffee?"

Stan came from around his counter with his metal urn. My

friend lit a cigarette, waving the smoke in front of his face.

"Menu?"

"I'm good, Stan. Now listen, Gordo, I got something up tomorrow night that I think you're really gonna dig. There is a weird little concert happening at the Apocalypse. And the best part, I've got free passes for both of us. So if we don't like it, no skin off anybody's nose. Are you in?"

My attention was split. I wanted to ask Joshua what he meant by skin, but the moss-man had left his seat and was now moving toward Stan. The owner of The Pearl had his back to him, having just spun the lid back on the metal urn. I rose from my seat in a fluid movement, stepping and then pushing Stan's body toward the row of stools.

"What gives, Gordo?" Joshua said.

Matching the moss-man's steps, I did a half-step and brought my hand down on his rising arm, stopping his movement, and then twisting. The man cried out.

"What in the hell?" Stan shouted.

I spun the man in the other direction; my hand on his shoulder held him firmly in place. I whispered in his ear.

"Gordo, let that man go. He's a customer." Stan moved toward me. "Gordo, let him go now. He was just trying to pay his bill. I'm sorry, sir, I'd be glad to offer you a free breakfast."

I straightened the man's arm and applied pressure. He had no choice but to release the blade he tightly held. It clattered to the floor.

"Son-of-a-bitch," Joshua said.

I rotated the man toward Stan, whose face reddened in anger.

"Wait. I recognize you. What in the hell do you think you're doing? Think I make enough for you to rob me? Here in my own place? I'll teach you a lesson, ya punk."

Stan charged. I held up a hand to stop him.

"Do you want to phone the authorities, Stan?"

"What? No, I want to cave this bastard's skull in." Stan

stopped suddenly, his hands balled into fists.

The other diners tried to disappear into the tall-backed benches, but there was nowhere to hide in the narrow room. A fat morning cloud had slid across and covered the front window, darkening the interior of The Pearl.

"The police . . . or does Gordo let him go? Stan?" Joshua asked.

Stan took gulping breaths and slammed his fists against his body, his face the color of a camellia.

"Screw it. Let the prick go." Stan turned and went back to his counter.

I ushered the thief into the street.

"Who are you supposed to be, some fuckin' vigilante?" His words were slurred as if his tongue were too thick for his mouth.

"I would suggest you don't come back. Unless it is to apologize and ask for Stan's mercy."

"What the hell were you whispering to me? What was that language?"

I pointed west, to where a streetcar rumbled on the tracks.

"Leave now."

I returned inside, to my place across from Joshua.

"The music tomorrow is played by this Lazerhawk person?" I asked.

"How did you know that guy was gonna do that? You took him out so fast."

"Just a lucky guess. As you have said."

"A guess?" Joshua leaned back in his chair, holding up a finger toward me. "Remind me not to pull anything on you."

"I will," I said.

My friend studied me. Stan came with a fresh tea for me, another coffee for Joshua, and a plate of sweet pastries.

"On me. You're always welcome here, Gordo." Stan's face had returned to its original color.

I smelled Stan's fear sweat. I nodded to him.

"Will you come to my place?" I asked Joshua.

"What? Oh right, yeah. I'll get you at nine, and we can walk together. These guys start earlier than usual for bands at the Apocalypse."

"Why?"

"Okay, you must have heard of Bill Monroe."

I shook my head.

"Bluegrass, Gordo! For shit's sake, you must have heard of bluegrass."

"I might have." It was not a complete lie. I had come across the word, though not connected to music.

"It's gonna be a trip. I think Monroe's in his eighties. But, man, he invented bluegrass music."

"I believe I'll like it."

I bit into the pastry. Like other things of its type, I was both drawn to and repulsed by the heavy sweetness. Still, it went well with the hot tea. I scanned the room—the diners had returned to their conversations, as if it was just another morning for them.

On the first morning of my arrival, I believed I had died and crossed over to the afterplace. I now understood that the City was far from my beginnings, across whole continents, and time itself. Hope of returning to my true home faded more every day I lived in a skin that was not my own.

This was my thousandth morning in the City.

Chapter Three

Joshua and I walked along Queen Street until we came to a brick building with windows that could not be seen through. Under a painted sign, which read *The Apocalypse,* Joshua handed his tickets to a thick man with rings in his eyebrows before we descended into a room with black walls. It was good to be out with my friend, if only to sit in a dark basement. A line of papers, red ink on white, were plastered on one of the black walls. As Joshua weaved his way through the tables, I studied the angled papers, their color so stark against the black, as if someone had sliced open the wall and let the entrails slide down. The red color was a large photo of a man in a curved hat, and the writing below, also in red on bright white, said he would appear for one night only.

Joshua signaled me with his hand. "Grab a chair, Gordo. I'll get us a couple of beers. This is Rain."

"Hey."

The woman was clad in black, her face ghostly white, with a smear of red across her lips that matched the posters on the walls.

"Hello," I said. "Did your father give you this name?"

"Fuck my father," the woman said.

She turned away from me, looking to the other end of the room, a raised platform where the musicians would take their place—I knew this from another evening when Joshua had brought me to a place where we listened to a different group of musicians. That place was aboveground, though the windows were covered in dark curtains. It was as if the people inside these places desired to be unseen.

I looked across the room to see where Joshua had gone. I thought about getting up to follow him, unsure what to say to the young woman clad in a color darker than the walls.

"Do you know Mr. Monroe?"

Rain grunted.

People filled the tables around us. Most of them were young, many wearing what Rain wore—black in a black room. I observed them, searching for joy in their expressions, but instead saw fear and anger. I questioned the safety of this gathering. Yet, I trusted my friend. He would not bring me to a place where I would be in danger. I waited anxiously for his return.

Two women had pieces of metal in their white skin. I had seen this adornment before. One appeared to have a large pin sticking through her cheek, and then clasped into a round latch. I had a distant memory of others piercing their skin like this, yet I couldn't bring it forward in my mind. I was about to risk asking Rain if she could explain this sort of skin decoration, when the white lights on the platform went out. The crowd murmured as the lights glowed back to life, changing the people to the color of the sea. Again, I wanted to ask a question, but I was stopped short by the sound of strings vibrating.

A group of four emerged from the darkness to stand at the platform, the light not strong enough to expose them in full clarity. A hand moved quickly back and forth, the source of the string vibration. A voice cried out, like someone calling from an impossibly long tunnel, trying to say something vital. It was a sad voice, but also beautiful, a sound that came from deep within a soul. The words were not words, just long vowel sounds, and then another voice joined, and another, the sound expanding like sun breaking through clouds. Words were formed, but the meaning was unimportant, as this was about the sound. The voices and strings wove together; the vibrations entered me and moved through my chest. The vibrations took me back to my last ride in the forest—the sounds were similar, but the place different.

Rain stared, her mouth slightly open. I gazed around the room. The light fell on the glowing faces of a crowd transfixed by the men in bright white clothes and tilted hats. Their music filled the room, and as if by magic, the walls changed color. Was it a trick of the lights, or perhaps a spell this group of men had cast upon us all? The men in white possessed a power over the crowd. Had these young faces ever seen something like this? I turned my full attention to the men in hats, trying to understand what we were experiencing. These men were only musicians, and yet together they created something mystical. I barely noticed when Joshua returned with our fermented beverages.

"How about that, Gordo?"

Rain held up her hand to silence him—doing it before I could.

"Bee-zar," said Rain.

"She sings with a group called the Insect Gods," Joshua said in a low tone, his face pressed against my ear. "I don't think she's ever heard anything like it."

"Neither have I." I lowered my voice and turned to my friend. "The old man, what is his instrument? I've not seen it before."

"That's a mandolin. And that, my friend, is the guy who invented this music."

I waited for Rain to raise her hand again, but she was lost to the sound.

"This is his?" I asked.

"Well, he pioneered it for damn sure. And check out the banjo player. You know he's been a fixture of the Nashville circuit his whole life, probably the Opry, or a studio musician for sure."

I didn't understand all the words Joshua used, but I didn't want to alter my experience by asking him more questions.

The men finished the song, then stood in silence as they looked out at us. Within the quiet moment, an echo of sadness reverberated in the room. Then without a breath, the man with a bow ripped a string of notes on his instrument, and the old man began to play.

"The true master of bluegrass," Joshua said.

The tallest man on the platform held what I knew was called a banjo, as Joshua had pointed that out another evening. This man put his notes in-between the others, adding to the tapestry of sound. All the men stood like alabaster statues; their powder-white hats and clothes illuminated the black-walled room.

The music went faster and faster, and the white-faced listeners made guttural sounds, whoops, slamming their drinks on already soaked tables. I didn't think the music could go any faster until the old man pushed things further. His fingers flew up and down the tiny neck of his instrument. I expected him to start spinning like a dervish—but he just tapped his foot. Tap-tap-tap-tap. That was all. A slow grin spread across the banjo player's face. He tilted his head, though his hat did not move, and he closed one eye. Joshua had done this, calling it a wink. I looked around, but could see no receiver of the banjo player's gesture. The man with the largest wooden instrument barked out sounds that matched the crowd's, urging the band on as if they raced across a field toward a great battle. Perhaps the music itself was the battle. There were no words to the song they played, just notes, many, many notes.

When they stopped it was as if everyone in the room held their breath. Then an ocean wave of voices, hands clapping, whistling, and so much noise that it threatened to burst out the sides of the black room. The men touched their hats.

"Much obliged. Now here's a quiet one before we take a quick break. Y'all make sure you tip your waitress."

The crowd hushed and the strings came to life. One of the men brought out a drum on a stand and a pair of sticks that were not sticks, but more like small brooms.

The music pulled me elsewhere. At first I resisted the movement, wanting to stay in this room. There was a shimmer in front of my eyes, my chest tightened, and I gave into the pull. I stepped into the clearing in the forest, where three old men plucked on instruments. The full moon rose behind them, casting long shadows across the clearing. I had come upon that trio in my escape from the shōen.

I had not been startled or threatened by the musicians, nor them by me. They sang together, their voices and instruments wove around each other, their plucked notes reverberated and were carried away on the night air. I moved quietly, not wanting to disturb the beauty. I sat on a rock and disappeared into their sounds. They played under a lantern moon, never turning to look at me. Their music was very different than this bluegrass—yet, there was something the two groups held in common.

I pulled myself out of that distant forest, and again studied the men on the platform, sending their gift of music out to the white-faced patrons of the Apocalypse. These men with their instruments stood erect, facing a sea of darkness. They had much honor. Like the men in the forest, with few words, their sounds told an ancient story. I now understood. The bluegrass men were samurai.

As was I.

Chapter Four

Unlike most of the crowd, Heather knew bluegrass. She saw in the punkers' and goths' faces the shock of the different sound, and then the delight. This made her love the music even more, knowing that great music of any kind has the ability to transform people. None of the regular patrons of a place like this would usually listen to bluegrass. Maybe it was assuming too much, but who comes to a basement punk club with black walls, hears "Nine Pound Hammer" or "Blue Moon of Kentucky" and doesn't walk right out? It was a helluva risk for whoever booked the group. It also might have been brilliant.

The men on the small stage were giving it their all. When the pierced and tattooed audience members saw those hands flying up the fretboard, they must have known they were just as skillful as some punk shredding on a Strat. Truth was, these guys were way better than the punks that usually played the Apocalypse—many levels better. Heather wished they'd balanced the band out with at least one woman, but this was likely what they were used to in Nashville, or wherever the group called home.

"See, aren't you glad you came out?"

"It's pretty damn amazing. The musicianship is incredible."

"Ha! Musicianship." Shauna clinked beer bottles with her.

"You don't think so?"

"I sure as hell do." The banjo player was in the middle of a scorching solo. "But trust you to analyze the musicianship. They're playing the hell out of this room. Stop thinking so much, Heather. Let the music carry you away."

Heather smiled. Shauna knew her too well, her tendency to overthink, breakdown and analyze. As the notes swirled, the room seemed to expand and contract, as if the walls were breathing. Most of the people were in their twenties like her, but they looked like early twenties, whereas she would turn thirty in two years. Bluegrass was her father's favorite music, and he'd play records for her when Heather was just a toddler. Even as a kid she knew who Bill Monroe was. It was amazing that all these years later she'd be watching him in a club like the Apocalypse. She wished her dad was there to see it.

At a table across from them were two men who looked closer to her age. With them was a goth girl whose white face caught the stage lights and cast its own glow. As the band announced another number, one of the men looked over at Heather. She looked the other way, not wanting to give him even half a thought that he had a chance with her. Oh yeah, you wanna come home and help me put my ten-year-old to bed?

When she turned back, Heather saw that he wasn't really looking at her, but past her, and past the people behind her. It was as if he was trying to see through one of the black walls and onto Queen Street. The light accented his eyes, like it had for his white-faced goth friend, and this intensified the effect of his gaze. He wasn't good-looking, a bit pale, a mop of red hair, but not bad either. There was a warmth in his expression. She studied him, while trying not to look directly at him. Not that it mattered—his attention was elsewhere. Plus, since Michael she had less than zero interest in starting something new.

"This is going to be our last number. We thank you so kindly for your support. We don't know when we've played to such a nice group of young people."

The place erupted in whistles and cheers. Monroe tipped his hat, and let loose a bolt of lightning on his mandolin. Her father would have loved it. A pang of guilt ran through her. She made a mental note to call him this weekend.

When they finished, Heather saw that the men had left. Only the white-faced girl remained, searching for something in her tiny purse.

"How's your time?" Shauna asked.

"Thanks, it was really a great time. Exactly what I needed."

"No, I mean for Zach. When did you tell the neighbor you'd be back?"

"Oh shit. What time is it?"

"Not sure, must be after eleven."

"I have to go."

"I'll walk you back," Shauna said.

The energy in the club had shifted, strains of bluegrass replaced with a churning beat punctuated with yells and screams. Lights flashed on a skinny girl and a much skinnier boy who gyrated on the square patch of dance floor.

"You don't need to. I'll grab a streetcar," Heather said.

"You'll wait forever."

"Then I'll walk fast—or go up to Dundas."

Heather swam through the crowd. Glancing back, she saw that Shauna had started to follow her, but was stopped by a tall man in black jeans. Shauna was doing her thing, leaning in close as she talked to him.

"I'll be fine," Heather called across the room, barely audible above the driving music.

"You sure?" Shauna mouthed.

Heather waved a hand, weaved around two drunk goths, and headed for the stairs. She spilled out onto the street, hearing the squeal of the Queen car already a block and a half past where she stood. She asked a pink-haired girl the time. She sneered at Heather. A large Asian guy with a soul patch said, "Twelve-oh-four." The numbers left his mouth as he exhaled a huge smoke ring.

Dammit. Shauna was right, this time of night she'd wait forever for another streetcar. She started a quick stride, calculating in her head how long it would take to get home. She considered calling Alice, but there wasn't a payphone in sight. Even if she ran, it was doubtful she could catch the streetcar ahead of her. She decided to cut up Euclid, walk fast and maybe get lucky with the Dundas car.

A half-block up, the streetlights were burned out.

"Oh great."

When she first got to Toronto a year before, she was leery of walking certain parts of the city at night. In her first week, she slugged a guy who rode by on a bike and tried to grab her bag. He teetered, swore at her, and sped off. Her dad had showed her how to box and break holds when she was a teen.

She had discovered that many neighborhoods in Toronto were full of people, walking, talking, and inhabiting the streets, so she felt less the need to always be on guard. Safety in numbers— maybe that's why they called it "Toronto the Good." Still, it was disconcerting to see the street ahead strangely empty.

She clenched her fist instinctively, and picked up her pace. Ahead, she made out the lights of Dundas.

"Yo, look at the ass on that one."

Two men stepped out from a corner, and then were joined by a third.

"Get out of my way."

Heather pushed past them. One of them grabbed her arm.

"Hey there, nasty."

She spun around, pulling her arm away from the grasp. They were more boys than men, with unshaven, acne-filled faces.

"Play nice with us."

"Ya, join us for a party, slut."

Boozy breath came from the tallest one with yellow teeth.

"Back off."

She took a step. Before she could take a swing, they grabbed her again, this time both her arms.

"You're not going anywhere."

"Bitch."

She opened her mouth to shout to anyone who might hear. Yellowteeth clamped a hand over her mouth and put a finger to his lips.

"Shh. No need to yell. Ain't no one gonna care, bitch."

She gauged the distance between them, tightened the muscles in her calf, and got ready to drive her knee into his crotch.

"Anyway. You c'n relax—we just after your money. I ain't risking getting the clap from a slut."

She made a fast plan to strike, a fast kick in the balls, and run before the others could react. She curled her foot up, already picturing the strike, and stopped. A figure, a man, standing by a dumpster from the direction she'd come—and now taking long strides toward her. The streetlight flickered to life, catching his face as he passed under it. Like Yellowteeth, he held a finger to his mouth. *Be quiet? Now?* As if he read her expression, the man gave a quick nod. The two boys holding her were still apparently unaware of the man's approach, as was the one whose yellowed maw hovered inches away from her.

"Now we gonna take whatever money you got. Then you can go on your slutty way. Just like that."

Yellowteeth jerked back, hooked by something, spun and flew into the brick wall with a crack and slid to the sidewalk. He didn't move.

"What the fuck?"

One of the men holding her stepped out toward the figure who'd just thrown their friend into a wall. The figure wore a denim jacket with a hood underneath, not unlike what the boys were wearing. There was a flash of metal as one of the two pulled out a knife and rushed. In a single fluid movement, the man caught the boy's arm, twisted him, and slammed his foot into the boy's knee. The boy hit the ground hard, and the knife clattered to the sidewalk. As the boy started to get up, the figure drew a long rod from his jacket like a circus illusion. He brought the rod around, spun it like a baton before slamming it into the chest of the boy on the sidewalk, who fell back writhing in pain. The man swung the rod again, catching the back of the boy's head. The one he'd thrown against the brick wall lunged and was met with another hard swing of the rod. The two boys had been knocked out. They couldn't be dead, could they?

The final boy was still holding on to her, but out in front like a shield. His grip was strong; she winced as he dug into her skin.

"Hey, back off, or the slut gets it."

It was an empty threat. She could feel his hands shaking.

When the figure swung the rod in a long spiral, she saw it was made out of wood, like a dowel her father would build with, but longer and thicker. She couldn't make out the man's features under his hood. He brought the wood to rest on his shoulder, one of the blunt ends pointing toward her and the boy that held her.

"I mean it, man. I will snap this bitch in two."

The man took a step toward them. She thought she knew the face by the light in his eyes. He said something softly, words she couldn't make out, like in another language, but one she didn't recognize.

"What'd you say? Speak English, man."

She stomped down hard on his foot. His yell was cut short by the wooden stick that shot out in a straight line and into his face. Heather heard his nose break.

He fell back screaming, blood spurting from his face.

A flash of fear surged through her. Maybe the man wasn't a good Samaritan, maybe he had defeated the others so he could have her to himself.

"Did they harm you?" the man asked.

"They wanted money."

"I think you could have bested them."

"Maybe." Her voice shook.

Adrenaline raced through her body. His words seemed to come out at a different speed. Again she visualized a hit, this time on the man in front of her. She could kick out a knee and then sprint.

He pointed up the street.

"Are you safe to leave? Should I travel with you?"

"No. I am close to home."

"I'll watch that you arrive," he said.

"It's okay. I'm fine."

Heather turned toward Dundas and took a few steps before turning back to survey the scene. The three men remained on the ground. One was on his knees, his hands cradling his face, another on all fours, and the last lay still on the sidewalk. The man with the wooden rod was gone. A streetcar squealed in the distance.

Heather ran.

Chapter Five

Both of them slept in, so it was a chaotic mess getting Zach out the door for school. Heather told the art director she'd drop the illustration off at ten, but she still had to mount it for presentation, grab the College car and then the subway to get to the magazine's office in time.

Of course, when she got to the magazine offices, the A.D. still wasn't in. Heather didn't want to drop the piece with reception and miss out on the personal connection, hoping like hell he liked the piece and would hire her again. But she also wanted to deliver it before the deadline, so she left it with the receptionist, asking her to please let the A.D. know he could call her if there were any problems.

"Uh-huh."

Heather was finally back home at eleven. The frantic pace of the morning had kept her from thinking about what happened last night. Sitting in her kitchen, reliving the scene, and considering what could have happened, caused her to shake. The phone jolted her out of her anxious thoughts.

"Hello. This is Heather."

"Hey, what's with your voice?"

It was Shauna.

"Nothing. I thought it was someone else," she said.

"I called you first thing this morning."

"I was down at *Toronto Life*."

"Did they like it?"

"He wasn't there. I dropped it off."

"You get home okay last night?"

"Shauna, could you come over?"

"Sure thing, you okay?"

"Just come."

—

"Shit, are you gonna call the cops? Did you call them already?"

"I've got basically nothing to tell them."

"You said they had acne, and one had yellow teeth."

She clenched her fist. "Even if they found them, I'm not sure I could identify them."

"You gotta report those fuckers!" Shauna looked around.

"He's at school."

"Oh right. Listen, those assholes get away with this sort of shit because people don't report it."

"Nothing happened, Shauna."

Her friend pulled away. Heather saw she was trying to be supportive, but she also heard the anger in Shauna's voice. Heather hadn't gotten to anger yet. The crying spell had come as soon as Shauna walked in the door. The thought of what could have happened kept racing through her mind. She imagined the phone call to her son from the hospital, and how it would be for him visiting his beat-up mom. Heather imagined telling him how they both needed to be strong, and how there were evil people in the world. She imagined too much. She always did.

"So tell me more about the hero, then."

"It's weird to call him that," she said. "I wasn't some damsel in distress."

"But if he wouldn't have shown up—"

"I know," she snapped. "Sorry, Shauna. You're right. I'm glad he showed up."

"So who was he?"

"I don't know, I'd never seen him—wait." Heather raised her hand and turned her head away. "I did see him before, in the club."

"In the Apocalypse?"

"Sitting a couple of tables across from us. With another guy and a goth girl."

"Oh yeah, I remember her. Wait. You think he followed you out?" Shauna stroked her throat and grimaced.

"I don't know. But he handed them their asses."

Shauna narrowed her eyes. "And then?"

"Then nothing. He offered to walk me to the streetcar, and I said I was fine."

"He didn't say his name, phone number? Give his Ninja superhero card to you?"

Heather shook her head.

"You could have kicked their asses. You're hard as nails."

"There's a part of me that thinks that way. I see myself kneeing them in the crotch and then bolting down the street. But I don't know."

An awkward silence descended. She appreciated Shauna a lot—she had looked out for Heather ever since she arrived in Toronto. Shauna was from North Bay, but had been in Toronto for a decade now. She bounced between server gigs, to waitressing, and now she sold supplies to all the retirees and the hopefuls trying to make a living from their art. She worked at the art supply store where Heather got hired part-time while she lugged her portfolio around the city.

Shauna had toyed with the idea of acting, and then singing, which she explained was the whole idea behind leaving North Bay. That and the fact that she would gouge her own eye out with a fork if she didn't escape her hometown. Shauna sang with a couple of bands, and often invited Heather to come listen. The gigs were in the same bars where Shauna used to sling beer. The sound was horrible, and the guitar player droned out most of Shauna's vocals. That was too bad. Heather had heard her sing along with the radio, and Shauna had a nice voice.

"I gotta go. I work at one," Shauna said. "You in today?"

"I canceled my shift. I want to be around for Zach when he comes home."

"You sure you're okay?"

"I'm really glad you came over. I always feel like I can call you anytime."

"That's because you can." Shauna hugged her. "But listen, if you come across this rod-swinging action hero again, you do me a favor and introduce yourself. Or damn, give him my number. He's a dying breed."

Heather laughed. "I'll be sure of it."

—

"Is this just red sauce?"

"Yep, like you like it. Ragu. Opened the jar myself."

Zach poked at it with his fork.

"You don't like it?"

"You usually put hamburger in it."

"Sorry, hon. I didn't get a chance to get to the grocery store. I'll get some for tomorrow, okay?"

He twirled it and slurped.

"If we can't afford meat, Mom, it's okay."

"What? Where did you get that idea?" Heather fought back the heat that began to rise up her neck. It wasn't unlike the feeling she got when she first showed her roughs to the *Toronto Life* junior art director.

"It's no biggie. I know we're not rolling in it. Kevin says you're a starving artist." Zach pointed his index finger in the air and twirled it.

"Kevin from your class? How does he even know that term?"

"Mom, I heard you say it, too. It's no biggie."

Heather went to the fridge to find some cheese to grate on the spaghetti but found only a two-inch chunk that had turned green. She grabbed it, and slammed it in the garbage.

Zach stared into his dinner.

"Shit. Sorry, I don't mean to swear, but shit, Zach. I need your help here."

"I can do the dishes, Mom."

"Not that kind of help. I just . . . I mean, listen, we're going to make it, okay?"

"Okay."

"Things are starting to happen," she said.

"Okay."

Heather listened to the clanking of their utensils and wanted to say something else, but she didn't know what to say. She did believe they'd make it, even if the odds were against her. And there was the palm reader.

Michael and her hosted the palmist at their house the summer before they left for Toronto. The plan was for him to do a bunch of readings and they would get 20% of whatever he collected. Heather thought the idea of palmistry was tremendously stupid and the guy was a con artist. Michael said it was all scientific, the guy was from India and had studied palmistry his whole life—he even had a slide rule that he used to measure and calculate lines on the hand.

"We also get a free reading," Michael had said.

"We could use the money. But, he's going to tell my future? Yeah, right."

"Why is it that you're the artist and you have a hard time believing in this? There's all kinds of stuff we don't know about the human body."

"And I think someone as smart as you should see through his bullshit."

Her comment annoyed Michael, probably insulted him.

Heather relented, and they were soon taking bookings. To her surprise, thirty people signed up. When it came time for her reading, she declined.

Again she relented, and sat across from the palmist in the back bedroom where he'd been doing the readings.

"This is not something to be fearful of," the palmist said.

He wore a well-tailored cream-colored suit. His hands were manicured, and his haircut looked expensive.

"I'm not afraid. I just don't believe in it." She waved a hand in the air. "Whatever this is."

"Belief is not necessary, Heather." His accent was slight, and he spoke with a formality that reminded her of programs from England.

The palmist went on about the history of discovering energy paths in the body, and how physical manifestations of one's life emerged in many different ways—including the lines in one's hands. He took her left hand, not gently, and without any sensuality, began to take measurements.

"Why my left?"

"I see that it is your dominant. The left is what you have been given. Some call it, potential. The right is what you do with this."

After each measurement, he wrote something in a journal. He was silent, no utterances or murmuring like from a doctor or psychiatrist, professionals whose voice assures you that an examination is taking place. She was relieved when he finally began to speak.

"You work with your hands, but it is not hard work."

"I think what I do is very hard," she said.

"Ah. No, I mean it is not physical labor, arduous work. You have a deep strength and focus. Something creative. Are you perhaps a writer, or no, a painter?"

"Good guess. Did you pick that up from the splash of cobalt blue I forgot to wash off?"

He remeasured two more lines.

"You had an illness as a child. It almost cost you your life."

"Uh—"

Heather was caught off guard, like the legs of her chair had dropped beneath her.

"I had a fever that was misdiagnosed, and then turned out to be meningitis. My father rushed me to the hospital. He saved my life."

"Which is why you are so close to him. But not your mother. She is no longer around, correct?"

"She—wait . . . you tell me where she is." Heather sat up straight.

"By your expression, I see that she is no longer alive."

Heather kept quiet. She leaned back.

"You have no other siblings. You've had many conflicts growing up. Relationships are difficult for you. Your father taught you independence, which you now carry. This is why you had . . ." He checked his journal. " . . . three relationships in close succession that did not work out and caused you pain. The first one, when you were very young, left you with a child, most likely a son, but maybe a daughter. Now, as you plan to leave your home—"

"Stop." Heather held up her hand. She fought the impulse to grab the journal out of his hand. "That's enough."

"Very well." He closed the journal and tucked it into an inside pocket. "I appreciate your hospitality—"

"Wait. How do you know I am going away?"

"Your hands tell a story of your life, mostly what has been, and yes, perhaps some of what may come. I have studied this science for many years."

"That's what the measurements were for?"

"Yes."

Her forehead was hot and she thought she might vomit.

"What will happen?" Heather's voice was soft, barely above a whisper.

The palmist's eyes were dark stones rimmed in milky white.

"It will be very difficult for you. You will come close to breaking. But if you stay, and endure, you will have success."

"How long?"

"Eighteen months. Then things will change for you."

"Can you be sure?" The room wasn't spinning, but it could have been.

"Again, it is all very scientific."

—

As she washed the dishes with Zach, she fought the urge to tell him that according to the palmist, they only had six more months. Right, and then she would tell him it was all very scientific. He'd think she'd totally lost it.

"You okay, Mom?"

"I'm good. We're good, Zach."

Chapter Six

I rose early and made tea. Staring out at the City as it awakened, I pondered the events of last night. The musicians and their bluegrass music had sounded an ache, a longing that reverberated deep inside me. The music reached back to my past, my true past, not the strange one I'd been living these last few years. Their music twinned in my mind with the musicians I'd come upon in the forest that fateful day that I died, only to re-emerge in the City, in the body of one Gordon Clement. What had happened to the soul and mind of this Gordon? Had he crossed over to my time? How strange it would be for a man from this City to awake in the shōen where I had spent most of my life.

I recalled my boyhood on the shōen. At ten years old, my young body was ripe with energy, without injury or pain, my flesh alive and fresh like grass shoots. At that age I didn't have the muscle that would harden on my frame, nor did I possess the awareness that would develop under my teacher's training. My body was now eighteen years past boyhood. So far away in time and in a City I'd never dreamed I would live in, I longed for the peace that comes with the innocence of youth.

I thought of my father, of my separation from him, and the tragedy of my brother. As the sun grew brighter in the City, my memory faded like too-fresh dye that spreads on a cloth. It was hard to retain the images in my mind. A heaviness grew in my chest, and there in my apartment I called out to my father in the language of the shōen. The syllables echoed off the walls of my small dwelling. A vision of my father appeared, his hand raised toward me. He uttered a single word, a name dear to my heart.

When I was banished from the shōen, I was told that my desires mattered to no one. Here in a gray City not my own, citizens cared even less for my desires. It had caused a deep sadness, one that cut through me like the blade of a tantō. I knew that somehow I must accept that I would never return to the shōen.

This bluegrass music from the night before had sent me into a reverie, and I barely recalled leaving the black-walled room or saying goodbye to Joshua. As I came out of this dream state, I found myself underneath a large painting of mice wearing clothes, brandishing knives and carrying bottles. Seeing the woman and the thieves that moved upon her pulled me out of the mist. A clarity emerged. I thought of the dear one I'd left behind, and imagined what my actions would be if she were the one in danger.

The training instilled in me by my teacher propelled me, and I prevented the men from doing any harm, then made certain that the woman would find her way home, following her until she had boarded one of the City's cars.

Last night I had dreamed of the shōen and of the mountain that climbed into the sky. Would I ever return to sit in the shadow of Ishizuchi?

I stood from my mat and went into the kitchen to make some more tea. As the water boiled, my father's voice rose up with the steam from my kettle, again repeating the single word. As on the day when I left to train with the samurai, my father spoke my mother's name. He told me, "Never forget her."

And there was another I didn't want to forget. She was the dear one for whom I was banished, and also the one that fueled the fire of my heart. More than the mountain, more than the memory of my dead mother, I needed to keep my love for her alive in my mind.

I cleared my head of all thoughts, both the sadness and small slivers of joy from the remembrances of my youth. With my mind clear from all distractions, the feelings of loss lessened— another idea had emerged. My master taught me that the telling of story is what puts roots in our being. I needed to tell my story.

I had to speak with Joshua. He would help me.

Chapter Seven

It had been a year since she'd left Garsen, and Heather still thought of the palmist, especially on the hard days and nights. Last night was one of the hardest. As she ran down the pitch black street, adrenaline surging, all her doubts about coming to Toronto resurfaced.

According to the palmist's prediction, she still had six more months before she would be successful. If that was even true. He'd been right about a lot of things, eerily right. So why not that?

She grabbed a bag of Oreos that Shauna had brought over and joined Zach in their living room, where he sat cross-legged watching *Knight Rider*.

She sat down and handed him a couple of cookies.

"You said me being a starving artist was no biggie. So tell me, what actually is a biggie?"

"Shhh. Michael's talking to KITT."

"Michael?"

"The guy on the show."

She watched the rest of the show with him, then they read *The Hobbit* together, she tucked him in for the night, and she went to her drawing table. Her notes for her next self-promo were taped to the surface. Last month's mailer had landed the *Toronto Life* job. She'd sent out a hundred postcards and got one job. Vince said that was about par for the course. He'd graduated art school when she was still in third year, and had been in Toronto a couple of years longer than her. Still, it was only last week that he landed his first cover from one of the trades.

"You'll get there, Robsen," he'd told her.

Vince could be a bit of an arrogant prick. She knew that he had zero interest in her, on account of her having a kid. He was also three years younger than her, having entered art school right out of high school.

Heather tore off a page from her sketchbook and started drawing, stream of consciousness, just to see where it would go. She'd left school near the top of her class. She didn't have superstar status like Vince, or Gary, who moved to New York and already had illustrations in the *New York Times Book Review*. She'd heard that the art director, Stephen Heller, had taken Gary under his wing, and gave him regular work in the *Times*. Stephen freaking Heller—the guy who judged all the big illustration awards. She was going to get one of her illustrations in front of him one day, she knew it.

She drew a male figure, lean, muscular, firm weight on the ground, the "s" curve of his body balanced perfectly. In his hands she put a long stick, like he was an ancient fighter. There was a lot of energy in the lines. Heather reached over and flipped on her radio. Bruce was singing "Hungry Heart," and it was perfect.

She grabbed her crow quill and the bottle of India ink. She went over the pencil lines she liked, fluid, nothing forced. It had taken her a long time to get comfortable with the flexible nib—she preferred the hawk quill with its stiff fine lines, but she wanted the work to loosen up. Again she forced herself not to think, flow, flow, flow. Lines across the face, a bit of pressure on the pen, suggesting eyes and a tight mouth. The figure grew stronger with each stroke.

The track had shifted to Cher singing about turning back time—a song she hated. She left the drawing to fully dry, thinking that tomorrow she'd pull a simple wash over it. As much as she loved it, she was doubtful it would make a good mailer—*Canadian Business* or *Saturday Night* didn't get a lot of calls for warrior illustrations.

She hadn't given him warrior clothes, no flowing robe or light armor. It was the stick that made him look like a fighter. On that dark street, his features were difficult to recall—still, she had nailed the expression.

She'd drawn the guy who saved her ass.

—

The next morning Heather could hardly wait to get back to her drawing table; she hadn't felt this excited in a long time. She got Zach out the door on time for once, with only a piece of toast for breakfast, promising him she'd make something good for supper.

She forced herself to bed last night, knowing she needed to be awake for Zach in the morning. The drawings from the evening session taped to the wall were fluid, alive, the ink line as confident as it had ever been.

She mixed up a few warm colors, a Cad yellow the color of farm eggs, and burnt sienna in another small bowl. She pulled single-color washes over the ink, giving them form and contrast, letting the lines of the drawings shine through.

Heather still thought it would be a risk to make a mailer out of the warrior drawings. But damn, Vince was getting a boatload of work with his little people metaphors, tiny figures walking across chasms, or climbing up giant chairs. She could use these, right?

She sat back. Her dad was right: the stakes were different

now. Her job at Grafite paid the rent, and her dad still sent a couple hundred bucks every month to help with the food. But it wouldn't take much to make it. If she scored a few jobs from some of the bigger national mags, or one of the city papers, she'd earn as much on one illustration as she would working a week at the art supply store.

Heather pushed away her anxiety over finances and focused on the work. She put on her Sade cassette, and drew to her sumptuous voice.

Why was she drawing this man, this superhero, as Shauna called him? She didn't recall much about him from the club, and then only saw him on a dark street, in a tense situation. The way he moved, with such confidence. This was a man who had trained his entire life. He'd spent hours at a gym, or some martial arts place . . . Dojos . . . that was the name for them. She recalled it from an old movie Michael made her watch. Her drawing tried to capture his assuredness in disposing of those assholes.

Her drawing instructor's voice, with his thick European accent, rang in her head.

"First you learn the proportion, then the movement, the S curves of the body, the weight and the balance, it all comes. And then last, there is the expression."

She pushed the voice away, and disappeared further into the drawing.

—

By noon, she had another row of energetic drawings with splashes of fresh watercolor.

She whispered, "Holy crap, these are good."

The phone rang at the same time, jolting her.

"What? Why are you calling me now? No. He's at school. No, this isn't a good time. Don't come over." Her pencil dug into her palm. "Look, okay, okay . . . I need to go to work in an hour. I've got Alice coming in to be with Zach. I can tell her you're coming over. Yes. Supper. You cook."

Heather went back to her drawing table and spun a couple of drawings around, looking at them from another angle. She put her pencil down and went to wash out her crow quill. Michael was coming over. Fine. At least they'd have something good to eat.

Chapter Eight

"**H**ahaha. Gordo. That's the eternal question."

Joshua wiped his face; he'd spilled coffee on himself with his first large laugh.

"And man, if I knew that, well, I'd bottle it up and sell it in Kensington market, or hell, Bay Street. I'd make a killing."

Joshua laughed some more while he drummed on the table with his fingers. Then he stopped.

"Ah, Gordo, I'm sorry. You're serious, aren't you? Ah, man, and there I go making you feel like crap."

"I do not feel that way. If my question is offensive, I withdraw."

"No, no. Wait. Shit." He called across The Pearl. "Stan, can we get a couple more coffees? Maybe another order of toast?"

"You want the toast or not?" Stan didn't look up from his grill.

"Damn, Stan, you know what I mean." Joshua turned back to me. "Gordo, is this why you wanted to have breakfast with me today? I mean, I love hanging with you. But when you called me this morning, there was something in your voice. I thought you were going to tell me you got diagnosed with some weird disease, or that your mom died."

"She died long ago."

"Oh right. Sorry, I forgot that."

The sky outside The Pearl was gray this morning. The patrons drank their beverages quietly, lifting food from plates in slow movements. I have noticed how light in the City affects its citizens, for on bright mornings the atmosphere is much more lively.

"I have not seen my father for three years."

"Right, you said that, too. But the deal is, I was worried about you, man. And then you tell me you want to meet a woman." Joshua collapsed back in the chair. "Well, buddy, you're full of surprises. What brought this on?"

"You told me you went home with Rain."

"Yeah. But it was a one-night thing, we both knew it."

"One night of what?"

Joshua's face colored.

"You know."

"You had sex with her?"

"You could say that."

"Then the two of you performed sex?"

"Okay, Gordo. Yes, yes. Man, you make it sound like something a doctor would do."

Stan brought fresh coffee and toast, fresh tea for me.

"Thank you, Stan. I did not order this."

"No worries, Gordo," Stan said and went back to his counter.

Joshua ran his fingers through his hair.

"You're his best buddy after taking care of that thug."

"Tell me about Rain."

"Sheesh, Gordo, it happens. It ain't unusual, you know, like the song?"

"No."

I didn't want to push my friend. I heard the annoyance in his voice. But I did want him to tell me how men and women met in the City. We had never discussed this topic before.

"Gordo, tell me where you grew up again."

"Mostly overseas."

"So you said. And you never had a girlfriend over there?"

"Men chose women to be with, or were chosen for them."

I watched my friend's expression, gauging his suspicion of me. I kept my own fear hidden. If I told Joshua about my true home, he might have no choice but to contact the authorities. I didn't want to put this upon him.

"Last evening, after you left with Rain, I met someone."

"You did? Why didn't you say so?"

I hesitated before telling the story of what had happened, again cautious of what might be revealed. When speaking of my stopping of the thieves, I did not dwell upon it.

"You took on three guys? Gordo, where did you learn to fight like that?"

"I learned on my own." I looked down, not wanting to see my friend's eyes.

Again, there was an awkward silence between us. I trusted Joshua, yet it did not seem safe to reveal my years of training.

"So she was all grateful, and . . ." Joshua paused, and I was unsure what he was about to say. He continued. "Well, I guess you saved her."

"She needed protection. I do not believe I saved her—I only helped."

"But after?" Joshua asked.

"We didn't leave together. I watched her walk away, then followed from a distance, ensuring she arrived home safely."

"That was nice. Maybe a bit creepy, but nice. All right, I get it. You want to find this woman again. But how? You don't have her number or anything."

"It's not about that woman. I want to meet someone to share companionship."

Joshua grinned. "Is that what you call it?"

"Am I not asking the right question?"

"Sheesh, Gordo, the way you explain things. Listen, I'm here for you. I'll be your wingman."

"Wing? Like a bird?" I rubbed my forehead. A heat had risen in my face during our conversation.

"Chill, my buddy. It's all good."

"Okay." I used the phrase I'd heard Joshua say that indicated affirmation.

"Listen, there's a great band playing this weekend at Sneaky Dees. We'll go together and see who we see."

"This is the group with the strings and the old man?"

"Totally different. You'll dig them. Folky California sound but with a psychedelic groove."

I nodded, willing the heat out of my face and the cords in my neck to release. Joshua checked his watch.

"Damn. I gotta meet a guy about a drywall job. I'll call you, and we'll set this up for Saturday." He placed his hand on my shoulder. "I'll help you find that companionship, my friend."

Joshua squeezed my hand as he liked to do, and walked out of The Pearl into the gray light.

—

I owe much to my friend Joshua. After I had lost Harry, he found me alone in the alley, weeping. If I'd carried a blade that day, I would have ended my life.

Joshua asked my name.

I told him Gordo, the name Harry had given me. Joshua asked me if I was hurt, and how could he help me. Taking my silence as an answer, he brought me to his small living quarters, which I now know is called an apartment. He fed me salted squares and soup from a metal can.

"How long have you been on the street?" he asked.

"I have not been on that street before."

"I meant the streets. Are you homeless?"

I knew the word, but had not thought of being "less" one. His question brought forth a picture of the shōen, and more tears.

"It's okay. You're safe here," he said.

"I was with my friend . . ." A very long pause before I could speak the words. "He has met death."

"Who was your friend? How did he die?" he asked.

But I did not answer.

Joshua asked me many questions I could not answer. He told me I could sleep at his apartment as long as I washed myself. His forced water spouts were similar to the shelter, except very clean, smelling of spring flowers.

His kindness was a comfort, yet I was still wary. Perhaps he was an authority, or was in contact with them.

"What was your friend's name?"

"Harry. He was my guide."

"Why do you need a guide? Are you hurt, or can't see right?"

"The drink no longer helped him," I said.

Joshua told me that alcohol, his name for the fermented drink, did not help people. Drink was an elixir for Harry. It lightened him at first, before he slid into a darkness. I left Harry in that street, covered with a thick piece of cloth that I'd found in a metal bin. I wandered exhausted until reaching the street where Joshua found me.

The memories of my arrival, and even of Harry, were darkened. There were days where I wondered if I'd always lived in the City, and the shōen was only a dream. This thought opened up a great chasm inside me. Did the shōen exist or had I only imagined it? What is home? Where is my home?

—

Joshua was very different from Harry. Not only did he have living quarters, but he had work as a painter of buildings and rooms. He was kind, and spoke in a lilting fashion that I found soothing. I learned that he was also a musician. He played and sang for me.

At the shelter, music came from a box on the wall, or from the people Harry called religious. Few joined in their singing, which was followed by stories about people who lived long ago. The stories told by the singing people rang of the tales my teacher spoke of, yet there was a force to theirs that I found distasteful.

Joshua's music had a lightness that matched his personality.

"Are you with this woman?" I asked as he sang for me.

"No, someone else wrote about Alison."

"Why not sing about a woman you know?"

Joshua's laughter echoed in the small room.

"Good point, Gordo. Good one."

Joshua was a good and kind teacher. I spoke of my time in the shelter, and my wandering with Harry, but I did not tell him about the ravine. Joshua was too gentle to press me in his questioning.

I also didn't speak with Joshua about the terrible shocks I had when I first came upon cars, or the larger machines called buses, which spewed smoke as they moved citizens. Nor did I mention my fear of the towering buildings made of unknown materials. When a strange bird soared overhead, I believed it to be a creature from the afterplace, ready to swoop down and exact justice upon us lowly humans. I now know of the bird's name—airplane.

Day by day, the jagged feelings in my mind subsided. I observed and experienced strange things. And then I accepted it all. This City was my home now. Joshua would teach me how to live in it.

Joshua was gifted with much patience. I surmised that he believed I was not in my right mind, thinking that I must have experienced a great tragedy. His word, trauma, was another new part of the language he taught me to use. Joshua took me to places of government, where authorities provided me with papers. I had squares of paper with me when I'd arrived at the ravine. These proved useful, as one had a representation of me on its surface. That is, the pale-skinned, auburn-haired body that I inhabited. Gordon Clement was a citizen of the City, named Toronto, and had recently been a resident of a different kind of home, one where he was cared for.

"You remember being in the hospital?" Joshua asked.

In my new understanding of this language, I saw that he meant a place of care. I said I did recall this time, if only to cease his questions.

"Yes," I said.

"Are you better now?"

"Yes, I am."

Once again, I was brought to wonder what had happened to this Gordon Clement. After my arrival, had he traveled to my true home? His entering into the shōen would be as disruptive to his being as the City was to mine, perhaps more. For him, there would be no metal vehicles racing down streets, or giant chrome birds in the sky. There would be no glass and wood boxes that displayed people engaged in all matter of strangeness. Perhaps, he would go mad. In my first year in the City, I feared the same.

Joshua helped me to find work as a painter of rooms. I earned wages, and after several months—how the City marked time—I filled out papers allowing me to purchase my own living quarters.

"Well, you're not buying anything, Gordo. But you give the landlord this money every month and you can stay here as long as you want. It's a nice pad, with a fire escape and everything."

"I will need to escape a fire?"

"No, no. That's what they call the stairs that run up the side of the building. They go right up to your place. You could make a fast exit if you wanted to." Joshua gave a broad smile.

"Why would I want to?"

"I'll show it to you, Gordo. You'll like it."

In those early times, Joshua spoke to me like one does to a child. I was thankful when he stopped doing this.

Chapter Nine

Heather came home from her shift at Grafite to Michael and Zach cooking.

"Michael made this awesome sauce."

"Of course he did," she said.

Michael tilted his head, gave Heather a smile, and then went back to stirring.

"Mom has a bunch of really cool new paintings. Wanna see them?"

"Zach, I don't think—"

"Sure, kiddo."

She took over the stirring of the sauce. Sipping it, it was amazing, as she'd guessed. Michael was a great cook.

"Nice stuff, Heath'. Get a job from a comic company?" Michael asked.

"What? No. What are you talking about?"

"Oh, this guy looks like some sort of badass."

"Michael."

"Sorry." He winked at Zach. "Something out of a comic book.

They hire people, don't they? Marvel, D.C., those folk?"

"There's Image Comics in the city. I'd have to send out samples to those big ones."

"Then do it. Go big or go home, Heath'."

"Just something I'm exploring." Heather looked into the other pot. "I thought the sauce was for pasta."

"Zach said you had that last night, so I peeled up the last of your potatoes. This sauce will go great with anything. Zach, can you set the table for us?"

"Got it."

As Zach rummaged in the cupboard, Michael spoke under his breath.

"You hardly have any food in the place. How are you doing for money?"

"I haven't had time to buy more groceries. And shh."

"You know I'd send you money if I had any. I barely made my rent this month."

"No whispering. Mrs. Nickle says it's rude," Zach called over his shoulder.

"Maybe you should look for another job. Something that pays more than the art store."

Heather held her finger to her lips again. She drained the potatoes, taking care to not brush up against her ex-boyfriend. They ate as Zach told Michael about school, and he told stories about working on the film set.

"Do you see famous people?"

"Sylvester Stallone."

"No way! He's Rocky! You get to work with him? Are you going to be famous, too?"

"Ha. No, it doesn't really work that way, kiddo. I just bang the sets together, and I'm not even in charge of that. I swing a hammer, do what they tell me."

"Maybe Mom could work on the movie. She could paint things. They must have painters."

"I don't think so," she said.

"I could talk to the art department, see if I could get you on the crew. Or even some P.A. work."

"What's that?" asked Zach.

"Production assistant. Kind of a Joe-boy gig, or in your mom's case, a Joe-girl."

"Jane-girl," Zach said.

"I'm fine doing what I'm doing. Just finished a piece for *Toronto Life*."

"What did that pay?" Michael asked.

Heather smashed the last potato on her plate and ladled sauce over it. Zach and Michael traded stories back and forth. Michael laughed hard at one Zach told about a kid who was scared of heights jumping off a slide.

"He was scared of sliding down so he jumped off?" Michael wiped his eyes. "Then what happened?"

"He landed on a kid! Flattened him."

"Oh no, was he okay?" she asked.

"The kid he landed on was fine. But the one scared of heights broke his arm."

Michael and Zach erupted into gales of laughter.

"Don't you have a book report due for Mrs. Nickle?"

"Not until Friday."

"As in two days. You gotta hit the deadlines, Zach. Life is full of them."

Zach started a whine that she finished with a look. He took his dish to the sink and then grabbed his backpack.

"Hey, Zach. Great cooking with you. You have a knack for that. Maybe you'll be a chef someday."

Zach gave a big smile and hugged Michael. "I wish you still lived with us."

"Uh. Yeah. Hey, good luck with that report. Reading's important, too." He gave Zach a playful punch. "Tell you what, I'll see if I can get Stallone's autograph for you."

"Really?"

After Zach went into his bedroom, Heather grabbed both

their plates and went to the sink.

"You shouldn't tell him things like that."

"Like what?"

"You always told me that the crew is not supposed to talk directly to the actors. And now you say you're going to get an autograph. Kids remember disappointments."

"Like you're one to talk. You teach him about deadlines? Shit sake, Heath', the kid's only nine."

"He's ten."

"Starting kinda early."

"The reality of deadlines was drilled into us at art school. I'm trying to prepare him for things."

"He's a great kid. You should go easy."

As they did the dishes together, she made sure there was no skin contact, or even an accidental brush against his arm while handing a dish.

"What's going on with you anyway?" he asked.

"Nothing. I'm doing dishes. What are you doing?"

"It's like I'm an electric current you don't want to touch."

Michael reached out and put his hand on her shoulder. She jerked back, then turned away, fighting the tears that welled up.

"Just do the fucking dishes."

They finished in silence. Michael grabbed his coat off the chair and left. Heather went to her drawing table, pulled out a fresh sheet, and taped it to her board.

"He's not a superhero," she said to no one and began another figure.

Her illustration instructor from fourth year, Blomsky, popped into her mind.

"Only the cream of the crop become editorial illustrators, Robsen."

"Yeah, well maybe I'm that cream," she said aloud at her drawing table.

Blomsky was an asshole, but a brilliant one. He'd puff on his beat-up pipe as students skulked up to his desk to ask for, and dread, his feedback.

"Brad Holland might actually be making some serious money, but it's not for newspapers—they pay shit. Some exec wants the company annual report to look edgy. Stupid fucking word that everyone loves to use and no one understands."

Heather remembered Blomsky ranting about the business of illustration. After talking with him, she always went back to her desk and scribbled down names of people he mentioned, like Holland from New York. She'd love to prove to Blomsky that her work was just as good. She wanted to prove it to her dad, too. She recalled the conversation they had before she left.

"Dad. Are you gonna be okay?"

"Hey, never better. Well, except the two loves of my life are moving across the country."

"It's not across the country."

Tears formed in his eyes. Her father was an easy cry, he always had been.

"I can do this, Dad. It's why I went to school."

"I know. But"—his voice caught—"but, it's going to be hard for you, even harder with a son to take care of."

"You took care of me when Mom died."

"That was different. I had to."

"And I have to do this."

"I know."

Her last mailing went to twenty magazines in New York. Why the hell not? She was good and she knew it.

Chapter Ten

The next morning, I entered into my meditation time thinking of Joshua. The roughness of the weave of my mat pushed against the thin fabric of the loose cotton pants that were a gift from my friend. The softness against the rough brought to mind the many hours I had sat on the ground, amidst the tall grasses of the meadow, studying and meditating. In these last months, I'd given up hope that I would ever return to the meadow. But the bluegrass musicians reawakened that which I tried to hide, reminding me of how I came to the City. I couldn't explain it to myself, but their presence held out the potential of my return.

In my meditation, I visualized the path that led from the estate into the forest, and then into the meadow where I used to meet my dear one. I called her face to memory, shocked that it took some time to bring her into focus. She was the deepest part of my ache. I feared the longer I stayed in the City, the more her face would dissipate, until she was gone forever.

As birds spiraled in the crystalline sky, I listened for the trio of forest musicians. They were the last people I came upon before I disappeared and awoke in the ravine. I heard music—but then realized it came from the apartment below. The notes drifted up through the floor, matched with a steady drumbeat, and an insistent deep voice. The apartment below often played this music, and I had grown used to it, even liked it, but it was different than the bluegrass men. I refocused, became aware of my breath, and searched for the simple strings of the trio in the woods.

How had I traveled to the ravine?

When I came upon the three musicians, their ringing tones sounded through the woods like the wind that rustled the leaves. I was doubtful they recognized my presence. This sort did not play for wages—their songs were prayers offered to the Creator. I considered if they were apparitions. Their soft voices and plucked strings soothed my racing heart. For those moments, I forgot about my escape from the shōen and disappeared into the music. Then their tones shifted, the melody in discord, a tension . . . time itself being squeezed. I needed to leave.

No. I needed to flee.

A group raced after me. Their steps came fast, and then arrows sliced the air, one sticking into a tree where a second ago my head had been. A searing pain exploded in my back. Thoughts, emotions, and physical senses fought inside me, crying out for primacy. Two arrows found their mark. I tumbled toward my certain death. Yet, still I ran. I waited, and did not wait, for the final blow.

From my first training as a samurai, I was told to reflect on this moment—the event of my death. No matter his eloquence or strength of mind, for a samurai to lose composure, and die in an unseemly manner, meant his life had been in vain.

"Is death such a disgrace?" I asked my teacher.

"No. But you must learn to be without fear when you consider it. Even if it is a lie."

My teacher laughed.

"I don't understand," I said.

"No one wants to die. Not even samurai. But when you accept the inevitability of your death, the wind on your face will feel different, a sunrise will never look the same, and every bowl of rice is cherished."

My teacher's voice followed me as I ran from the archers. Far in the distance, the sounds of the musicians echoed in the air. Perhaps that is what happens when the line of life and death is straddled—space itself grows smaller, and everything comes within reach.

The third strike came, and in those scant seconds I yelled that it was not yet my time. No matter how deep the arrows pierced me, I would not perish. I would live, and return to the shōen, if only that I could hold my dear one, and our child that she carries. A final flurry of musical notes rushed forth and cut through the air. All went dark.

I awoke in the ravine.

The trees were not so different, and yet completely different. I had never seen such a forest. Was this the afterplace? Had death come so swiftly? Had I crossed over?

A man in strange clothing approached. He spoke to me in an unknown language. My teacher had shown me many dialects, though this man's speech had nothing in common with any of them. The man held out his hand to me, sprawled on the ground. His expression was open, like his hand, emitting kindness. If this was the afterplace, then this man must be the greeter of the recently dead. Yet, why didn't he speak my language? And why did he look so different, his skin lighter, his eyes round, thin lips and a thick wash of hair under his nose? It was not like the facial hair I'd seen on elders, or had tried, and failed, to grow on my own. This thick caterpillar of deep brown hair danced as the man spoke his strange language.

Then the air shifted, and my ears were opened. A phrase I knew came out of his mouth.

"Are you hurt?"

I reached for his hand, and he pulled me upward. I stared

into his eyes, watching the insect move above his lip. Then I spoke in a language I didn't understand. Somehow I spoke in his language, and in my mind I knew the meaning of these foreign words.

"I was dying," I said.

"I can get you some help. Are you injured?" he asked.

The pain from the arrows had disappeared.

"No."

A woman joined the man; they seemed to know each other. They spoke in fast voices, and I could not follow—yet, they both seemed to want to give me aid. Others walked along pathways in the ravine, all dressed in strange clothing, some accompanied by animals. I recognized the beasts as dogs, but they had lines on them that ran up to the men's and women's wrists.

"What is this place?" Again my words came out in a foreign tongue.

"Toronto."

I had never heard this word uttered in my life. The sound was close to words I had known, but the meaning was lost to me. If this was a waiting place, would this man and woman take me to meet a great being? I was never taught what happened after death, only to be ready for it.

I had so much I wanted to ask about the crossover. Then I saw my sleeves, covered in a material made of black and red squares. I raised my arms and studied the clothing wrapped against my skin, my legs in a heavy blue material and my feet encased in footwear with thick strings. What had happened to my hitatare? Was this the clothing of the afterplace?

The man said something and gestured. He pulled out a black square, opened it, and presented it to me. Then he pointed at my clothes. My leg coverings had pouches in the front and the back. He nodded, encouraging me. The woman smiled, but her face was strained.

I reached into a pouch in the back of my leg coverings and pulled out my own black square. Opening it, I discovered papers within. The colored ones had intricately drawn faces. Other smaller, square papers were hard, like pottery but made of a material I'd never felt. I handed the black square to the man. He took out one of the small hard shapes.

"Gordon Clement."

The sounds were similar to the name I was called on the shōen, but not the same. How had the hard shape told the man this information?

As I peered upward, feeling the heat upon my face, small lights appeared. And then I was falling again. The man and woman reached out to catch me.

All went dark for a second time.

—

It has been three years since I awoke in the ravine, and I have learned much. My first guide Harry was followed by Joshua, and though I never again revealed my true self, I counted him as my friend.

Chapter Eleven

When I first received messages on paper, I found it very unusual. The messages were never personal. Most often it was a company offering me something. When it first happened, I took the letter to Joshua, who told me to rip it up. He said I didn't need a credit card. A long conversation followed on what such a card would do to my life.

I discarded almost all these messages. Joshua helped me make sense of one I deemed important. It appeared to be from a government.

"It's a new health card. You must have had one of these to get into the institution, uh, I mean the hospital you were in," Joshua said.

"I lost it."

Joshua pursed his lips. I saw his body stiffen for a moment, and then release.

"If you have to go to the hospital again, you show them the card, and they'll take care of you."

"Why would I need to go to the hospital?"

Joshua sighed. "I dunno, if you get sick or hurt, or just, you know, need an operation."

"An operation of what kind?"

"Who knows? Surgery or something serious."

"In surgery they cut into your skin and remove part of your body. I wouldn't allow that."

Joshua had taken me to a library in the City, where I now spent many hours reading in this new language. I read about the medical procedure of surgery. It seemed a very bad idea.

I believed that Joshua saw me as someone with limited intelligence, and my way of speaking was not as fluid as his. There were moments that I wanted to finally reveal the truth to him. Yet, that revelation held a danger for me. My fear came from a caution that Harry had once spoken to me, even though I did not fully understand his meaning.

"Don't lose this one, 'kay?" Joshua said.

"I will put it in a safe place."

I showed Joshua the other messages that had arrived in the box with the key.

"Why are all these people contacting me?"

"Trying to sell you stuff, Gordo. Same as everyone."

"I'm not trying to sell anything."

"That's why I like you," he said.

I wanted to understand the City so that my reliance on Joshua would lessen. His kindness was a gift freely given, yet I wanted independence. Along with this desire came a sadness. If I fully became a citizen in this new land, would my previous home cease to exist? When a memory fades, are the people and land forever dead?

I cannot allow my memory of the dear one to dim. I continue to hope for a return to the shōen.

—

After my day of working with the painters, I entered my building and retrieved the day's messages from the box. I reminded myself to call them *mail* or *letters*—using the language of the City lessened Joshua's fears of my mental ability. Today's mail consisted of a letter from a merchant, another from a place of finance, which promised me a form of currency I still did not understand, and a card for something called *Vogue* magazine. A fourth piece stood out from the rest. In dark blue ink, my full name was written in large letterforms on the front of the enclosure. This writing did not come from a machine, as did other letters I had opened. This message was written in someone's hand, in a style that was rigid with hard slashes cutting across the T's.

ATTN: GORDON CLEMENT

I'd never received anything like it before.

—

Heather sat in the Second Cup and stared across at the glass tower where an art director was viewing her portfolio, or so she hoped. When she talked to him earlier in the week, he promised her an in-person meeting. When she got there on time at 9:30 a.m., the receptionist said the art director was in a photo shoot. She told Heather to leave her case and she'd give it to him when he returned.

"Do you know when he will be back?"

"No idea. Just put it over there with the others."

Looking at the stack of black cases on a side table, Heather considered walking out. She had learned from Vince that some art directors only did drop-offs, and he said it was always better to go through the book together.

"Why?" she asked.

"So they know you're not a flake, and can hit a deadline."

Heather had been trying to get her work in front of someone at the national news magazine for months. Believing this might be her only chance, she placed it next to the others.

She didn't feel like going back to her apartment. She decided to head over to Queen West, have a long coffee, and then browse a couple of her favorite bookstores. After a couple of hours, she'd phone the magazine and see if the art director had viewed her portfolio. She didn't need to be home until Zach finished school, and her next shift at Grafite wasn't until tomorrow.

She finished the coffee, then walked over and caught the College car. She didn't want to show up a sweaty mess if the art director wanted to talk about her illustrations. When she got off by the university, a breeze picked up and blew through the trees scattered across the campus. She stopped at a Chinese convenience store to get an Orangina. There was nothing like that amazing drink back in Garsen—she'd discovered it when Shauna brought over a couple bottles.

In Pages Books, she thumbed through the stacks, noting a number of novels that looked interesting, but she had to keep to her budget. Pages had a huge selection of discount art books, something she could never afford at full price. Last time, she'd picked up a book on John Singer Sargent. She'd poured over that book, copying figures into her sketchbook, marveling at the way Sargent played with light on flesh tones and folds of drapery.

She believed the warrior drawings would work their way into her style. She hadn't felt this passionate about a series of drawings for months. She put two of the warrior sketches into her portfolio, labeling them "personal work," and placed them on opposite pages. One had the figure in a long flowing fabric, and the other in a suit that a Bay Street banker might wear, right down to the four-button vest.

She wasn't sure why she'd put the warrior in the robe. It probably came from studying Sargent's drapery. The man who'd stopped the creeps that attacked her had an angular face, and his skin was white like hers, whiter, actually. She imagined him being from some other culture. Heather thought it unlikely she'd see him again, but if she did, she'd have a lot of questions.

—

I ripped open the message with my name inked on the front, reading quickly, then again more slowly. A person had been trying to reach me. They had only written a few lines, asking if I was the Gordon Clement they were seeking. The sender must have sent a number of these letters. It read that if I knew of another Gordon Clement, I should pass this message on to him. There was an urgency even in the handwriting, which began formal and structured, and then became looser as it progressed. I was most struck by the last lines.

> *Gordon, call me as soon as you receive this letter. You are a danger to yourself, and to others!!!*

At the bottom of the message were the letters *A* and *S*, separated by dots. I knew these letters identified the sender. There was no other name on the letter or on the enclosure it had arrived in. Only the name Gordon Clement. My name.

I had never received anything so personal, or so alarming. Who was this writer looking for? Perhaps this citizen whose body I inhabited was in my shōen, where he had gone mad—or he no longer existed, or was trapped in a void that he could not escape from. Perhaps he was dead. Was this writer looking for the one I inhabited? Or were they actually searching for me? I went to the phone to call Joshua. He would advise me.

I let the phone ring a long time. No answer. I tried again. After three attempts, I knew he was not at home. I reread the letter. The words shouted at me from the page.

I pushed the buttons on the phone, entering the numbers transcribed on the letter.

"Who is this?"

The person, a male, was aggressive in tone.

"Are you looking for me?" I asked.

"Who the hell are you?"

"Gordon Clement."

A long silence.

"Are you still there?" I asked.

"Yes."

Papers were rustled. Something heavy fell. I pulled the earpiece away.

"I received your message. A letter."

"Which Gordon Clement are you?"

"I am the only one I know."

"No, you idiot. What's your address?"

The words rushed out of me. I told him where I lived, instantly regretting it.

"I'll be right over."

"I don't think that's . . . hello?"

I set the phone back on the cradle and sat down to wait. What else was there to do?

Chapter Twelve

I did not know whether to wait, to run, or to call Joshua again. I decided I needed to face whatever was coming to meet me. Who was this man on the phone? And why did he ask me which Gordon Clement I was? I had planned to tell him that I was not Gordon Clement at all. And yet like the foolish one who exposes his next move on the battlefield, I had already revealed too much.

I believed only misfortune would come out of this meeting.

My mind swirled as I imagined countless scenarios, but I stilled myself. My teacher had taught me that when emotions pushed in, demanding attention, I needed to listen to my body, my breath, and most of all, my heart. I felt the thrum of the energy that beat within. I made tea to further calm myself. As I put the kettle on the stove, a buzz came over the small box, jolting me out of my stillness. A new thought raced through me. I would exit the building by way of the fire escape if need be. I steeled myself and depressed the button.

"Yes?"

"Let me up."

The voice was harsh, made more so by the distortion of the box.

I went downstairs and let the man into the area known as the foyer. He was slightly taller and broader than me, his hair pulled back tight against his skull, with a dusting of white at his temples. He wore a dark suit with a white shirt that seemed to have a light of its own. He had a black case with a handle, something I'd seen people of business carry. His eyes were an intense shade of blue rimmed with black.

"Gordon Clement?"

"Yes."

"You live here?"

"I think that is obvious. Otherwise, why would I come to let you in?"

He shook his head as if stung by an insect.

"Take me to your apartment."

"Can you tell me what your business is?"

"Not here. Let's go."

Though I wasn't in his way, he pushed past me and headed up the stairs. I followed.

"I am on the third floor," I called after him, but he was already a dozen steps ahead.

"I know."

As I opened the door, I had an urge to slam it shut and run. But where would I go? And why?

"I was about to make tea. Would you like some?"

"Green or that tepid Canadian shit?"

"It's green. I bought it in a market, and it is good."

"Fine."

I poured hot water into the teapot that was a gift from Joshua, and dipped the ball of leaves in. I brought out two fresh cups, setting them on the table in front of him. He slid the pot to the side and set down his case.

"Sit," he commanded.

He unlocked the case; the sound of its release made me step back.

"Relax." He searched for something in the case.

I was unable to ascertain his emotion. There was something in the cadence of his voice that was familiar, yet that was impossible, as we had never met.

He brought out a brown folded paper that held more papers. He flipped through them, took a pen from a hidden pocket in his suit, and started to write something. He looked up at me and then around the apartment.

"How long have you lived here, Gordon?"

"Are you from the government?"

"Answer the question."

I said nothing. Reaching over, I started to pour the tea.

"Let it steep. Weak tea is worse than no tea."

I sat back and crossed my arms, cursing myself for not contacting Joshua before responding to this man. He let out a long sigh, then put his paper and pen down on the table.

"How did you know I was on the third floor?"

"I know all about you."

"We have never met."

"But you also feel like you know me. Right? I can see by your expression that you believe this. Should I tell the story or should you?"

A tingling sensation crawled across my neck and down my spine.

"What story?"

"How long have you lived in Toronto, Gordon?"

He said my name like it was an accusation.

"A few years. Three."

"Uh-huh. And where were you before that?"

"I was overseas."

The man laughed.

"Of course you were. But that's a lot of places, Gordon. Just where overseas were you?"

Now he said my name like he was taunting me. I picked up the teapot, expecting him to stop me, but he didn't. I poured us each a cup. He brought it to his nose and smelled.

"Hmm. This is good."

"Why are you asking me these questions? If you are not from the government, are you a member of some other authority?"

"Listen to yourself talk. You really believe you're him."

The tingling on my spine intensified, sending sparks throughout my body.

"I'm sorry, I don't understand."

"Yes you do."

"Who do you think I am?"

He laughed like an opponent who knows he has won.

"You are Gordon Clement of 66 Baldwin Street, Toronto, Canada. But that's not who you believe you are."

"Who do I believe I am?" My voice was but a whisper now.

The man's eyes were so dark it was as if they swallowed all the light around him.

"You believe you're a warrior from another time and another place. Japan, say, late twelfth century. And more than just any warrior, you are samurai. I can't say what your samurai name is because you never told me."

I stood up from the chair and knocked over the tea, spilling it on the man's dark shoe.

"What do you mean I told you? We have never talked before this moment."

He pulled a cloth from another hidden pocket and wiped up the liquid.

"Sit down, Gordon."

"You should leave now. My friend Joshua is coming over."

"Sit down. No one is coming."

I again pictured running from the room, before easing myself back into the chair. The man with no light in his eyes took two long sips of tea, finishing his cup.

"Seeing as there's a large gap in your memory, let's start at the beginning."

"The beginning of what?"

The man opened the folded paper. "In 1980, you were brought to me by your mother. An old woman."

"My mother died . . ." I paused. " . . . a long time ago."

"1982 is not that long ago. What year is it now? Do you know it?"

"Of course. Joshua invited me to a celebration. It is 1984. But my mother died . . ."

I stopped. I didn't know what year my mother left our family. She traveled to the true afterplace, not this City. I strained to bring it to memory. I tried to picture the soft curve of her face, the melodies she sang when I was a small child. We sat together, under the shade of the sakura. Our mountain rose high above the farm outside the estate where I would one day train. A figure appeared in my mind, but I couldn't make out the features. Hot tears slid down my cheeks.

"All coming back to you?"

Then I saw my father and my lazy brother. We lived on the grounds of the estate. There was the lord's main house with its lush green grass and scarlet flowers. She had died long before that time.

"My mother . . . I cannot find the year."

The man rose and went into my kitchen.

"You got something besides tea?"

I heard the icebox door open. The man came back carrying two bottles of beer.

"Those are my friend's. He keeps them here, so when he visits he can drink them."

"He won't mind."

He opened the beer with a metal hook from a small knife he pulled from yet another pocket—a strange thing for someone to carry.

"Drink. I'll fill in the gaps. Maybe more information will jar something loose."

I'd drunk beer before with Joshua and liked the taste. But today, in the presence of this man with his probing questions, its bitterness assaulted my tongue.

He pulled out a paper and brought it to his face.

"Twenty-five-year-old Caucasian male with red hair and pale complexion, first visit October 16, 1980. Brought by his mother, likely in her seventies. Subject reports delusional thinking, false histories, and other strange behavior."

"What does that mean? What is false? Who is strange?"

The man pulled out another paper.

"Subject lives in a world of his own making. Sees himself as a Japanese warrior, samurai class. Claims to have lived in the twelfth, or maybe the cusp of the thirteenth century, somewhere on the island of Shikoku. Subject does not believe he's a reincarnated historical figure. He believes he is presently this person. Saying he traveled in time and place to come to Toronto in the twentieth century. He doesn't know how he arrived, or how he came to inhabit his body. When asked why he'd come to this time, he said he didn't know."

He looked up at me to gauge my expression, and then continued.

"Subject can describe the look, smell, and culture of Heian or maybe the early Kamakura periods. Can speak some phrases that sound Japanese, but when a tape was played for a known language scholar, the dialect was not modern-day Japanese, but a much older form. Language likely picked up from arcane books. Subject possesses above average intelligence, is in good physical condition, and speaks in a formal, stilted fashion."

I watched the man's mouth move around his many words. I searched my memory for his face, and the sound of his voice. Had I met him before? There was a familiarity, but my mind had entered a fog, as when I tried to recall my mother's face.

"You are a doctor," I said.

"Yes, Gordon."

"The subject . . . you are talking about me."

"Coming back to you now?"

"What is your name?"

"Good. You're finally figuring it out."

The man held his beer bottle upward, reached over and touched my bottle with a clink, a move Joshua often did, but this time it was unsettling.

He told me his name was Dr. Alex Shepherd. He studied my face for a reaction, then proceeded to tell me more things about myself that were written in his papers. His rapid speech was difficult to follow. At one point, it sounded like he had moved into the language of the shōen, but I decided that my comprehension was clouded by the storm of internal fear that churned within me.

The Doctor repeated that my mother had died in 1982, and my father was gone before he first met me.

"Gone where?"

He ignored my question and continued to recite what he called "the reports." I wanted to tell him that my father was still alive back at the estate. I had a moment of terror, as I considered what the lord might do to my father because of my actions.

"So you agree?"

I realized the Doctor had asked me a question.

"Yes," I said. And then added, "No. I don't know what you are asking me."

"Thought I was losing you. Where did you go just now?"

"I didn't go anywhere. You see me before you."

"You went back there. Listen, where you're going is not real. Look at you. You're as white as I am. Ha, whiter. You're not who you think you are, Gordon."

"What about my mother?"

"She's been dead for two years. She told her lawyer to tell me to take care of you. But then you disappeared. Boom. Right off the map. Good thing I found you."

I didn't say anything for a long time. I set my half-full beer down and walked to the window. There was the squeal of a streetcar winding its way across College, or Dundas, I couldn't be sure. A teenage boy gave his female friend a playful push. I closed my eyes—the street sounds quieted, until someone yelled something in a language unknown to me. But then, a face grew in my vision. Eyes, and bowed lips came into focus. I heard a sung melody. The music emanated from a face I knew—my mother. She was there in the garden with my father. They had often worked together before her illness. This was not the old woman the Doctor spoke of—this mother was the one from my childhood home. Yes, she was still dead. But the vision made her alive again.

I turned back to the man calling himself a doctor. His voice became louder, filling my apartment like the rushing wind of a kamikaze. His lips moved quickly, but the words being emitted did not match what he was speaking.

"Are you speaking Japanese?"

He dropped one of the papers, then snatched it up from the floor.

"Listen to me. Concentrate. What are you hearing?" He touched his own ears and then his lips. "I don't speak Japanese. And you don't either—except for some phrases you must have picked up from books in the library."

His words were slower now, speaking the language of the City again. Had I imagined that he spoke the language of my shōen?

"Hey! Am I losing you again?"

The Doctor reached into his pocket again.

"Stop. You must leave now."

I grabbed his arm before it could exit his clothing. He shook off my grasp, and so I clutched again, this time with more force.

"Go easy now. Breathe, Gordon. You're outside of reality."

He jerked his arm out of his suit. He held a long needle. I'd seen one when Joshua had taken me to an actual doctor. He struggled to rise from the chair, while pulling a cap off the needle, exposing the point. I slid my hand down his arm and applied pressure. The Doctor yelped in pain, and the needle fell to the floor. I twisted his arm behind him, pulling him upward and rotating his body. His other hand flailed, trying without success to strike me. I pulled on his arm, putting it at the angle I knew to be most painful.

In this strange dance, I pushed him to the door, then down the stairs. He stumbled, almost falling at one point. All the way down he said my name, as if reciting a single-word poem, and then he began to curse. A neighbor on the second floor opened her door.

"What the hell is going on down there?"

"It's okay. We are friends. Close your door. All is fine."

The Doctor let out another loud curse. I applied more pressure to his arm. I felt his strength, and understood that if not for my better position, he would strike back.

"Be still," I said. "I will break it—you know I can."

The last few steps, he relinquished and no longer struggled. I pushed him out to the street in front of my building.

"I'll be back when you're not in this state," he said.

"I am in no state. You are not welcome to come back."

I left him on the street, going back into my building and checking that the lock was secured. When I was up a few stairs, I peered out the second-story window. A young man rolled by on a wheeled board. The Doctor was gone.

Once inside, I picked up the needle from the floor and threw it away. He had left his case and papers behind. I gathered them, scanning the pages as I placed them in the case. The vision of my mother revealed that all the Doctor had uttered was a lie. In spite of the familiarity I had felt, we had no prior relationship. I was not sure what to make of his double language.

Many of the Doctor's pages were filled with rows of numbers. More than half of the pages had no markings of any kind. He had pretended to read these blank white sheets. The Doctor's goal was deception, to create a myth, though I did not know why.

Chapter Thirteen

Heather left the bookstore, walked down Queen, past Grafite and the small diner next door. She asked herself if she wanted a plate of fries and gravy at The Pearl, but decided against spending money and that she needed to stock the fridge with food that Zach liked. She planned to head to Kensington and splurge on some coconut tarts for the two of them, but something caught her eye across the street.

The last time she'd seen him it was dark, but his movements as he walked out of the shadows that night were burned in her mind. The man on the south side of the street moved in a similar way, not aggressive, but with purpose. It had to be him.

She wanted to call out, but she didn't know his name. How would he react to something like that? She turned and followed him from her side of the street. She took a step onto the street, and a car honked its horn. She glared at the driver, who was moving so slowly she could have easily made it across.

She quickened her pace, keeping her eyes on the warrior. He looked like an ordinary person today. Possibly his strength was hidden underneath the clothes that any young Canadian man would wear. How old was he anyway? She couldn't tell in the dark, but she'd thought they were around the same age. Still, his head had been covered by a hood that night. She raked her memory of him sitting at the table in the club. Did he have red hair?

The warrior talked with someone in disheveled clothes, maybe a street person, or no, wait . . . what was going on? Was he being attacked? Heather took a fast look around, trying to see if anyone else was seeing what she saw. Cars moved in front of her, blocking the intersection where she wanted to cross. More car horns. A streetcar jammed full of people squealed to a stop. When the doors opened, a group tried to squeeze onto the car. There was an altercation—someone pushed a young man wearing a backpack, and he toppled into an older woman laden with shopping bags.

Heather crossed the street. Moving around stopped cars, she held up her hands to the angry drivers who were heating up inside. The warrior had stood outside a hardware store, where now the disheveled man who'd accosted him was laid out. Two other people yelled at the man who was sprawled on the sidewalk. How could she have lost him? Heather looked back to the other side of the street, scanning, until she caught sight of him again. It was as if he'd flown over her.

She went back across, gathering honks as she moved—one car lurched forward, nudging her leg. She slammed her hand on the hood.

"You can't fucking move anyway!"

The driver flipped her the middle finger, and the driver in the car next to him shouted over. Heather couldn't tell who was yelling at who. She made it to the other side, the warrior moving fast ahead of her, now into the next block. He strode as if he was either escaping something—the situation in front of the hardware store—or he was trying to catch someone.

"Hey!" she called out. And then again, "Hey!"

People moved aside, not wanting to block the crazy lady.

"It's okay. I'm just calling to a friend," she said to the street.

No one cared. He was a lot farther away from her now. Heather started to run, weaving around people, saying "excuse me" and "sorry" to a few, nothing to the ones that swore at her. A tall man came into focus, moving quickly ahead of the warrior. Was this who the warrior was trying to reach?

Ahead of her, they rounded the corner on Spadina, and for a second Heather thought she'd lost him for sure. Adrenaline coursed through her body as she pursued a man she didn't even know. Finally, he stopped outside of another packed streetcar. There was no sight of the taller man who he'd seemed to be following. The doors closed, and those not able to get on stepped back as the car rumbled up the street. The warrior stared at the streetcar as it lurched away.

As she caught her breath, a wave of thoughts swooped in. How had she got so caught up in this? It was ridiculous. Heather walked toward him, his back to her, trying to form a sentence in her mind. "Thanks for saving me that night. Can I buy you a coffee?" or "Excuse me, do you remember me? You helped me that night." Or just "What is your name, because I can't get your image out of my brain?"

And maybe it wasn't even him.

Heather stepped on the streetcar platform.

"Sorry, can I talk to you?"

He stepped off and headed toward the street.

"Hey! Were you at the Apocalypse?" She chased after him. "You and those men on the dark street. You stopped them. Was that you?" she called after him.

The warrior turned toward her, but looking through her. Just like that time in the club. It was definitely him.

"Do you remember?" she asked.

The warrior raised his hand to her, eyes closed. Was that a bow? She observed him closely—a white man with a pale complexion and red hair. For a half second, he looked Asian.

But was he?

In a voice that cut through all the surrounding noise of Spadina Avenue, he called back to her.

"Yes. I remember."

Chapter Fourteen

The next day was Thursday, as the denizens of the City called it, one day before the end of the week. Time seemed so important in the City, marked by months, weeks, hours, and minutes. People continuously checked timepieces, strapped to their wrists, to situate themselves. I tried to recall if the Doctor wore what they called a watch. The Doctor also spoke of time. His talk was of years. His assertions swirled in my head: the year of our first meeting, when he proposed that I was in his care, the year of my mother's death, and most of all, that I was not from the shōen. His words assaulted me, cutting my skin in a hundred places.

I went through my morning rhythm like nothing had changed—except everything had. Walking through the park, the children's laughter sounded harsh. The wind stung my cheeks, and the sun did not dare show its face. Entering The Pearl, I studied the other patrons. Did they also believe me to be this Gordon Clement? Of course they did. I had given them no reason to think otherwise.

My friend Joshua greeted me in his usual exuberant manner, and Stan brought me some tea.

"So you're in for the concert tonight, Gordo?"

"Have you been away?" I asked.

"Oh yeah, had to drive out to Newmarket to see my aunt. She's not been feeling great. Ended up staying for supper and came home late. Why?"

"I tried to phone you," I said.

"Oh, sorry. Was it something important?"

"No."

I smoothed the fabric on my clothing, then, unsure what to do with my hands, clasped my fingers together.

"Are you all right, buddy? You don't look so hot."

"What is tonight?"

"The concert, man, the one I told you about. The psychedelic groove band."

In that moment, I decided to not tell Joshua about my visit from the false doctor yesterday. I needed to deal with the Doctor on my own. Telling Joshua would only create fear and confusion for my friend. If this man came to my apartment again, I would refuse him entry. He spouted lies, though I was not sure of the reason.

"Oh yes. I do remember," I said.

"Are you up for it?" Joshua waved his hands in front of my face. "Gordo, hello? Earth to Gordo. Where are you, man?"

"Sorry, Joshua. My mind is somewhere else this morning."

"I can see that. Did something bad happen yesterday? Why were you calling me?"

"I was not feeling well, so I went to my bed early. I'm okay now, thank you."

"I hope you're not getting that flu that's going around. That mother is vicious. I think that's what my aunt had. Hey, if you can't make it tonight, no problem. We can do it another time."

Stan came to refill Joshua's coffee and poured more hot water into my small kettle. The clinking of metal on cups and plates soothed my ears. I was in a safe place. The people who came to The Pearl were good people.

"I'd like to go to this concert," I said.

"Excellent. And I did line something up. I called a couple of—"

"I don't mean any offense. I would like to be alone for a while."

"Oh, okay." Joshua took a long gulp of his coffee, wincing, and then finished it. He put on his jacket and stood to leave. "You sure you're doing all right?"

"Why do you keep asking me?"

"Well, for one thing, you're kicking my ass out to the street."

"I am sorry."

"Relax, Gordo. I'm just giving you the gears. I have mornings like that, too." He extended his palm to me, and I hit it with my palm as he had taught me to do. Joshua called it a five.

"Thank you."

"I'll be by your place at nine. Doors open at eight, but people won't start showing up until closer to ten."

After Joshua left, the thoughts I'd been holding off rushed into my mind. I closed my eyes and tried to focus. I sensed Stan coming over to me, most likely asking if I was okay. Ever since that day I helped him with the thief, he had taken special care of me whenever I came into The Pearl.

I held up my hand. "It's okay. I have a headache this morning."

"Ah yeah, hungover again. That's what you get hanging out with the likes of that one. I tell you what, I'll break an egg into some tomato juice for you."

"Thank you, Stan. I need to go to an appointment."

I got up to pay, and Stan waved off my money.

"I cannot keep coming here for free."

"You had tea. I'm out like twenty cents. Can I get you an aspirin or something, Gordo?"

I shook my head at Stan and left The Pearl.

Thoughts about the Doctor bombarded me as I made my way along Queen Street. I passed people eating their morning meal as they walked, the smell of coffee and cigarettes acrid within my nostrils. The street was lively as usual: men in suits similar to my age walked alongside couples wearing short pants, the women adorned in headbands and beaded jewelry. A long-haired man shouted at me to buy a watch, and another stood in front of a stand of shirts with patterns of color or crudely drawn animals. A woman in tight short pants danced to music coming from a device on the sidewalk. Joshua called them boomboxes, which I thought sounded more like a weapon. The woman wore one of the T-shirts that also hung on the stand. Her shirt fitted closely around her form, the fabric bright red, with white letters that read, *Nanu, Nanu*. I had not come across these words before.

Queen Street's din of activity pulled me away from my spinning mind. When the Doctor came back, would I have the force needed to repel him? What if he entered my building by another way? What was in his needle?

"Hey, if you're enjoying the show, cough up some dough," said the man selling shirts.

"Excuse me?"

"Yeah, these tits don't come for free." The woman gave a fast shake to the music and grinned at me.

"Oh, sorry. I don't need a shirt. Or a tit."

"Well, then head on down the street, man. Make way for the paying customers."

The woman shook again, and I drifted away from them before crossing the street. Cars filled the gray lanes, and everything moved like a muddy stream, including the streetcar that I saw further east. I bumped into a Chinese man carrying a box of vegetables, most likely rushing to a merchant in nearby Chinatown. He wore an apron made from rough cloth. I wondered where he'd picked his vegetables, strange long tubers in rich purples and yellows—certainly nothing I had seen grown in the City. I knew that we were of different backgrounds, yet I felt a kinship to his kind. His features and movements reminded me of the people from my true home. When I first discovered this Chinatown, so close to where I lived, I was gladdened. Yet, in my attempts to speak with the merchants and patrons of the neighborhood, I was met with either empty conversations or indifference. We did not share ancestors, yet in their faces, and the color of their skin, they seemed familiar to me. In the pale skin I now wore, they saw no similarity at all.

I cursed myself for not telling Joshua about the Doctor. I could tell him tonight, but there would be music, loud music. I now recalled our conversation about meeting other companions, and presumed that is what he was about to tell me. I decided to go find Joshua at his work, and tell him about the events of yesterday, but suddenly I spied someone walking quickly on the north side of Queen Street. The man weaved around people, bumping some as he strode past. A young man in a bandana swore at him. It was the Doctor.

I watched this all from my side of the street, under the awning of a store that sold pieces of metal and tools to fix machines.

"Hey, you okay, man? You don't look so good."

A skinny man with a patchwork beard stood next to me under the awning. He must have been there before. I didn't see him walk up to me.

"Thank you for your concern. But I am fine."

"Cool, cool." He reached into his jacket and pointed something at me within his pocket. "In that case, you gonna want to hand over your wallet."

"Why?"

"No whys, just the wallet, man. And it's all copacetic."

"What's in your pocket? Is that a weapon?"

"The wallet, motherfucker. Or you get a big hole in your stomach to match the one in your head."

I was now more surprised that I hadn't noticed him. His body stench was unmistakable.

"How will you attack me here on the street? With all these people?"

He shifted his look to a spot behind me. It did seem as if this part of the street had fewer people.

"Hand over the wallet or I'll gut you like a fish."

"I do doubt that."

His hand came out of his pocket fast, and I grabbed his wrist and twisted. The blade fell to the street. I spun him and brought his arm back behind him.

"Ow, ow, ow. Let it go, man."

I pushed his arm further, knowing the point at which it would break. My teacher had shown me that early in my training. The stench of the man flooded my nostrils. Rivulets of sweat ran down the back of his neck. Wait. Where did the Doctor go? Why was he on this street? Had he followed me . . . or did he know my morning routine?

The skinny man with the stench screamed. I released him and he collapsed on the sidewalk. Lost in thought, my control had wavered. One more inch and I would have broken the bone. The merchant rushed out from the store.

"What the hell?"

A smaller and thicker woman joined him. "Has this man assaulted you? Peter, call the police."

"Son-of-a-bitch tried to break my arm."

I picked up the knife, carefully folding it inward, and handed it to the shopkeeper.

"He is a thief. He attacked me with this. I stopped him."

"Is this true?" The woman's voice went higher.

I was halfway across the street as the trio behind me began to yell at each other.

The woman called out to me. "Hey, come back. Don't you want to press charges?"

I focused on the street ahead of me, quickening my pace. The Doctor's movement was unmistakable, fast, forceful, like a shark swimming in a sea. He was the predator, and nothing would stop him. Except, I was behind him. He couldn't have seen me—so now the hunted pursued the hunter.

My gait moved into a slow run, as I scoured the street for his shape. I ran the last block before turning north to Chinatown.

"What's your hurry, man? How about a dog?"

I ignored the vendor, making my way up Spadina. Ahead, a streetcar jerked to a stop. A long line of people were sucked into the car. There, at the head of the line, and now up the stairs . . . was that him? He towered over the others, or perhaps that was an illusion.

I ran to the platform, reaching the streetcar just as the doors closed. I scanned the crowd jammed inside. Perhaps I'd imagined his presence. And then, at the last window in the car, his dark-rimmed eyes peered at me. As the streetcar pulled away, the Doctor pointed at me, mouthing words that I understood.

"I am coming."

Someone addressed me, a woman's voice, behind me on the platform. But the Doctor's words had so shaken me, I was unable to respond. She seemed oddly familiar. I nodded to her. Pursuing the streetcar on foot would serve no purpose.

The woman called to me again. Her lips quivered, and I wondered what had caused this feeling.

I had to ask what she wanted of me.

Chapter Fifteen

He walked back across the street and met her on the platform as another streetcar pulled up. Heather stepped aside to let people pass, but he did not move, letting others go around him like a boulder in the middle of a river.

"I'm sorry to rush up to you. But I saw you a few blocks ago. It looked like you were in a fight."

"There was no fight."

They were the only two left on the platform as the car closed its doors and headed up Spadina.

"Sorry . . . it's not my business. I just wanted to thank you."

"Why?"

"Why? For saving me the other night—after the concert. From those asshole—sorry, creeps."

"There is no need for so many apologies."

A flush crept across her cheeks, and she turned away. "I'm going to—"

"It's a nice morning. Where were you going?"

"Excuse me?"

"I must apologize now. I've been very distracted. I'd like to honor your gratitude. My name is Gordo."

"Heather."

"Like a plant I have heard of." Gordo pointed back to Queen Street. "There is a place nearby where I like to spend some time in the morning. Would you like to go with me?"

"I should let you go," she said, taking a step further up the platform.

"Where?"

Heather didn't have an answer, it was just something people said when they tried to get out of a conversation. He walked off the platform. Watching him cross the street, she realized that she wanted to keep talking—she needed to know more about him. She jogged across the street, joining Gordo on the other side.

They came up to the diner she'd passed, and he entered The Pearl. The morning rush was over, and there were many empty tables. Gordo walked to a spot at the back.

"Hey, back again. You change your mind on that egg, Gordo?"

"Hello. I'd like some more tea, Stan." Gordo gestured to the seat across from him. "What do you drink? My friend Joshua likes the coffee here."

"I'll take a coffee and an ice water," she said to the man who'd addressed them.

Sitting in the diner with the man she'd called the warrior was like meeting someone out of a book, or from her imagination.

"Who was the man you were following?"

"He is someone who I've met before. A doctor."

"Your doctor?"

"No."

Drinks came, and Heather dumped in a creamer without tasting the coffee, assuming it would be the bad diner stuff.

"I wanted to thank you for the other night, but I don't want to butt into your life. Let me buy you some breakfast."

"I am only having tea."

His movements were languid, even in the way he poured the tea from the small kettle.

"Why did you do what you did? You could have been hurt."

"Those men meant to hurt you. I didn't want that to happen."

"The way you fought them—where did you learn to do that?"

He didn't say anything for a long time, and Heather worried that she had offended him. He spoke English as if it were not his native language. There was another quality to his speech that she couldn't identify.

"I believe you would have been okay. You have an inner strength," he said.

"Are you kidding? I wake up in the night thinking about what could have been."

"I understand. But you need to release those thoughts. Focus on what is now, what is in front of you."

"Why do you think I have strength?"

"I sense it."

"Can I ask you something?"

"Yes." Gordo sipped his tea.

"Where are you from?"

"I am from the City, like you."

"No, no. Originally?"

"You believe I am from somewhere else?"

"Well, you look like you're Canadian, but you don't sound like it."

"Please explain."

"Your way of talking, it's different. Eastern Europe, maybe? Or some country I've never heard of? Geography's not my strong suit."

"I am from here," he said. "But I've been overseas."

"For how long? And where?"

A burst of noise came from the front of The Pearl, two men swearing at each other. One of them threw a punch before Stan ran over to them. The diner owner pointed his finger like he was scolding children.

"This is a violent city," Gordo said. "Many people are unhappy."

"There's some good people. But I agree, it's a lot different from where I grew up."

"This isn't your home?"

"I've been here about a year now. I'm from out west. A small town no one's heard of."

"Why did you leave this small town no one has heard of?"

"I came here to try to be an illustrator." Heather took in Gordo's blank look. "Like an artist for magazines and books. It pays well if you can find the work."

"Being an artist is a high calling. I've trained in the arts, but I no longer practice."

"Really? What did you do?"

"I painted symbols with a brush. Calligraphy is the name for it. I was not as skilled as some, but I admired the beauty and practice of it."

She looked at the man that before today she'd called the warrior. As she'd sketched his figure on her drawing board, the scene after the bluegrass concert became more and more dreamlike.

"Gordo, were both your parents white, or, like, of a different ancestry?"

"My mother is dead. I fear my father may also have died."

"Oh, I'm sorry. I'll stop prying into your life. I should go. I need to do some work before my son comes home from school."

"You have a son?"

"Yes. He's ten, his name is Zach. Such a great kid."

"Will your partner also be at home?"

"My what?" She touched her throat. "Oh, no. I'm not married. I don't even live with anyone. Just me and Zach."

"I am sorry."

"Don't be. We're good."

"Tell me about your son."

"He's ten—oh, I told you that. He's great, maybe been around adults too much. I'm trying to help him just be a kid."

"What else could he be?"

"Gordo, your way of asking questions, I mean . . ."

"My way is what?"

She looked at her hands. "I shouldn't comment on how you speak."

The sun pouring in through the front window illuminated Gordo's face, his smooth white skin glowing. He clasped his fingers together and closed his eyes. Heather had a thought that he was about to pray.

He opened his eyes. "Would you like to hear a story?"

"Um, yes. Sure."

He smoothed his napkin, placing his spoon on it, and then began to speak in a slow, measured voice.

"One morning, a young boy studied a caterpillar stretching its body on a bright green leaf, slowly eating its way to the edge. His father called to him. He was to meet a man with a bow and quiver strapped across his back. The boy knew this man was a retainer, in service to the estate owner, the lord of the shōen. The boy rose slowly and walked to where his father and the retainer stood. He did not bow.

"Even in the way he moves, he shows himself," the retainer said.

"You must show respect." The father raised his hand to strike the boy, but the retainer touched his arm.

"Bring him to the house tomorrow—we'll start training right away."

"You've observed his insolence. Are you sure?" the father asked.

"Come after the sun has risen."

The father and son watched as the retainer grew smaller on the road. The boy asked why he had come to see them.

"The estate was attacked and several men were killed. A young one being trained by the retainer was amongst the

dead."

The boy asked if the retainer was a samurai.

"You already know this. And you will be trained by him."

"What about the farm?" the boy asked.

"Our family will now live with the lord. Your brother and I will work the grounds of the estate."

The boy knew that no one in their family had come from samurai.

"How is this allowed?" he asked his father.

"They are in need. The retainer knew of our farm, and that I had two sons without a mother."

The boy asked why he was chosen ahead of his brother, though he had already guessed the reason. His brother was lazy and had little skill of any nature.

"And what if I do not want to go?"

"What you want does not matter," his father said.

At the farmhouse, they found the boy's brother slouched against a sakura tree. The mountain that stretched into the sky cast a shadow on the three of them. None knew the tragedy that awaited their family.

Just like that, Gordo was done. Heather sat in silence. It was as if all the other sounds in the diner had quieted while Gordo told his story, though she was the only one listening. Someone dropped a utensil on the floor, and her body jolted.

"Is there more?"

She waited for Gordo's reply, but nothing came.

"It sounds like something from long ago. Did you read it in a book?"

"It is just a story."

"Why did you tell it to me?"

He didn't answer.

"Will you tell me the rest? What was the tragedy?"

"Another time. Would you like to meet tomorrow?"

"Of course—I mean, yes." Heather glanced at the clock behind the diner counter. "I start my mornings with some work after Zach goes to school. But I can come tomorrow, around ten-thirty. Will you be here?"

"I am often here much earlier. Yes."

"Will you tell me the rest of the story?"

"Perhaps."

Heather left The Pearl quickly, not wanting to appear rude but needing to be alone to try to understand the meaning of the story, and more than that, the mental state of the person who told it. She walked to Yonge Street and then up to College, all the while repeating the story in her head. From a payphone, she called the magazine, and the receptionist said her portfolio was ready to be picked up.

"Was there any message from Mr. Shipley? For me, I mean?"

"No."

Chapter Sixteen

I waited for Joshua to arrive and contemplated whether or not I wanted to join him in going to the concert. I had wanted a female companion to tell my story to, and now that I had found one, I didn't need to meet another female. I was unsure how the woman, Heather, had received the telling. The expression on her face, and then leaving The Pearl so quickly, told me that she was troubled by it—or perhaps, she needed time to understand.

It felt good to tell someone of my beginnings, even if I didn't reveal the truth behind the story. I would meet her again, and observe her emotions when I told her more. I did not want to cause her discomfort, as she seemed very kind. Releasing this information about my true self to another was like taking deep full breaths after being constrained for so long.

Joshua arrived, smelling of something sweet, but not a flower. I understood this was the herb that he rolled into a cigarette and smoked. He gave me a small amount once, along with a ceramic tube to place the herb into. I had yet to do anything with the gift.

I did not invite my friend in, worried that he might see the

Doctor's case, even though I had hidden it in my bedroom—
still, he might see something amiss that would make him ask
questions I did not want to answer.

We walked to the place known as Sneaky Dees, yet another
place in the City with a strange name. The music was pleasant,
a bit loud, but I liked how the rhythm made the room feel like
it was pulsing. A man sat on the stage in front of a machine,
pushing buttons. I wondered when people with instruments
would take the stage.

Joshua pointed to a spot against the far wall, where under a
greenish light, two women sat at a table. I could tell one was tall,
even though she was sitting, with long dark hair spilling down
her shoulder and back. The other was a medium build, light hair
formed into points like I'd see on an animal. I'd seen this type of
hair before; a lot of women had it. The green light lit their faces,
making them less attractive than I guessed they were.

"Gordo, this is Rebecca and Sky."

"Hello."

"I'm going to get us some drinks. Save my seat, Gordo."

I had heard the expression about saving before, but did not
remember the proper response.

"So, J's friend. What do you do?" Sky asked.

"J?" I asked.

Sky laughed. Her pointed hair did not move. "So, what, he
dragged you off the street because he needed a wingman?"

"Joshua is my friend. He asked me to join him here."

"Joshua?" the long-haired one, Rebecca, asked. "That's his
name?"

"Of course."

"Where are you from?" Sky asked.

"Overseas."

Both of the women laughed together.

Joshua returned with drinks. "What'd I miss? I'm guessing
you were talking about me."

"Hey, Joshua." Sky elongated the *shhh* sound.

"Yeah? Oh, right. Gordo calls me that. That cool with you?"

I heard the tension in my friend's tone. I couldn't be sure if the others recognized it.

"Hey, who wants to dance?" Joshua asked.

"There's no band yet," Sky said.

"There's beats," Joshua said.

Rebecca swept back her hair, crossed behind us, and went to an area in front of the platform. Joshua followed her. They moved in time to the man pushing buttons. Joshua moved well— I'd seen him do this dance before. The words that accompanied the music were repetitive, men and women asking, *Do you really want me, baby?* Hearing this type of song previously, I learned they were not about infants.

"You're a talkative one."

"I was thinking about the music," I said.

"Thinking you hate it? I heard the band coming on later is even worse."

Sky reached into her bag and pulled out a case. She lit her cigarette and offered one to me.

"I don't smoke."

"Well, what do you do?" She leaned her body over the table, taking on a cat form. Her eyes narrowed, and I expected her to emit a feline sound.

My attention shifted to raised voices by the place where we had entered. Two men formed a wall on either side of the door, speaking loudly to someone I could not see. The Button Man must have hit something because the music changed to a faster and much louder beat. Joshua gyrated in front of the tall woman, whose hair spun through the air like thick waves of water.

Voices rose above the music, then another man joined the pair at the door. Bodies shifted and jerked, but it was not a dance.

"You're a lot of laughs. I'm going to the can."

I was barely aware of Sky leaving the table. My senses focused on the sound and movement coming from the entrance.

I left my table, moving toward the men at the back. Bodies hit against each other, flesh was slapped, blows were exchanged in the semi-darkness. A tall man burst through the wall of men.

I recognized him immediately.

"That's enough, asshole."

One of the men grabbed the tall one's shoulders, while the other, a short thick man, drew back to strike his stomach. My teacher had me train at night, when moves are felt more than seen. Even in the dark, I knew the man drawing back to swing his fist wouldn't complete his punch.

The tall man moved, grabbing the fist as it came toward him, and twisted hard. The shorter man yelled and hit the floor. In the next moment, the man from behind lost his hold, was spun and then flipped onto a table. Glasses shattered, followed by yells and a high-pitched scream. The music went on. Somehow the Button Man was too transfixed.

The Doctor stood in the middle of the floor; two men stayed down, moaning. A man with a wide back and mountainous shoulders approached.

The Doctor's voice cut through the music. "Who the fuck says I can't come in here?"

The wide-backed one raised his hands.

"Settle down, cowboy. We're just doing our job. You can't come in here with a weapon. My friend tells me our pat down showed you were packing."

"Why would you think I'm a cowboy? You're a moron."

"How about you go up those stairs and out to the street before the cops get here? No harm, no foul."

"You spout nonsense."

The Doctor clenched his hands and released. Under his suit jacket, I imagined the tension of his muscles. His feet were spread. He was coiled, ready to spring out. I'd seen this stance in my teacher.

"You guys need some help down there?" a voice called down.

Had the Doctor seen me, or was I just another figure in a

sea of bodies? But why had he come? How would he know I was here?

The Doctor turned to the voice upstairs, and the mountainous one made his move. It was a mistake, and in a blur he was on the floor. Between the beats, I heard a bone break. This time the shouting alerted the Button Man. The music stopped. Out of the momentary silence, sirens sounded. The Doctor flung another who'd come from behind against the wall. Another one he smashed in the face. A man stepped out from the gathered crowd, but then changed his mind.

In the doorway, the Doctor twisted back, and caught my gaze. A grin spread across his face. He pointed a finger at me, mouthed something, and then disappeared up the stairs. No one followed him.

The authorities would arrive very soon, but I was certain the Doctor would be gone. I returned to the table. Someone walked onto the platform and took the microphone.

"Sorry, folks, uh, listen up." He waited for the crowd to quiet. "We had a bit of trouble with someone who didn't want to follow club rules. Toronto's finest are going to do a walkthrough. Please cooperate with them, and we will get this party going as soon as we can. The Phantoms will be coming on a bit later, so freshen your drinks, and everybody stick around."

Joshua arrived back to the table. The spike-haired woman was nowhere to be seen. The long-haired one gauged the situation and headed for the door.

"Hey, where you going? The band hasn't even started," Joshua called after her.

"Let her go," I said.

"What?" Joshua sounded out of breath. "What the hell's going on, Gordo? Did you see anything?"

"I saw everything."

Chapter Seventeen

Heather drank her coffee at the small kitchen table, hoping the music playing on the tape player would push away the strangeness of the day before. Gordo's story still reverberated in her head. Why had he told her that story? Something in the way he told it made her wonder if he confused reality with the things he read in books. The way he said the *boy* or the *father* suggested this story was about someone he knew. But how would he know people who were samurais and carried bows and arrows? Maybe he was just a bit strange. It didn't mean he was dangerous and that she shouldn't meet him again. She released her tight grip on the coffee cup.

Zach dug into his Cheerios, slurping and humming.

"Hey, turn that one up, Mom. I like it."

"Hmm?"

"That's the Head one. You've played them before. I like his voice and the drums. It's cool."

"Oh, right. Sure."

Heather turned her tape player up a couple of notches. She

listened to David Byrne sing about home, which made her think of her dad.

"You okay, Mom? You look sad."

"Hmm? No, I'm fine."

"Was it Michael? Did you guys fight? I don't like it when you fight. He doesn't have to come over."

"You're such a sweet kid. How'd I get so lucky?"

"Knock off the mushy stuff, Mom."

He shoved the rest of the banana toast in his mouth and chewed madly with his mouth wide open.

"Oh, so nice," Heather laughed. "You're also very gross."

She reached across and tweaked his nose, making him laugh and spit toast crumbs out on the table. Then they both started laughing. The song switched again. It was one of Heather's morning groove tapes, and the heavy bass of Peter Gabriel's "Sledgehammer" came on.

"You're a pretty cool mom. None of my friend's moms have this kind of music, or are artists."

"Yeah, but they probably have good jobs and take their kids on trips to Mexico."

"I don't want to go to Mexico."

She gave a half-smile. "Well, it's a good thing."

"Can I stay home this morning?"

"It's the end of the week, Zach. One more day and then you've got the weekend to hang out with your artsy mom."

Heather checked the clock above the oven.

"Shit. You better get going, you'll be late."

She ran and got Zach's backpack, shoving his lunch bag into it, gave him a big hug, and pushed him to the door.

"You said the 's' word."

"Yeah, yeah. Write a book about me when you're older."

Heather loved her mornings with Zach before school, or at least when they both got up early enough to spend time together. She didn't really care about vacations or buying Zach expensive toys or clothes. She just wanted him to be fed, clothed, and free of worry. Okay, maybe a trip to Mexico would be nice, too.

She turned up the tape player, this time to Paul Simon, loving the polyrhythms of "Graceland." Heather danced over to her drawing table, where she'd taped a piece of watercolor paper to a board. Last night after Zach had gone to bed, she drew more sketches of the warrior. Now that she'd met Gordo, the warrior had become something separate, a character that lived in her imagination. She drew the warrior on the streetcar platform, giving him long black hair tied back in a ponytail. Then she erased that and sketched in a traditional top knot she'd seen in Japanese art. There were other drawings of younger warriors on the paper, one that looked like the boy from Gordo's story.

Heather knew she should be working on a new promotional piece, a guy in a suit on a bridge, or something like Vince would do. Last week she'd invited Vince over to give her advice on her portfolio, tell her what she could do to improve her chances.

"You gotta give them something they can use, Robsen."

"But what do they want?"

"If I knew what A.D.'s wanted, I'd be swimming in work," he said.

Vince was getting work. He'd just scored his first cover, so Heather wasn't sure if he was being humble or if he was holding out secrets. The running joke between Vince's friends, all of whom were trying to break into the business too, was "How many illustrators does it take to screw in a light bulb? Six. One to do it, and five more to say, I could have done that." Heather had met a few of them, and though they tried to hide their competitive natures, they all had one. Whenever one of the newish crop of illustrators from one of the art schools scored a big job for a magazine, or even better, an annual report that paid thousands, they all pretended to be happy for them. Really happy. Fucking happy.

She knew she was just as competitive as they were. That was the reason she plied Vince for tips about how to get work from art directors. She wanted to score a cover, and then they could all be happy for her.

Heather darkened the lines of the warrior's long robe. A Toronto tourism ad was taped to her desk—a streetcar rumbling down King Street. She still planned on going to The Pearl to meet Gordo, but wanted to do a bit of work before she headed out. She grabbed her palette and began to mix a deep red to fill in the streetcar. Just as she was about to lay in a wash, the phone rang.

"Shit."

She quickly rinsed the brush, immediately sad for the lost pigment, but she wasn't about to let it harden on her Winsor 7.

"This is Heather. Oh, yes, I dropped it off last week. To be honest, I wasn't sure you liked anything, you didn't leave a— Hmm? The personal piece . . . yes, something new I've been working on. I wanted to show another side to the style. Half page? Really?"

She bit back the shout rising in her throat.

"Yes, yes, the budget is fine. Love to do it. I can come pick up the story this morning. Oh, what's the deadline? Sure."

Heather shook with excitement. Holy crap—*Canadian Business*—she never thought she'd get in there. They wanted a half page and it paid $750 for a feature, the most she'd got since she arrived. Okay, Vince, it turned out that wasn't such a bad idea to include the warrior drawing.

She tried to do a bit more work on the piece on her table but was too wired. The A.D. never told her when to come, so why not now? She skidded into the bathroom for a shower and was out the door in twenty minutes.

Chapter Eighteen

After exiting the club, we were questioned by authorities on what we had witnessed. These were given the name, the police. I told them that I knew the man as a doctor, saying that he had forced his way into my apartment. This brought them much concern, and they asked if the force was of a sexual nature. One of the taller police was aggressive to me. He had a lighter complexion than the other, with the red line of a scar running across his cheek like someone had drawn it on.

Joshua told me I didn't need to tell them anything, and not wanting to cause my friend concern, I told him that I would just explain what we saw. The police told me they wanted to ask me more questions and instructed me to get into their vehicle.

As the police drove me away, I spotted Joshua mouthing words to me.

"Where are we going?"

"We're going to take you to the station. Won't keep you too long," the shorter police, who was driving, said.

My pulse quickened. Was the station their word for what

Harry called the crazy house?

At the station, which seemed to be simply a place of gathering for other police, they asked me a number of questions. Then they asked if English was my first language and suggested that maybe I was the one that needed a doctor. I was uncertain what they meant by that. They did not offer me a ride, but simply sent me back onto the street.

I had a fitful sleep, as I thought about the Doctor and his presence. I knew that I would see him again.

—

Heather ran down Queen Street, gripping the envelope with the *Canadian Business* story. She'd been so excited about the job she'd completely forgotten about her meeting with Gordo.

She burst into The Pearl, too loud, she realized, as several people glared at her. At the back her new friend lifted his head and gave a barely perceptible nod.

"There is sweat on your face."

"Sorry. Something came up and then I almost forgot. I ran to get here." She took a breath, trying to release the tension in her chest.

"You did not need to come. Was there an emergency?"

"No, nothing like that. I know it's late—if you have to leave, it's okay."

"I have time."

The Pearl owner came and took her order of coffee, toast, and eggs, and poured more hot water for Gordo. Heather told him about the new assignment from *CB,* and how it was a huge step for her. Gordo listened intently, nodding and asking questions about her art. His soft voice added to the sincerity of his questions. She told him that illustration was more than a way to make money, but a way to express herself. But of course she had to make an income to support her and Zach.

"Tell me about your son. Is he also an artist?"

Heather laughed. "Hard to tell. For now he thinks his mom

is cool, but that will change."

"Why?"

"Teenagers always reach that point where their parents are the most un-cool part of their lives."

"I'm not sure I fully understand what is cool, though my friend has tried to explain it to me."

Heather rolled her eyes. "No one knows."

"Where is your son's father?" he asked, seemingly unaware of the forwardness.

"No offense, Gordo, I don't want to talk about that."

Gordo cast his eyes downward. "I am sorry to have offended you."

"No, it's okay. I just . . ." Her voice trailed off as the Queen Streetcar went by, washing out the sounds of knives and forks on plates. "Gordo, will you tell me the rest of the story you started yesterday?"

He took a sip of tea, lifted his head, then closed his eyes. Heather waited in the awkward silence, wondering if she had crossed over an invisible line. At least when her food came, she had something to focus on.

"You don't need to—"

"The lord and owner of the shōen visited the boy's small farm on the edge of his estate. Men brought him on a kago. He never left the perch as he spoke to the boy, his brother, and his father. The boy's mother had been gone for six years on that very day. The lord asked about a samurai. The father said yes, one had visited, and they were honored that his son would become one of the lord's retainers.

"Perhaps in time. He will need to be trained," the lord said.

"The lord of the shōen was from nobility, but things were much different in the farmland than in the courts in Heian-kyō. In that city, the lord would not have even granted them an audience.

"The family moved into living quarters on the estate, and the boy began his training. The samurai who gave the teaching

had held the chief position of retainer for a long time. The boy was unschooled in not only general knowledge, but in the physical, mental, and visual arts. Even at the boy's young age of ten, the world around him opened. He was so hungry to learn.

"Earth, wind, water, and fire. Do you know these?" the teacher asked the boy.

"Of course."

"You know little. I will teach you to respect them, and then to harness their power."

"The teacher noted the boy's patience and determination. The boy's mother had spoken of his perseverance. It was one of many fond memories he had of her."

Gordo stopped the story suddenly, clasped his fingers together on the table, and took long, slow breaths.

"Are you all right, Gordo?"

"Of course. It is just a story."

He quickly unfolded his hands and widened his eyes. The abrupt end of the story made it feel like it was time to go. She made up an excuse of needing to get back home, then wrote her number on a piece of paper and slid it across the table. Gordo studied it, but did not pick it up.

"I am here every morning."

"Okay."

Heather left The Pearl, walking into the din of drivers honking, and hordes of people trying to get across Queen Street.

Chapter Nineteen

The next days were full of work with the painters. I did not usually paint on the days known as weekends, not that it mattered to me. I welcomed long days of applying color to walls, if only to escape my fear of the Doctor's return. My thought of him grew distant as the days passed.

As the first day of a new week began, I awoke with her face floating above me. I reached out for her as she faded in the morning light. I had dreamed of the time before, when we sat together in a wide meadow. I was still a boy then, but two years of training had moved me closer to adulthood. Her beauty and poise were already evident in her youthful face. The breeze lifted her hair, and she laughed as she pinned it back into place. I asked her why she was laughing.

"My silly hair. It comes undone so much, that's all." Her expression changed. "You look sour."

"I don't think it is a time for lightness."

"Why? It's a beautiful day. Do you have a pain, or ate something bad from the table? Oh, I see . . . you are thinking of what happened."

Her voice was like a song that rose and fell.

"He was very young, only a few years older than me," I said, speaking of a tragedy that had happened on the estate.

She tilted her head. "Yes. And so?"

"And now he is gone."

"No. He is dead."

Her eyes narrowed as they did when she spoke in her teacher manner. Even though she was only a year older, she often took that tone with me. When her father passed by, he saw his daughter practicing her gift of wisdom with me, so he had no reason to suspect anything happening between us. I was a samurai in training. She was a teacher.

"It could happen at any time. To me or to you." I pointed at her, and then quickly lowered my finger.

"That is how death is," she said. "Did you think it was only for the old? Ha! I thought you were being trained in all things."

Her laughter at me brought color to my face.

"I do not mean to insult you," she said, the melody of her voice returning.

"It was an accident. It saddened me that it happened to someone so young."

"Are you afraid to die?"

"No," I replied.

My answer hung in the dry open meadow, a long echo rising into the sky, before it vanished in the clouds.

"I don't believe you," she said.

I gazed into the sky. I wanted to speak, but was silenced as she held a finger to her pursed lips. She pointed at my mouth. Sunlight glinted off her bottom lip like a luscious apple.

A gong sounded. The deep thrum came from the main house. She rose quickly, and I stood and jumped back. The gong rang again. Thunder rolled and the sky released a torrent of rain onto the meadow. We ran through a glorious sun shower back to the house.

I bolted upright in bed. I searched for the smell of flowers and rain, or her scent of citrus and sweet lavender. Her face, the meadow, everything disappeared. I was alone.

I moved into my morning rituals, beginning with a time kneeling on my mat and attempting to again distance myself from the spectre of the Doctor. In the meditation, another face appeared to me. Why had I chosen to tell her of my life? The woman, Heather, was very different from Joshua, but still there was a threat of revelation. There was always a threat of revelation.

Harry had been the one who told me of the place called the crazy house, where they took those who were unlike the other citizens, those the authorities deemed dangerous and in need of imprisonment. If I told Joshua or Heather of my true self, would they call those authorities? Would they think I was not of right mind?

Perhaps I had started to tell Heather about the time before so I could revisit it. The visit from the Doctor had pulled at the very fibers of my being, stretching my mind, body, and soul across a vast chasm, and I had begun to doubt my own thoughts. I did not want to forget. I was determined to return to my dear one. Once again we will run in the rain.

Arising from my mat, knowing that my mind would not be emptied this morning, I left my apartment.

To prepare to meet the Doctor again, which I surely would, I needed to return to my training. I saw what the Doctor had done to those men at the club when I was with Joshua. To keep my body in condition, I practiced movements in my apartment. But it was not the same as training with my teacher. As I walked along Queen Street, I recalled a place in this area that purported to be a school of training. A sign in their window read "Blue Sky Dojo." The dojo seemed a word that I should know. I had passed it before, and looked in the windows. It had the shape of a training place, though the materials that clad the floor and walls did not seem right. It was very different than the house where my teacher instructed me.

Perhaps today I would enter and ask about this dojo, find out their methods and beliefs. Was there a master? If I were to battle the Doctor, I needed much more than exercises and movements in my apartment.

I looked in the window, but the lights were off in the Blue Sky place, and a closed sign was placed in the window. I moved and peered into another window, one of the many coffee shops that lined the streets. I considered stopping to see if they had any tea, wanting to feel warm liquid in my body. A troublesome thought entered my mind. What if the Doctor had already returned to my apartment? What if he was there right now? I quickened my pace.

It was as if a current of energy pulsed through my body. I scanned the entryway to my apartment building and studied my window, searching for light or any sense of movement inside. Had he entered somehow, and now awaited? Entering my building, I remained alert. While standing on the platform where the keyed boxes were kept, a man in the apartment on the lower floor called up to me. I knew his voice from other times he'd spoken to me.

"Mail here yet?" the man asked, his voice rough and often punctuated with a cough.

"I will check for you," I called back.

He appeared in front of me, dressed in a shabby robe, a cigarette dangling from his lips. His name was Louis. I turned my key and opened the small door to my mailbox to find a single letter. It was addressed to "Occupant," which I had learned meant nothing.

"Yes, it has arrived," I said.

There were shuffling noises and more coughing. Louis stared at me, and I wondered his intent until I understood I was in his way.

"I'm sorry."

"Somebody came lookin' fer ya," he said.

"For me? Who was it?"

"Damned if I know. I let him in because he banged on the effin' door for fifteen minutes."

He pushed past me to the mailboxes and inserted his key into the tiny lock.

"Did he say what he wanted?" I asked.

"Nope. He said your name and what you looked like. I pointed upstairs. I told him you probably weren't home. I also told him to not bang on the doors."

"How did you know I wasn't home?"

"I hear people come in. You learn a person's sounds. You're real quiet when you enter, like you don't want anyone to know."

"You sent him to my apartment?"

Louis took out a small bundle of mail. "Well, you weren't there anyway. You sound nervous. You owe this guy money?"

"No. I am not sure I even know him. What did he look like?"

"He looked like a pain in the ass 'cause that's what he was. I'm not standing here in the hallway to jaw about him. You got problems, deal with him. But tell the son-of-a-bitch to stop banging on doors."

"I'm sorry. I will tell him if I see him again."

"Yeah, yeah."

Louis went back downstairs. I looked upward to my apartment, but did not venture up the stairs. This was perhaps the energy I had felt. He had been in my apartment, and maybe was still there. Louis hadn't said if the man left, and I hadn't wanted to irritate him further, so I climbed the stairs to my apartment. I forced my muscles to loosen, but to remain poised, ready to react if needed.

My door was locked, and there was no sign of entry, no wood slivers on the floor or scratches on the handle. I opened the door and pushed it away from me. My teacher told me to always be aware when entering a room, and to imagine the person on the other side, ready to strike. I stood there, watching for shadows, listening for any movement, even the sound of a breath. With proper concentration I was able to hear the heartbeat of another.

On my apartment floor lay a yellow square of paper with thin lines. Bending at the waist, keeping my gaze upward, I picked up the paper. I carried it with me, aware that there was writing on the other side, but not reading it until I could be certain I was alone.

I went into my empty kitchen, filled a kettle for tea. Finally satisfied that no one was in the apartment, I steeped the tea. The message must have been slipped under my door. I breathed in the rich scent of green leaves, willing the fragrance to calm my mind. I began to read.

Gordon,

Our first meeting went badly. I was probably too aggressive, but I needed to be sure you were who you said you were.

You misunderstood what I wanted from you.

You were in that nightclub last night. I meant to talk to you. But people in this City are assholes.

We have to meet again. I came by your apartment but you were gone, maybe on purpose. Meet me tomorrow afternoon, at 2:00, on Yonge Street near Dundas, by the row of chess tables. I'm sure your friend knows where it is.

Don't disappoint me. Come. Unless you're already happy with your life.

It was signed at the bottom, *A. Shepherd, MD.* And under his name a line, and the words, *"Bring me back my case."*

The message was written in black ink, in small precise letters. Even though it was written in the City's language, it reminded me of the calligraphy I studied for many years.

. . . who you said you were. What did he mean? And why had he not mentioned the encounter by the streetcar? Surely he saw me. He said my friend knew where the chess tables were. Did he mean Joshua? If he saw us together, it meant that he'd been following me.

I sipped at my tea and read the letter again, this time more slowly. My face grew hot. Why would he say that about being happy with my life? Heat from my face traveled down my neck, shoulders, and into my arms and fingertips, transferring onto the yellow square of paper.

Meeting the Doctor on the street felt safer than in my apartment. The area he named was one of the most congested parts of the City. I had seen men gather there to play the game of chess on the concrete boards. I understood the game, yet in another form. Some of the players were old, while others, young and full of bravado, smoked cigarettes and slid their hands through long greasy hair.

I should warn Joshua—but how to explain? If I went and met the Doctor, heard him explain the nature of the work he believed we needed to continue, then it would be over. Though I had no idea why there was such urgency, I would grant the Doctor an audience.

I finished the tea, folded the letter, and put it into a drawer where I stored other important pieces of mail. I retrieved the Doctor's case from under my bed. I opened it and studied a few more of the pages. They revealed nothing.

Tomorrow, I would go to Yonge Street and face him. This day, I would resume my formal training, as so much of my discipline had faded.

Chapter Twenty

I felt in my body the rigorous training that I'd begun last night. Perhaps I tried to do too much too soon. Still, I needed to prepare for whatever awaited me. My first meeting with the Doctor had shown me that my senses had dulled.

Leaving the subway and carrying the Doctor's case made me feel like someone I was not. How similar this feeling was to when I arrived in the City, when I learned that people did not see me in my original form as a citizen of the shōen. When I first observed my reflection in a glass, it was a shock. How did I inhabit this skin? Now, more than a thousand days later, carrying a case that wasn't mine, I was about to confront a person that might know my other self. The blank pages in the case were a lie the Doctor attempted to push upon me. I knew that my true self was trapped within this skin I wore.

I made my way through the crowd, up the moving stairs, and out into the bright afternoon sun. No one took notice of me. An older woman held my gaze for a moment, but then quickly turned away. This was the way of the City. I was foolish to think that holding a black case would change how the citizens saw me. Yonge Street was a river of people, entering and exiting onto the tributaries, places of business lit with garish signs. Merchants beckoned the pedestrians to enter and purchase their wares of electronics, foods, or cheap metals. The movement and general din was not dissimilar to the marketplace near the shōen.

The chess tables were nestled beside a large building with tall windows. The area by the building was lit by a giant spinning red disk. Joshua had brought me here several times. The glowing disk represented the small disks that were sold inside. This was where Joshua bought his plastic boxes with ear pieces that produced the music for his personal listening. He offered to buy me such a device, but I told him I preferred the sounds of the street, or silence, over the constant din of music. I may have insulted him, though that wasn't my intent.

I stopped in front of the music place, scanning the people within, hoping and then not hoping I would see Joshua inside. I didn't want to expose my friend to the danger of the Doctor. I believed this man held a knowledge that could cause harm, not only to me, but anyone in his proximity. When I turned the corner, there he was, seated at one of the concrete tables with chess pieces laid out. He still wore the dark suit and white shirt, but now had a red strip of cloth draped over his shoulders. It struck me odd that he wore what Joshua called a scarf. I'd seen other men wear them, but only during the winter months.

The other tables were full of players, and a few onlookers who smoked and watched the games. As I brushed past one, he muttered something I couldn't make out. I sat across from the Doctor, the pieces arranged in their original places, as if anticipating this moment. I set his case next to my stone chair.

"You play?" the Doctor asked.

"My friend has shown me the moves. I am familiar with the game."

"Ha. I bet you play Shogi."

I studied the Doctor's expression. His eyes were blue suns

rimmed with black, his mouth a straight line.

"Have you asked me here to play chess?"

"Something to do while we talk."

He moved a pawn forward, to which I responded.

We played our opening moves in silence. The people nearby punctuated the air with their voices. At one point, one of the onlookers came to our table. The Doctor raised his arm and waved him away. I thought there would be a confrontation, but the other man made a scoffing sound and left us for another table.

"I'm not who you think I am," the Doctor said.

"Perhaps you should explain your identity."

"You've got my case. Did you look at the papers?"

"Many of them are blank."

"So you wondered how I read them?"

I moved a knight into position.

"I did not wonder. I saw that you were lying. You don't know me, and you never have. And you are not a doctor. You are playing a game, as we are now."

Another onlooker turned his face away from a game to look at us. The Doctor ignored him and made another move.

"Don't you wonder who I am? Or why I asked you to come here?"

"Yes. But I have little patience for this. If you're here to tell me something, or accuse me, then do it. I came as you asked, and I am open to your words. But if you threaten me, it will be you who is in peril."

The Doctor laughed. "Listen to the way you talk. *You who is in peril.* Do you talk to your friends like that? Look, you're as pale as they are. Hell, you even have that God-awful red in your hair."

The Doctor slammed down his bishop.

"Pinned your queen."

"What?"

I studied the board to see that the Doctor already had the

upper hand.

"I came to see you because I know who you are," he said.

"You came to threaten me with lies. Saying you were a doctor and that I was under your care. You tried to make me doubt myself and question my mind."

"But you saw through it, Gordon."

There was nothing I could do to save my queen. My mind was not focused on the game.

"What do your friends call you?"

"My friend calls me Gordo."

"Then I'll call you that. I come as a friend."

"Then explain why you carried a medical needle? Or why you forced your way into the music club. Had you followed me? Or what about your taunt from the streetcar? Explain that and tell me you are not a liar."

The Doctor leaned back, twisting his body from side to side, the bones emitting cracks.

"Gordo . . ." He waited to see how I would react to this name, then continued, "Like I said, I'm not who you think I am."

"I already know you are not a doctor."

"I'm also not an enemy. We're more alike than you realize. And now that I know you're the Gordon Clement I was looking for . . . well, we can help each other."

"How did you come upon my name?"

"I was told it by someone."

"Do I know this person?"

"I doubt it. Just another one of the sheep that roam this shithole."

I didn't know what to ask next; without my queen, I'd already lost. I castled on the left side. We played in silence, the pieces clicking on the concrete table and the voices of other players the only sounds present.

The Doctor picked up my king and rotated it in the air, then pointed the wooden crown at my eyes.

"Gyokusho. You know the name?"

I breathed deeply. Behind the Doctor a milkweed bloomed, its purple flowers a stark contrast to the gray stone.

"I've heard of it," I said.

The smell of burning tobacco, the smoke from a bus, and the sweat from the other chess players filled my nostrils. These scents kept me alert, kept me prepared.

"And why do you know this name?" I asked the Doctor.

"As a young boy, my grandfather taught me the rules of Shogi," the Doctor began, "a more complex and much more rewarding game than this Western impersonation. How old were you when you learned?"

The Doctor's words assaulted my mind, as he tried to force me to reveal myself. Again I focused my breath on that which surrounded me.

"Am I losing you? I said how old—"

"My father taught my brother and I."

The Doctor's mouth curved upward. "Well, well. Look at us two white Canadians both being schooled in the ancient game. How likely is that?"

"I don't have the patience—"

"Fuck patience." He slammed the king back down on the concrete board, cracking the wooden piece. "Tsumi. Or if you'd rather, checkmate."

One of the onlookers turned quickly and came to us. The man's jeans were ragged, streaked with white lines. When he saw the broken piece, he laughed. He stood over the board, puzzled by what he saw.

"It's a pisser. The only game where you can feel like a genius one moment and a moron the next. How about I play the winner?" the man asked.

"There are no winners," the Doctor said.

The Doctor scooped up the pieces and pushed them into a bag with a drawstring. He flipped his scarf over, reached down, and took his case back.

"Hey, I was just asking," the man said.

"Fuck off."

The man stepped back as if he'd been struck. He looked like he was going to respond, but must have seen something in the Doctor's eyes that made him stop.

I held up my hand to the man. "I'm sorry."

The Doctor grabbed my hand and pushed it down.

"Let's go. I'll show you the one good thing I've discovered here."

Chapter Twenty-One

I followed the Doctor down Yonge Street, taking long strides to keep pace with him. He swung his case back and forth like a pendulum. I had the thought to turn the other way and disappear up the clogged street, but I wanted to learn what he knew about me, and how he came by this information.

"This is it. Not the best, but good for around here. The best is on Harbord, but that's too far of a walk."

We entered into an eating establishment. This one, like many in the City, served the disks of cooked flour, tomatoes, meat, and cheese. I had eaten pizza with Joshua, and after the initial surprise of heat and flavor, I neither loved it nor hated it. The City seemed to exist on it.

"When I go back, I'll carry the knowledge of this food."

The Doctor set down two triangles on one of the small tables.

"Go back where?" I asked.

"Have you had this? It's fucking amazing. That's what they say." The Doctor took huge bites, chewing and savoring.

"Not from here. But yes, I've eaten this before."

"Ha! Still only rice and fish, right? I'll eat this three times a day—especially the good ones."

The pizza was particularly flavorful, much more than others I'd tried. The Doctor's demeanor had shifted with his apparent delight of the food. His body was looser, his shoulders eased. Watching an opponent move like this, I considered that either their focus had drifted or their confidence was so strong they thought themselves invincible.

I forced my shoulders to relax, doubting that he would attack me in such a place. But doubt can lead to a loss of readiness, and then to defeat. "You say you will go back. Explain where. And you still haven't explained how you know Shogi."

"In a moment. I need another. You?"

I shook my head.

On his return, he set the pizza down and inhaled deeply. His eyes returned to their intensity shown during the chess game.

"Gordo, I've been in this place for ten years. This spring will make it eleven. I know you've been here for a much shorter time. When I found out about your arrival, it took a while to track you down."

"My arrival from where?"

"Cut the bullshit. That's another thing they say here." The Doctor's mouth spread into a grin. "I know what happened to you because the same thing happened to me. You could say I made it happen. Ha."

The Doctor picked up his pizza and took a deep bite. He wiped the tomato sauce from his chin.

"What did you make happen?" I asked.

"The crossover."

Words sprang into my mind, but I didn't say them. I studied his face, trying to see inside him.

"You are from my home?"

A tremor moved through my soul.

"You still call it home. Well, that's something."

"I don't understand."

The Doctor made a heavy sigh. "I gained some information, first by accident, and then I sought after it."

"What kind of information?"

The Doctor took two more huge bites, ignoring my question, and continued.

"You ever think of living forever, Gordo?"

"I don't know."

"Of course you have. Everyone does."

He waited for a reaction that I did not give, then continued.

"Okay, you want to be dense. I'll lay it out for you."

"Please do."

"After a series of events, I found myself amidst a great battle."

"What kind of events?"

The Doctor put down his food and stared at me, again looking for something in my gaze. He twitched as if something had bitten his neck.

"So, I'm in the service of my land-greedy lord. He decides to put pressure on the other village twenty miles away, or kilometers, or who knows how the hell we measured things back then. The longer I stay here, names and numbers slip away from me. So the lord wants all of his retainers, including me, to go find the champions in that village. You know how that was done?"

I did not respond. His speech was rushed, smooth, like others talked in the City.

"Then we were ambushed. The bastard of a lord knew we'd be attacked. Not that he cared. Most of us were struck down right away. My friends drowned in their own blood in an empty meadow. Myself and three of the strongest fought back. We were beginning to turn the tide, and get the upper hand, when the arrow pierced my neck."

"But how—"

"Exactly. Observe." The Doctor tilted his head. "Not a mark on this body. I guess it worked."

"What worked?"

"The deed I executed made this possible."

"I don't understand."

"The darkness came upon me. Music came from somewhere, the sky, the ground, who the hell knows? Then a flash, an explosion of light, and then a flood of bright green color."

The Doctor's lips parted as he mouthed something unheard.

"What are you saying?" The tremor inside me grew. "I can't hear you."

"I spoke in a language you know."

"What language?"

"I said the same happened to you. Ha, I see this on your face. When you crossed over, you believed you'd come to the afterplace. Am I right?"

I said nothing.

"There I lay, on my back, clouds swam across the sky, the music had silenced. Just like you, I expected some of my ancestors to come and greet me."

"But they never did," I said.

"No. And neither did yours, because we were not dead. We had crossed over."

The breath I'd been holding escaped into a long exhale.

"You are samurai."

"Just like you, Gordo."

The establishment was empty except for the woman with dark hair and a stained apron, who pushed another pizza into the large oven. She averted her gaze when I turned to her, so I couldn't tell if she'd been listening.

"You've not explained how you found me—or why you told me I was not in my right mind."

"You don't have to talk quietly. No one around here gives a shit. We can say anything we want. People in this city say crazy things all the time."

"Why did you pretend to be a doctor?"

"I told you. I needed confirmation."

"Of what kind?"

"You think you're the only Gordon Clement in Toronto? Shit, I was beginning to think I needed to try another city—until you called me."

"Who gave you this name? My name."

"Doesn't matter. But I'll tell you, one guy I found didn't take my doctor routine too kindly. Fucker pulled a knife on me."

"There is another Gordon Clement? Where does he live?"

"Again, doesn't matter." The Doctor looked over to the counter. "You know her?"

I shook my head.

"Hmm." The Doctor studied the woman before turning back to me. "Listen, I didn't know if you were going to be another crazy fucker with a knife. So I told you about me being your doctor, and if things got rough, well . . ."

"You would inject me with the needle."

"Sure." The Doctor faked a smile. "But forget about all that. You were the one I was looking for."

"On the street, you saw me outside the streetcar. And then at the music place with my friend . . . you've been following me."

"I'm playing the long game. I wanted to intrigue you, have you come looking for me. And here you are."

"You said my life depended on it."

"It does. Your old life. How'd you like to return to it?"

So many images rushed into my mind I had to close my eyes to regain focus. How could he make this offer?

"This is something you can do?" My voice held the tremor that had grown inside my body.

The Doctor smiled.

"Not yet, but I'm putting it together. I see you finally believe me. How does it feel to be a little less alone?"

I jerked my body back as if I'd touched a flame.

"I did not say I believed anything. I am a man living in this City. I've been overseas." I spit out the words, a flush moving across my face and down my neck. My hands clenched.

"For fuck's sake, Gordo, you asked if I was samurai."

The Doctor crammed another bite of pizza in his mouth, staring at me as he chewed and swallowed.

"Besides the pizza, I do like their profanity. Fuck is an excellent word. Now look, I've found another who is like us, but much older. He has told me things."

"We are not like each other."

"He's been in this shithole longer than me. Much longer. But he arrived here the same way as us."

"I did not arrive in any way."

"Stop it. I know who you are and you know it. I met this man and he told me a very similar story to my own, except it was many more years ago. He also ended up in a field wondering where the hell he was. He crossed over. Just like we did."

It was as if I was balanced on a thin rope above a high chasm. This man who called himself a doctor could either save me or push me into the darkness.

"Even if the fantasy you speak of is true, then what of it? Why do you need me?"

"Death. It's about death, Gordo. That's how it happens."

"I don't understand."

The Doctor slapped the table with his open hand; the woman pulling a pizza out of the oven glanced toward us. The Doctor lowered his voice.

"Okay, you want me to spell it out? Me and you, we return to this old man, and we create our own opportunity."

"What opportunity are you suggesting?"

The Doctor took in a long slow breath. "We kill him. Then we go back home. As simple as that."

My breath was trapped in my chest, as my desires were ripped in opposite directions. If what the Doctor was proposing was true, and all it took to return was the death of one old man . . . could I do this?

"You still with me, Gordo?"

Flashes of light appeared in my peripheral vision. When the

chimes of the door sounded, I thought I was imagining it all, until I saw a woman walk in. I recognized her immediately.

Why her, why now?

"Excuse me, I'm sorry to interrupt you—"

The Doctor raised his hand to wave her away like he did to the chess onlooker.

"It's okay. I know her." It was a struggle to speak, as if I were swimming out of the depths of a lake.

"Well, I don't. See him another time," the Doctor said to her.

"Oh, I'm so sorry. I'll go," she said.

"Wait, wait, wait." I forced air into my lungs. "You don't have to leave. Join us."

"What the fuck are you doing? This woman is of no consequence."

She turned her head quickly. I saw tightness in her shoulders.

"There's no need to be an asshole. I said I was leaving," she said.

The woman from the counter called over. "There a problem? You people can take it outside."

My head throbbed with pressure—it was as if the room held its breath.

"I need to think," I said.

The Doctor stood.

"You hopeless shit. This is more important than anything else you are involved in here." He flipped his hand toward me. "Fine, speak to this woman."

"Don't talk to him like that," she said.

"Contact me when you decide to be serious, Gordo."

He brushed past the woman toward the door.

"How will I contact you?"

"Not my problem."

And with that he was gone into the street, swept up in the river of people. My chest relaxed, and I took my first full breath. The room eased its tension, and the lights in my peripheral vision were extinguished.

"Sorry I broke into your important conversation. But your friend didn't need to be a jerk."

"He is not my friend." I held out my empty palm toward the chair. "Join me."

"Are you sure?"

"Do you like pizza, Heather?"

Chapter Twenty-Two

"Yes, I do like pizza—but I feel bad that I chased your friend away," she said.

"He's not a friend."

"Who is he?"

"Not a good man," Gordo said.

He got up from the table to order a slice for her.

"You don't have to do that."

The small pizza place was like a hundred others she had walked by, mostly catering to take-out, with a few round tables. At least this one had actual tablecloths as opposed to plastic or bare wood. She was surprised to see Gordo inside, and had rushed in without thinking who he might be with.

"Anyway, I'm sorry."

"I am glad you arrived. My time was done with that other man. He told me some upsetting things."

"Like what?"

"It matters little."

"Was that man the one you said was a doctor?"

Her words rushed out of her. She wondered if she'd interrupted some sort of therapy session.

"He's a man that I don't care for. But I am forced to communicate with him."

"Sorry. I'm out of line."

"There is no need to apologize about lines. I see that your pizza is ready."

Gordo brought it back to the table and put it in front of her.

"Some people like to put this on it." He slid over the shaker of Parmesan.

She didn't tell him that she'd eaten about a thousand slices since she'd arrived in Toronto. She bit into the hot pizza and burned the top of her mouth.

"Ow!"

"It's best to wait."

She laughed. "Ha, it seems you're right."

Gordo leaned back in his chair as she ate. Two teenagers, a short boy and a girl with her hair tied back, came into the pizza place and sat at the table across from them. Gordo looked at them, then suddenly dropped his gaze and sat up straight in his chair.

"I've sat too long. Do you want to walk with me?" he asked.

"Uh, sure. Where?"

"Just to walk. You can bring your pizza."

Heather shoved the rest in her mouth, then smiled, aware she looked like a chipmunk. She thought he would laugh, but he simply stood and walked out of the pizza place. She crumpled the paper plate and went after him.

They walked the noisy stretch of Yonge, weaving their way in and out of the throng, and past the shouting prophets in front of the Eaton Centre.

"I used to stop and listen to them," Gordo said, "but then I realized they were speaking nonsense."

"End of the world stuff," she said.

"They talk of a God coming. And how this God will destroy

many, and save few. That seems very unlikely. I don't know how they would come upon this knowledge."

"I think they had rotten childhoods, or bad drugs, or who knows what."

"Perhaps. I learned nothing of this kind of God."

"Did you go to some sort of religious college?"

Gordo didn't answer her. He studied a man in a long coat who had been speaking very fast to the crowd. A man in a brush cut, wearing a leather jacket, told one of the prophets to fuck off, and grabbed the man's black coat. The fast-talking one swung out at the brush cut man and clipped his forehead. Gordo took a step forward.

"Don't," she said.

"I can stop this without harming them," he said.

"I know."

She put her hand on Gordo's hand. He pulled back and turned to her. The brush cut man flipped off the fast talker, stepped back, and walked quickly away. The prophets returned to shouting out their warnings.

She took her hand off of Gordo's. "Okay if we leave? These guys give me a headache."

"Yes. There's a park where I often go. If you don't mind the walk, we can go there and continue our conversation."

As they moved away from Yonge, the number of people thinned, as did the noise. Heather's curiosity burned in her, creating a physical tingling as they walked and talked. She knew he was a bit odd, he might have some problems, or he could even be quite ill. But she also found him deeply intriguing.

She had a million questions, including where he learned to fight like he did the night after the bluegrass band.

"I visit this park every day. Unless the weather is bad."

They entered into the small park on the Grange: children climbed through a tunnel and onto a set of geometric boxes, a pair of women chatted on a bench next to the kids.

"I've walked by, but never spent any time here. It's lovely."

She followed Gordo over to a bench under a canopy of elm trees. A light breeze rustled the leaves above, mixed with the sounds of children laughing and squirrels chittering. Except for the streetcar rumbling down Queen Street, she could imagine being back home in the park that ran alongside the river in her small town.

"Have you been reading more of that story?" she asked.

"Reading?"

"The one you were telling me about the boy becoming a samurai."

"Oh yes." He picked up a leaf, twirling it in the air. "Why do you ask?"

"I liked it. I've actually been working on some drawings. Someone I call the warrior."

When he didn't respond for a few moments, she feared that her question had triggered something within.

"It is a sad story," he said.

"That's okay. Stories that mean something often have a sadness."

He held up the leaf to her.

"The lines that radiate out have such a beauty." He paused, then added, "Would you like me to tell you more?"

"I would."

She followed his gaze past the leaf he was holding and over to the children.

"The lord of the shōen had a daughter. Though his family suspected nothing, his teacher had observed the boy's growing interest. In the middle of a training session, the teacher told the boy to be careful of his steps. The boy feigned confusion.

"Then show me how to step," the boy said.

"The teacher told the boy it was not his walking, but the path he was on. The lord's daughter was one year older than the boy, and like a lotus in morning, she was opening into a young woman.

"The boy fought against the urges, swimming in the cold

lake outside the village—twice, three times a day even. His lazy brother asked what he did that required such frequent bathing. The brother and father laughed, knowing that a boy of that age would experience sexual temptation. Had they known the source of temptation, they would not have found it amusing. The boy put his entire family at risk.

"His teacher taught of two kinds of willpower, one without and one within. The boy felt he had neither. Living on the same grounds, the boy and the lord's daughter came across each other often. This was different than in the courts, where men and women were isolated. On the shōen, far away from the Imperial Court, daily lives overlapped. Over the years, glances became stares, looks became words, and then a touch of a hand on a robe, or a bare arm. They met together under the trees within the estate."

Gordo pointed to the canopy that arced above them.

"Very much like these trees, though the leaves were of another shape."

"Please go on," Heather said.

"The lord saw the boy with his daughter. He believed she shared her gift of wisdom as part of the boy's training. The father did not know of their conversations in the shade of the trees that bordered the outer walls of the grounds.

"The teacher corrected the boy during lessons, telling him he'd lost focus. One late afternoon, after a long physical session, there was a confrontation. The teacher saw what burned within the boy, and how desire obscured the true danger. The boy promised he would focus, telling his teacher he did not mean any dishonor.

"This is not about honor."

"He looked like he was about to strike the boy.

"Have I not taught you how to detach from your desires? Following our desires is the path to destruction."

Heather heard Gordo's voice quicken.

"The danger is not in your becoming a samurai. It's in your

not becoming."

"I'd never heard my teacher's voice so full of anger. I felt as if . . . I mean, the boy felt as if—"

Gordo stopped suddenly. His voice had gotten louder as he repeated the teacher's words. The women on the bench were looking in their direction and gesturing.

"Gordo. Who is the boy?"

"What do you mean?" His eyes widened. "He is just a boy."

"Who is this story about?"

Heather kept her voice quiet. She wanted to touch his hand again, but held back.

"I'm sorry. I need to go now. The story is about no one. It is like you said, something I have read. In a library."

Gordo jerked up from the bench and headed toward the entrance to the park. She watched his fluid stride. As much as she desired it, she knew not to follow.

Even before he'd made the slip, she had guessed. This was Gordo's story—or that is what he believed.

Before

Chapter Twenty-Three

Shikoku, 1185

My teacher had been giving me instruction for six years, and we—my father, brother, and I—were settled on the lord's estate. I sat alone under a beech tree outside the shōen, and from the long grass, I plucked a yellow flower and twisted it in the sunlight. In the distance, I spotted my father walking the road toward me.

"This is how you spend your time now? Daydreaming in the middle of the afternoon while your brother and I sweat?"

"My teacher is traveling. He will be back tomorrow," I said.

"That gives you the permission to sit on your rump and look at flowers?"

I tossed the small plant behind me.

"What do you want, Father?"

My father knew that increasingly I paid more attention to the words of my teacher than his.

"Why do you assume I want something? You languish under a tree as if the world is your own. Have you risen so far above us?"

"It was your choice that I go with the samurai to train, and then eventually work for the lord."

"We all work for the lord. Your brother and me included."

"I doubt my brother works much."

My father scowled at the remark. Not looking at me, he spat on the ground and walked away.

That day, I left my spot under the beech tree and followed my father out of the estate, onto the road leading to a village where there was a market. I recall some of our conversation from that fateful day, but parts of the talk have been cut out like squares from paper.

Arriving at the market, smells arose from cooking pots of food mixed with sweat from the merchants and their animals, the clang of blades being sharpened, fabrics hit with sticks, the buzz of flies, the briny scent of fish—I delighted in it all.

My father spoke with a merchant about a basket of fruit.

"The freshest pomegranates you will find anywhere," the merchant said.

"I do not mean to insult, but last week the number in the basket was greater," my father replied. My father often engaged in these conversations. Swapping stories of the growing seasons of different fruits and vegetables—subtly asking, so as to not insult, for a slightly better price.

"Are you from the nearby shōen?" the merchant asked.

"Of course. We have spoken before."

"Ahh, then you work for the lord. So you must know the season is ending."

Around us, voices rose and fell, swallowed up by the sound of other hawkers and shouters. In one spot a hooded man sat across from an old man with a long mustache. The older one stirred a boiling pot of what smelled like tea leaves, or perhaps an earthy herb. I moved away from my father's conversation with the merchant to get closer to the two men.

"You are here seeking work," said the older man to the other, giving the pot a stir with a wooden stick.

I knew this one: he was Sanjo, a giver of prophesies. The hooded man wore a deep red sash around his waist, the tail of which dangled away from his black robe.

"No. Try again." The hooded man's voice was deep.

Sanjo stopped stirring.

"So you are escaping from somewhere . . . the North. And now you find yourself in need of shelter."

"Guesses in the wind. You know nothing, old man." He reached across and grabbed the old man's stick. "Enough prophecy. Tell me if you've heard of the family for which I inquired."

"Yes, I know of them."

"And they come to this market?" The hooded man looked at me, his eyes intense. I turned my head away to the basket seller in the next stall.

"Yes. I've seen them here," said Sanjo. "What do you want from them?"

"There is a young boy, almost a man. He has something I desire."

I looked over my shoulder to see Sanjo ease the stick out of the hooded man's hand and return to stirring his dark liquid. He held out his free hand to receive a gold coin from the other.

"Yes. I've seen this boy today. He has the wide shoulders of a man. Long, unkempt hair. Dressed in robes the color of dirt."

He could have been talking about me, yet no one would call me almost a man, would they? I moved my body behind one of the baskets.

"And where will I find him?"

"I saw him by the southern edge, in the direction of the animal pens."

The hooded man moved so fast he toppled the chair.

"Go."

Had the soothsayer spoken to me? I looked quickly around and saw no one else. Sanjo pointed in the direction the hooded man had run. He stared into my eyes.

"Go."

I jumped up, pushing my way through the crowd, eliciting shouts as bodies pressed back on me. The man's red sash fluttered behind him as he strode through the market. I moved through the sea of people, anticipating openings in the crowd, sliding between bodies, getting closer to the hooded man. All the while, Sanjo's command rang in my ears.

"Go."

Ahead of me the booths became more spread out, the crowd thinner. I stopped short, almost running into the back of a woman carrying a sack of food. She cussed at me. I thought I'd lost the man, until, a number of yards away, I saw that he'd taken off his sash and wrapped it around his hand. His back to me, he spoke to another young man, about my height but broader in stature. The hooded man, clad in black, stepped to the side. I found myself staring into the profile of my brother.

Why had he come to the market this day? Why hadn't my father told me he was here? Had he planned to meet us? He should have been back home on the estate. This was the day my father and I visited the market by ourselves. He should have been back at the lord's place, doing his work. Instead, my brother was in the market, talking to the hooded man. What business could they have? My brother looked in my direction, but he didn't acknowledge me. Perhaps I was too far away, or the sun was in his eyes. But then my brother began to walk toward me. At the same moment, the hooded man turned and unraveled the sash from his wrist.

My brother opened his mouth to speak when the man stopped him short, the sash twisted and wrapped around my brother's neck. His eyes widened. He opened his mouth, trying to speak, and his tongue reached for air inside his too-black mouth.

I held out my hands to my brother, frozen in fear. The man gave the sash a final twist. My brother's eyes went dark, and he slid to the ground. The man untied the sash and wrapped it like a serpent's tongue around his waist. I was only a few hand-lengths away, and yet the distance seemed a vast field. I wanted to move, but the wave of shock paralyzed my young body. I was only a boy, what could I have done to prevent the killing of my brother?

The man lowered his hood and spoke to me, only two words—

"Too late."

Then with several long strides, he slipped into the crowd and was gone.

Chapter Twenty-Four

Toronto, 1970s

He awoke on a field of grass. Only moments before, he'd been on the battlefield, surrounded by men without limbs, their moans echoing like a never-ending gong, the smell and taste of death acrid on his tongue. His body was pierced with arrows, his lifeforce draining onto the cracked ground. In his third decade of life, he believed his time was over. But instead, he now stared into a sky so bright it hurt his eyes. He was no longer bleeding, nor did he feel pain.

Where was he?

He thought back to what had happened. The old man in the market, Sanjo, had talked of a crossover, a way to extend his time far beyond old age.

"However, this only happens to those from samurai lineage," Sanjo had said.

"I am samurai."

"I hear the lie in your voice. But no matter. What is your reason?" Sanjo had asked him.

"Ha, idiot! Why wouldn't one want to live forever?" He had fought the urge to grab him by the throat.

"The crossover is not living forever, but a similarity. There is a cost, which in time you will realize," Sanjo replied.

The old man had spoken in riddles, right up until he slit his throat.

But now. Where was he? And what of this promised immortality? Why had it failed? He did what was required. He killed the boy. Sanjo had lied.

Rising from this new field, he understood that death had brought him to the afterplace. Given the life he'd led, he knew a punishment from some form of deity awaited him. Except there was no trial or punishment. This was not the afterplace. He had not died, but had awakened into a city full of wonders never before witnessed, nor even dreamed.

In those first days, the strangeness of the City bore down on him, with its odd language, strange machines, structures that rose into the sky, and constant barrage of noise. He stumbled through the streets, needing to steal from markets to get food, to defecate in hidden places, and wash in a lake of brown water. Wonders and dreams turned into nightmares as he struggled to stay alive in a City full of mindless citizens who chattered and raced around him.

As the years passed, his disorientation moved into understanding, and he began to unlock the mysteries of this place. He didn't know how or why he had arrived in this City, but he no longer wondered. As his knowledge grew, he came to understand that as mind-numbingly inane as its citizens were, this civilization had advanced far beyond anything he'd encountered in all his travels.

Considering the new world he lived in, two thoughts emerged. First, how might he harness this power, control it, and master its unbelievable strength to destroy others? And second, how would he return so he could unleash this power?

He set out to learn as much as he could of the City, notably what he came to know as *science*. Along with the gaining of this knowledge, he worked to unlock the secrets of the crossover. However, the secret of how he had traveled over a huge span of time existed outside of the laws of nature. Still, he was a man of tenacity. He believed he could discover how such a thing happened.

He spent many hours in buildings that were repositories of information. He spoke, read, and now comprehended the language of the City. He had picked up the citizens' way of talking with their clipped sentences and curse words. In his study, he came across the word "doctor." This type held the balance of life and death of the citizens in their hands. He decided it was fitting that he take on this name.

A decade passed in the City. The vast knowledge he had gained would give him a power more deadly than any land owner, daimyo, or even an emperor. But he still did not know how to return. In the last year, a new idea had emerged. If he'd made the crossover, others would as well. Perhaps some had already arrived. Sanjo told him they would be samurai. He believed they would easily stand out in this city of mindless serfs. The Doctor, as he now called himself, would acquire information from them—even if he had to rip it from their bodies.

Chapter Twenty-Five

Toronto, 1981

I awoke from a sleep of utter darkness, void of any dreaming. No longer in the ravine, I was stretched out on a bed and covered with a thin blanket that scratched my skin. Who brought me here? Next to me were other beds, some occupied with sleepers, several of which snored loudly. One of the beds had another bed resting on posts above it. There a man sat, his head and shoulders drooped, whether out of exhaustion, sadness, or apathy, I couldn't tell.

The strange language once again flowed out of me.

"Is this the afterplace?" I asked.

"Ha. Yes siree, buddy. It's the place after you ain't got nowhere fuckin' else to go."

He had a thin roll of paper shoved in his mouth. I observed that it was on fire, and when he removed it from his mouth, he exhaled smoke.

"Have you been in this place long?" I asked.

"Long enough to know it sucks."

The man abruptly swung his legs around and jumped off the high bed. He stared at a small reflective device that was strapped to his wrist with a piece of leather.

"Lunch's up. Let's go see what they're slopping on plates."

When I didn't move, he grasped my hand and shook it violently.

"Harry Strothers. Don't wear it out. You from some other place, boy? You got a funny voice. Newfoundland? I had a buddy went out there once and couldn't understand shit. And they were supposed to be speaking Canadian."

"I am Gordon C—"

"Damn glad to meet ya, Gordo. And it don't matter a shit how you talk around here. All ya gotta do is show up when they start slopping it out."

He released my hand and walked toward an open door. I followed, as did two others, including one of the snorers, who had stopped in mid-breath and risen from the bed as if by some magical spell.

That first day was a completely new world of surfaces, fabrics, and devices that did things I did not think possible. What was this world where I had awakened? I was like a man dropped in the middle of a strange forest, where every plant, animal, and even scent was foreign.

"You have no other home?" I asked Harry.

"Nope. And by the looks of it, neither do you."

"I do, it's just . . ."

Soon, I learned they called this place the shelter—though I am not sure what we were sheltered from. Perhaps the other residents of the City. The man in the ravine had given it the name Toronto, a word that still seemed curious to me.

The foodstuffs that Harry called slop proved a challenge. The soups were mostly fine, though the liquid held more salt than a cup of sea water. Layers of fat coated my tongue when the food was cooked in oil and covered in some sort of hard material. I watched the others pour gelatinous liquids out of bottles that were red as a fresh cut, and then dip the hard shell into it. I discovered meat buried within, though I could not guess the animal.

My stomach burned as waste flowed through me like fire. The first altercation I had with another man happened during a mealtime. He stepped ahead of me, eager for his slop.

"I am here," I said. I had become accustomed to the City's strange language.

"Fuck you."

There were shoves and jabs. In truth, I wasn't even hungry. I'd recently spilled my lunch in the waste facility. But a tremor inside me flared. I put the man in a hold. He struggled and I applied pressure, too much perhaps. Still, he wouldn't stop moving. I heard the crack of bone. Someone laughed. The man's face whitened and I let him slip to the floor.

I was taken away from the eating area by two men with large frames. They talked to me in calm but forceful voices.

"You can't do that, Gordo. If you get charged with assault, we can't help you."

I wanted to tell them that I didn't belong here, that this was not my home. I wanted to ask if they could help me return to the shōen.

"But I was there," was all I said.

I knew from the sound that I had broken the man's arm. I was told to go to the room where Harry and I slept. There I found my friend listening to a square device that projected voices and music.

"Turn that radio up, Gordo," Harry said. "I like this one."

I rotated a dial as I'd seen Harry do. The lilting melody was not unlike the musicians I recalled from the grove. The singer pleaded for something, a lost lover or a dead relative. Perhaps he also wanted to go home.

"I heard you got into a brouhaha," Harry said.

"I don't know what that is."

"You gotta be careful out there, Gordo. You act like that

and they'll cart you away to the hoosegow and throw away the fucking key. Or worse yet, the crazy house."

"Where are those places?"

"Keep a lid on it. That's all I'm saying, my red-haired friend."

I did not fully understand the threat, but I trusted Harry's saying that I would not want to go to those places. In my bed at night, I willed myself to return to the shōen. I had tried this many times—I always awoke in the shelter.

Though it was the middle of the day, I fell asleep after breaking the man's arm. Upon opening my eyes, I stared into the face of a woman. Not hearing her enter my room suggested that already my training was slipping away.

"Gordon. Are you okay?"

I sat up in my bed.

"We need to know you won't do this again," she said. Her lips were thin, but covered in a deep crimson color. "This is a safe place for all."

The two large men who had removed me from the eating area stood behind her.

"Are you here to take me to the hoose place?"

"The where?" she asked.

I decided to not repeat the question. I did not want to ask about the crazy house.

"Can I go now?"

"Leave the shelter? No one is keeping you here, Gordon. But if you need to be here, you are welcome to stay."

"Okay."

Time passed. The days had a sameness to them. Then one morning I awoke to find that Harry had left the shelter. He left without saying goodbye or telling me where he was going. I worried that he'd been taken to one of the places he warned me about. I asked the men who lived at the shelter, but they knew nothing.

"Who the fuck is Harry?" one of them said.

I was afraid to ask the large men who watched over us. They

may have been responsible for Harry's disappearance.

Every day I waited for his return. Seven days passed, and then a man threw hot liquid at me. I busted his nose. My fist shot out, a blur, and smashed into his face. A fountain of blood erupted, soaking the man's face, the table, and one of my sleeves. Men drew away from me. A tremor formed in my loins, crawled up my stomach, and into my throat. It was like an animal shrieking in the woods, long and loud.

"Gordon!" It was the woman with the painted lips.

I swallowed the scream back into my body.

"You are out," she said.

The large men took me by the arm and led me out of the shelter.

"I do not want to go to the crazy house."

I tensed my body, then willed it to soften, as I prepared for battle. One of the men had the name Mark, which I thought strange, like an animal sound. He spoke softly to me.

"Gordo, you can come back when you've settled down. A few nights on the street will chill you out."

They turned and went back into the shelter. I walked down the street, in search of Harry.

—

I walked the streets of the City, moving farther and farther away from the shelter. After a few hours I had lost all of my bearings. Since my arrival, I hadn't ventured far from the building, and never without Harry. I came across men that looked like Harry, even a woman who wore a coat and had features similar to him, but he was nowhere to be found. I traveled the City, now understanding that if this was the afterplace, it was a dark form of it. It was so unlike the stories of the underworld that my teacher had told me. In this place, the citizens shuffled along in a daze, most of them in a hurry, though I couldn't understand where they were all going at the same time. Harry had been my guide to this strange place. I desperately needed him.

If I asked anyone on the street about Harry, I was met with a grunt, a quick turned face as they looked away from me. Many citizens simply pushed by, pretending to not hear my question. I kept my face open, trying to project safety as I asked a slim woman with a large black bag attached to her shoulder.

"Get back. I don't know you." Her eyes and lips squeezed into an unpleasantry.

"Have you seen Harry? His family name is Strothers. He is—"

She reached in her bag and threw some paper at me.

"—my friend," I said.

I stood in the middle of the street, musing that if Harry would have stayed in the shelter, the place he called the stink pit, I might not have broken the man's nose. Then I would have had a place to sleep, with a scratchy blanket to cover myself.

I looked down at the paper the woman had thrown. It was the currency that I'd seen before—my own black leather square had similar bills, all gone now, shared with Harry for his fermented drink. He let me try the drink, and the burn was familiar, like strong rice wine, but much, much worse.

I was unsure of the values of the currency, but doubted it was enough to pay for lodging. Eventually, I found a place that had the feel of an inn. There was loud music and raucous talk. I approached the long high table where men were gathered, drinking from dark bottles and clear glasses. I observed few women in the place.

"Do you have rooms here?" I asked the man behind the table.

"You looking for company, buddy? I can set something up." He looked behind me, and then to his right. I followed his gaze. "Fifty bucks for an hour. Includes the room." His tone had dropped, and I strained to hear.

"I only want the room."

"What?" He leaned back.

"I just need a place to—"

"You some sort of perv? You go over to Wellesley if you want that sort of action."

"Action?"

Another man appeared from behind. His shirt was rolled up to show thick arms covered in inked drawings. I knew others who had painted themselves in this way.

"What's the deal with this guy?"

"Wants a room but no hooker. Jack his monkey in private. Or who the fuck knows what."

"Hit it." He pointed to the door I came in.

One of the men came from around the high table and shoved me toward the door. I spilled onto the street, the sun brighter than before in contrast to the dark inn. Ahead of me, I spied a figure in a hat shuffling in a way that I recognized.

Thinking that I might be fooled again, I walked quickly to catch up to the man. Only steps behind, I kept my voice low.

"Harry."

He stopped, looked upward, and then kept moving, almost stumbling.

"Harry. It's me."

This time he stopped and turned; it took a moment for recognition to set in. His eyes were bloodshot, and his lip drooped as it did when he drank the fermented drinks.

"Well hey, Gordo. Where the hell you been?"

When he spoke his name for me, my chest softened.

"I don't know," I said.

—

Harry took me under his care. He had no home or bed to offer me.

"No way they're letting me back in the shelter," he said.

He taught me the ways of survival in the City, showing where to find food in the waste bins, and which ones had the highest chance of being unspoiled. We were not always successful. After one meal, I painted the alley with vomit, and my stomach burned for a full day after.

The days piled onto each other, and I grew weary of the sameness. We were like foragers, but instead of a forest with plants and berries, we searched the streets for a lower quality of food. After a week of eating this way, I longed for the thin soups of the shelter.

I wanted to tell Harry of my true home, and how wonderful the food was, but the thought of it saddened me. I kept many things to myself.

"Hey, Gordo, you don't happen to have any spare bills tucked away somewhere, do you?"

Seeing the longing in his pale unshaven face, I wanted to help Harry as he was helping me, but there was nothing I could do. So, we begged.

On the corners of busy streets, we stretched out our hands. Harry told me to put a shake into my palm. When he found a piece of cardboard in a bin and some ink pens, he made a placard, which we set in front of us with Harry's upturned hat.

"This paper says you have no work. What disease do you have?" I asked.

"I must have worked somewheres. Hell if I remember." Harry laughed and then gave a tremendous cough. "Let's go with cancer if anyone asks. No, wait. Let's say blood disease. Very rare."

I admit I was surprised when the placard brought us more coins.

"Look more sick, Gordo. Slouch down."

"I am not sick."

"Sure you are. We both are. On death's fucking door."

We slept in alleys, huddled against brick buildings, or waste bins, or wherever we could be sheltered and unseen. The nights were warm, but as the humidity dropped and dew settled on our bodies, the damp chill sank into my bones. When the leaves on the City trees began to turn, I sensed colder weather would soon arrive.

I asked Harry why we needed to be unseen in the night,

why we hid in the shadows. He mumbled something I could not make out. The next night I learned the reason. After I'd fallen asleep against a bin, two other street wanderers came upon us. They kicked us awake.

"Whattya got? Out with it."

Harry awoke with a start, threw a string of obscenities at them before they pushed him back to the ground. They laughed when he struggled to rise.

"Stay down, old man. Give us what you got." The taller one opened and closed his hand quickly.

I held up my hands to them, slowly rising, and showing them first my empty hands and then my pockets. Harry always kept whatever meager coins and bills we'd collected hidden in a place inside his coat.

"Out with it, you old turd."

The shorter one kicked at Harry's leg.

"You can kiss my ass and go straight to hell." Harry spat at them.

My training had prepared me for the wave that rose inside me. My teacher had taught me to focus my emotion, gain control over it, and to channel the anger into a force to be used on my enemy.

As the men lunged toward Harry, in three fast strides I met them. I grabbed the short one by the arm and swept him back. He turned, faster than I thought possible, and his fist shot out at me. Still, I'd anticipated the blow, and moved away from it with ease. I slammed my elbow into his throat. In the side of my vision, Harry remained on the ground, kicking at the taller one, missing him by several feet. The tall one stood undecided between striking Harry or moving to where I stood over his companion, who had crumpled to the hard surface of the street, gasping like a koi out of his pond.

In his hesitation, I spun my body with my foot extended. My shoe connected with the side of his face. The crack resonated in the night. Somebody yelled faraway. The tall one held his jaw like a fractured plate. His eyes widened, the lone streetlight casting a beam on his white face.

Both men moaned and yelped like animals. The shorter one caught his breath long enough to vomit onto the street.

I helped Harry up, and we walked away from the scene.

"Well, Gordo, why the hell didn't you tell me you could do that?"

—

In that swirling time of my first year, I spent long hours trying to understand why I had traveled to the City. Was this some punishment visited on me because of my love for the lord's daughter? Or was I being castigated for leaving her behind? If I had stayed on the shōen, made my desire to be with her known to the lord, there could have been only one outcome. The lord would have had me killed.

Was my transformation into another man's skin because of my failure to accept death?

Harry was not a great man. But he was my guide, and my friend. In his own way, he understood my pain, as he lived in his own prison.

One night, full of fermented drink, Harry asked, "Who are you, Gordo?"

"I'm your friend, Harry."

"No, no, screw that. *Who* are you?" His words were slurred.

I had seen this expression on Harry's face before. Usually I let it pass, thinking it was simply his roaming, inebriated thoughts. This day I decided to tell him the truth.

"I'm not from here," I said.

Harry coughed and spit on the sidewalk. "Well no shit, Sherlock."

We were sitting against a waste bin in an alley, as twilight moved into evening. Soon we would begin to search for a place to sleep. A layer of sweat was painted on his brow, and he shivered as he took another drink from his glass bottle. Over the last few days, his skin had taken on a greenish pallor. I feared that he would not recover from whatever sickness had invaded his body.

"I am from a place that is not here. We don't have any of these structures, or lights, or your way of talking and eating. Even the way people move on the street is different."

"You sure are different, Gordo."

"In my place there are no cars, or buses, or planes in the sky. Everything is greener, more vibrant. The air is sweeter, and we can drink from the stream outside my house."

Harry's eyes widened. "Can we go there?"

I said nothing for a long time. The one who had been my guide was slipping away. His crossover would be to a place unknown to me. Did the people of this City have their own afterplace, or did they disappear into a black void? I could not imagine the latter, and so hoped that Harry would travel to a place where he could enjoy his fermented drinks without pain or worry.

Finally, with my friend's last breath, sweat running down his forehead, he asked,

"Gordo. Are you an angel?"

"No, Harry. I am samurai."

Chapter Twenty-Six

Toronto, 1980

It took the Doctor a year to find a samurai who had crossed over. He had come close to giving up, believing Sanjo had lied and no others had traveled from the long ago. Then someone in his building told him about a dying man who talked nonsense. He had let it be known to the other inhabitants of the building that he was a doctor, a lie they never questioned, so they asked him to look in on the old man and his gibberish.

He sat by the old man's bedside and listened to his ramblings. Unlike those other inhabitants, he understood what the old man meant.

"So now you will cross over again?" the Doctor asked the dying samurai.

"I do not know."

"But another will come take your place. You're certain?"

"Yes. There are always the same number as musicians. Three is the number."

The samurai's ragged breathing told him that time was

short.

He pressed. "Three on this side, right. What about a doorway? Is there a doorway?"

"Of a sort."

"Where is it?"

The old man went silent, and the Doctor thought he'd lost him.

"You must be from a family. The musicians only allow those to cross over."

"What kind of family?"

"Of samurai lineage," the old man said.

The Doctor clenched his fists and drew in a slow breath.

"Could I follow one when they cross over?"

"The youngest open the doorway the widest," the old man replied.

"What? What does that mean?"

Again the old man was quiet. And then he spoke his final word before expiring: "Koen."

After the death of the samurai, he spent a year searching for any mention of the word Koen on buildings, signs, or gardens in the City they called parks—a name as stupid as everyone who lived here. Thick books held the names and places of the City, but he found no mention of the word. Finally, he learned of an eatery that formerly had held that name. There he found another old man, though this one was still healthy and vibrant, who owned and lived in the eatery with a younger woman.

He visited the eatery a number of times before he was certain of the owner's identity. The place was empty of patrons in the mid-afternoon, so he chose that time to approach the man. Upon entering the eatery, the Doctor flipped the lock to the outside and turned over the sign. The room held only three tables with chairs, and a line of stools set against a tall counter. Behind it was a grill, some pots, and baskets holding different foods, oddly shaped tubers, and spiked fruit. Gray squares of light formed on the dark walls behind the counter, where the woman stood. There were no others in the room.

The Doctor confronted the owner, called Riku, telling him that he knew his true identity, and that he knew of the crossover.

"The story you tell is one of fantasy. Perhaps there are doctors you can speak with to help you," Riku said.

"When a samurai dies in this City, another comes from the other side. There are always three."

"Three what?" Riku asked.

"Don't think I'm an idiot. Where is the doorway?"

"I am sorry—"

"Yeah, yeah, fantasy. I think I'll shove my blade in your ribcage and then you can tell me what you know."

Riku studied his face. "You are not samurai."

"No. But you are. And the old one who died in my building was samurai. He was the one who told me about you. How long have you been here?"

Riku placed his fingertips together, then peered into the Doctor's eyes.

"I no longer keep track," Riku said.

"Bullshit. You probably know right down to the hour. I do."

Riku let out a deep sigh, and then made a sound like a whistle as he breathed. His body rustled in the loose clothes, as if made of rye grass.

"Let us drink tea. It will relax your mind," Riku said.

"I don't want your fucking tea. Tell me what I ask or I'll open you up right here."

The woman let out a sharp sound. Riku raised his hand to his head and made the smallest of movements. The woman, at least a decade younger than him, brought over a yellowed bottle and two short cups. She wore similar loose clothing.

"It's cold. I don't drink cold sake."

Riku shrugged and reached for the bottle, but the Doctor grabbed it from his reach and filled both glasses.

"When someone dies in the City, does the crossover happen immediately?"

Riku drank slowly and then set down his empty cup.

"I knew the samurai in your building. We have talked," Riku said. "He told me the timing of the crossover is never the same."

"So another one is already here?"

"Perhaps. I had no knowledge of your arrival."

"Then another samurai is already in the city," he said.

"It is likely. But why does that matter?"

"Because then I'm too late. I need to be at the door when a new one arrives."

"Why?"

"To cross back, you idiot."

"You want to return?" Riku asked.

"Of course. If another samurai is already in the City, I need to find him."

"And kill him."

"Will that open the doorway? The old one said if they are young, the door will open wider. What does that mean?"

He saw something flit in Riku's eyes.

"You know who the new arrival is." He grabbed Riku's shirt and pulled him close. "Don't tell me his name, then. I can end this right here. Young or old, it will achieve the same result."

Riku cleared his throat. "The death needs to be natural. Killing me, or the one who has arrived, will do nothing."

He released Riku, then leaned back and laughed.

"You're a fucking liar."

The woman, once again behind the counter, hit a small metal bowl. The reverberating ring filled the room.

"She is protective," Riku said.

"Well I don't give a shit. Does she know that phrase? It's one of the many I've learned since I've come here. If she gets in the way, she'll die before you do."

"Again . . . killing us will not allow you to cross."

"Idiot. How do you think I got here?"

Riku refilled his cup. The woman rubbed a cloth over the clean counter.

"You are not from one of the families, so you must have come another way," Riku said.

"What families?"

"If you have spoken to the old one, you know the lineage of those who cross over must be samurai."

He made a guttural sound and pointed at Riku as if he were aiming at a target.

"Tell me the new arrival's name or I'll shove a blade through you and she can watch you drown in your own blood."

"Your threats mean little to me," Riku said.

"Maybe killing you won't do any good, but killing her will have an effect." He swung his hand in an arc, pointing to the woman. Then he downed his sake and refilled his cup. "The expression you're trying to not show tells me I'm right. You fucking samurai think you can hide everything."

"Perhaps you were trained as a bushido. That is how you were able to cross," Riku said.

"Bushido is bullshit, and we both know it. My training came in another way."

"And what was that way?"

"It doesn't matter. Tell me the new samurai's name or watch the woman die."

The woman was at the table again.

"What the hell do you want?"

"Do you want some food?" the woman asked.

"Do you have pizza?"

"We do not," Riku answered.

"Cook me something, I don't care what. I'm going to be here for a while."

The woman didn't respond until Riku nodded with a small head movement. The Doctor reached across and grabbed the old man's hand, squeezing it hard.

"You've led a violent life. And I see you continue to live one now in this city." The old man's voice was soft.

The Doctor increased the pressure, but again, the old man

expressed no pain.

"I've seen things in this garbage pit of a City that make my other life seem peaceful. People here care for nothing but themselves. They help no one. They're all swimming upstream to see who will get to the mouth of the river first. They don't care who they hurt along the way."

"You were given a second chance. That is what the crossover is. You should understand this gift. Especially as someone not from a chosen family."

"Family means nothing. And fuck the second chance," he said.

The old man's hand grew hot under his grip. There was absolutely no look of pain or even discomfort. He considered breaking a finger, but then let go and pushed away the hand as if it was a piece of fruit gone bad.

"And what will crossing back achieve?" Riku asked.

"When I return with what I have learned, they will treat me like a god."

"Or a demon."

The woman brought over plates of steamed vegetables and rice in small black bowls.

"Thank you, beibī." Riku touched her arm and she smiled.

No more words were spoken until the food was gone. Then he swung the back of his hand, smashing into the old one's face, knocking him to the floor. The woman rushed to him, but was stopped by the Doctor's raised hand.

"Take another step and I'll finish it here." He kneeled down, pulled out a long blade, and held it over the old man's eye.

"Tell him," she said. "Riku, tell him."

The old man stared into the blade. "Even if you find a way to return, you cannot stay there."

"Another lie, but go on," the Doctor said.

"I can guess that you killed someone on that side. In the before time. Where did it happen?"

"A market."

"After that killing, did you immediately cross over?" Riku's voice remained calm.

"No. It was later. We counted time different then, you know this. Maybe a month."

"The one you killed must have been samurai, or from a family of that class."

"Yes, the soothsayer in the market told me they were."

"So you did know about the families. How did you find this out?"

"I was told by another. But I believe I killed the wrong son," the Doctor said.

"You must have also learned about the balance of three."

"Yes, yes, three on each side."

"So then—"

"Enough. Now, give me the name or die."

"Riku," the woman said.

"In this city he is called Gordon."

"And the family name?"

"Clement."

"The names here are stupid."

The Doctor brought the blade a hair's breadth away from Riku's eye. He drew back to strike. The woman rushed in, less than seconds, almost too fast to be possible, and she fell to the floor. She lay across her partner, raised her arms, and crossed them in front of the Doctor, wrist to forearm. The Doctor stepped back from the pair, folded the knife, and slipped it into his coat.

"Tell me this, old man, have you tried to return?"

"I am content in this city."

The Doctor laughed.

"For a samurai, you're a fucking liar."

He kicked over his chair, left the small eatery, and moved into the street where hundreds of people swam in an aimless flow.

Escape

Chapter Twenty-Seven

Heather got home from downtown just as the courier rang the doorbell downstairs. Still sweaty from the fast walk from College, she signed and grabbed the envelope from the driver. She couldn't believe that the A.D. had sent it out that fast. She swore at herself for lingering too long at The Pearl to see if Gordo would show up. She had checked the last three mornings, but since their meeting in the park, she'd not seen him.

She ripped the envelope open and slid her drawings out. They were marked up with red notes.

Like the direction here, but too vague. Needs something to tie it in.

Then in two circles, the words *Money Symbol. Stock ticker.* And a third circle read, *But not.*

Shit. The art director had turned down her idea, well, not completely. His phone number was at the bottom, asking her to call him if she needed more direction. Dammit. She was not going to fuck this up.

She went to the sink and splashed cold water on her face,

then tied her hair back. Shit, shit, shit. She needed to focus. Why wasn't Gordo at The Pearl? He said he went there every morning.

She taped the drawings on the board and began to write down another set of words. It was the classic problem that Vince always talked about.

"They say they don't want another bag of money or a picture of a bank, but most of the time that's exactly what they want."

"And they say they don't want it?" she'd asked Vince.

"But they do."

Vince was right. When she paged through past issues, the magazine was full of dollar symbols, clichéd Roman columns, money bags, and the worst: piggy banks. She needed something that said money without showing money. No problem, right?

Why did not seeing Gordo bother her so much? She had taped a fresh sheet of paper to her desk and started a new sketch when the phone jolted her.

"Hey, Heath'."

"No time to talk."

"C'mon. Don't you need a break? Zach's at school—what are you so busy with?"

"What do you want, Michael?"

"A cup of coffee. You spare me one of those?"

"I'm on deadline."

"New promotion piece?"

A wave of heat flashed up her neck. It wasn't for a fucking promotion.

"Goodbye, Michael."

"Wait, Heather. I—"

Instead of slamming the receiver down, she waited.

"What?"

"I'm in trouble. I, uh . . . really am."

She let Michael drift in the silence, listening to his breathing. She'd heard that tone before, but there was a real quaver in his voice.

"What kind of trouble?"

"Can I come over? I won't stay long. I'll be gone before Zach is done school. Promise."

Again she let him hang.

"Heath'?"

"Yeah, yeah."

—

She finished a couple of new roughs that she was happy with before she had to go downstairs and let Michael in.

"You got here in a hurry. So what's the big emergency?"

They sat at her kitchen table, and she gave him a glass of water to get rid of him quicker than the time a coffee would take to make and drink.

"What you working on?"

"*Canadian Business.* Half-page."

"Whoa, nice. How much does it pay?"

"What do you want, Michael?"

He downed the glass of water. "You wanna make some coffee or something?"

"No. What do you want?"

"Geez, Heath', relax."

There was a redness around the tips of Michael's fingers she'd never noticed before.

"I'm on deadline. And Zach will be home—"

"How's that little guy doing? I miss hanging out with him."

She didn't want to tell Michael that Zach also missed him. One of the reasons she liked him in the first place was how good he was with Zach.

"I don't have time for this," she said.

"I'm in trouble. I fucked up."

She sighed. "How this time?"

"You sure I can't have a cup of tea or something? Or do you have any wine?"

"What happened, Michael?"

"It's hard to talk about." He rubbed his hands together, tugged at a fingernail with his teeth. "There was a guy on set, he was connected to someone who took bets."

"Yeah, so? Oh shit, are you telling me you lost money?"

"I was doing pretty good with the NFL, had some winners. And then I made some on baseball, which you know I don't know as well. And well, things kinda went south."

She got up from the table and filled the kettle with water. When they lived together, Michael told her about a problem he'd struggled with years ago, before they'd met. Though he never named it, she guessed it was an addiction.

"You have a gambling problem." She started to pace. "That's what you never wanted to tell me."

"It's not a problem, Heath'. I've had a string of bad luck."

"So pay the man off and walk away. You said you've been making money."

"The Stallone movie wrapped, and I won't have anything else for a while. The guy who had been letting me know about productions dropped off the planet. I don't even know if he's in Toronto anymore. I've been looking at the job boards, which never have much. I could volunteer for some construction on sets, but I don't have time to work for free."

She tapped her fingers on the counter. "You told me that you can get onto crews by volunteering."

"Heath' . . . I don't have time."

Michael wrung his hands like he was trying to stop himself from hitting something. The kettle hissed in the background.

"Wait. Did you come here to ask for money?" She threw her head back and laughed. "For fuck's sake. You know I'm scraping to make the rent."

"Just a small loan. I need to do something."

"And where am I supposed to get this money? And what do you mean 'do something'? The 'something' is paying off the scumbag that's been pressuring you."

"How do you know he's pressuring me?"

"Isn't he? You said you were in trouble."

He placed his thumbs over his eyes and pushed. A streetcar squealed outside, and someone yelled a name.

"Do you think your dad would wire you some money?"

"What? Are you out of your mind?"

"Sorry, sorry."

He caught her watching his trembling hands and jammed them in his pockets.

"I need to find some money . . . I mean . . . the guy's been pressuring."

"Who is he? You telling me some mobster or loan shark was working the set with you? This is something out of a movie, Michael. A bad one. How much do you owe?"

"A lot."

"How much a lot?"

"Maybe ten grand."

She slammed her hand down on the counter.

"Are you kidding me?"

"I know. I know. I fucked up."

"How did this happen? You can't pay that back. You don't have that kind of money."

"There's a game tonight, Jays against the Yankees. You look at the stats, especially with Alexander pitching, it's a no-brainer."

She stood across from him, hands on her hips, mouth hanging open.

"That's the something, Michael? Betting on another game? You need help. Have you had counseling? You need counseling. For Christ's sake, Michael, this is serious."

"Heather."

She hated when he called her by her full name.

"I was wondering . . ." Michael held up a finger, still slightly shaking, and pointed at her hand.

She followed his gaze to the ring on her hand, the one he gave her before they came to Toronto. He'd told her it wasn't an engagement ring, but one that showed his commitment to her. She wanted to smack him in the face.

"You still wear it. I was going to ask about it the last time I was here. Does it still mean something to you?"

"I got used to wearing it. But no, it doesn't mean anything. We don't mean anything, Michael."

"Could I borrow it?"

"You mean hock it."

"It's just for a short time. Just until . . ."

She spun the ring around on her finger. It had a beautiful green stone. He'd told her it was his grandmother's, that it was worth a lot, that he wanted her to have it.

The kettle began to sing. Heather unplugged it, keeping her back to him. "You need to leave."

"I'm sorry."

"No you're not. Just go."

"You won't help me?"

Steam rose from the kettle, fogging the window. She spun around, whipped the ring off her finger, and slammed it on the table. "Take it and don't say a word. I don't want it back. Take it, sell it, I don't care. But get the fuck out of my apartment."

He pocketed the ring and left. She grabbed a pencil and began another drawing.

Chapter Twenty-Eight

A high-pitched note reverberated through my apartment when I awoke this morning. Sitting upright in my bed, I could not tell if the sound was real or imagined. Had I been dreaming? Images swirled within me—they were from the time before. In my apartment, an ocean of space and time away from the market, the hooded man's words echoed within my small room.

"Too late."

I'd always wondered . . . what was I late for? Too late to save my brother's life? Or was it something else? I believed that I would never be able to answer this question.

The man at the chess tables wore a fabric that I had seen before, in that exact hue. My breath quickened. His face was different. And like me, the skin was different. There could be no mistake. It was the Doctor's voice who had said those words in the market.

"Too late."

All these years later, after being chased by those intent on ending my life, and then entering a City I never knew existed, I had my answer. This was the same man who killed my brother.

I forced myself to slow my breathing. Like a flash inside my mind, I understood that this man held the answer to the crossover.

His question to me in the pizza place sounded in the room alongside the still reverberating note. He spoke in the parlance of the City.

"Your old life. How'd you like to return to it?"

—

Seeking the fastest exit, I raced down my apartment's fire escape. It was half a block before I stopped and listened to my breath, but only for seconds before I ran again. I thought of only one thing—find the Doctor.

He said I should contact him when I decided to be serious. He killed my brother. He knew about the crossover. What opportunity did he mean? Perhaps the ache in my center could finally be eased. Perhaps there was a way to return to the time before.

I jumped at every sound like an animal charging. Then, I was in the middle of the street, and a large truck was shouting at me. The machine blared its horn, the driver's square head hung out the window.

"Get out of the way, numbnuts."

I leapt to the other side of the street, almost knocking a woman over who was carrying bags and wearing a hat too large for her head. More words were shouted at me. I took long strides, holding myself back from running, still unaware where I was going. My teacher said that if a feeling bursts inside, you must follow it.

"But first you need to contain it, control it before it controls you," my teacher said.

The voice was so clear that I looked into the open door of a shop to see if someone had spoken. A man smoking a thin cigar scowled at me. Music drifted from the shop, someone singing about the moon and New York City—a place I'd heard of, another large city, but in a different country. I slowed my breathing and my pace.

Questions swirled in me like the wind currents of a kamikaze. If the Doctor could travel back, then I could too. If I traveled back further than my original crossover, I might be able to prevent the death of my brother. Would I meet my younger self in the market? That seemed impossible, as I could only exist as one person in one time. The circle of logic spun inside my head, creating both excitement and fear.

What about my father? He had aged much in the recent years, and I worried about his health. He was still alive when I was chased by the archers. Was he still alive on the shōen? Or worse, had the lord made him perform the ritual of seppuku to pay for his son's shame?

What of the dear one I left behind? If I returned before our night under the moon, then I could stop the events that unfolded. But her father might still banish me, and the archers would find their mark. My heart became a field stone in my chest as I considered all these things. My breath had shortened, yet not from exertion.

I stopped my thoughts and noticed the eating establishment in front of me. This was the place I'd eaten pizza with the Doctor before Heather interrupted us.

"Oh no."

I said it aloud, and a tall black man repeated the words, laughing as he passed by me. In the park I had revealed too much in telling my story to Heather. My exclamation was from remembering the concern I saw in her eyes. She had guessed the truth in my story. But I couldn't think of her now. Finding the Doctor was more important.

I entered the eatery. "Can you help me?"

"You wanna slice?"

It was the same person from the other day, a woman with

skin the color of earth and older than me by at least a decade. Her thick hair was tied back, and she wore the same red-stained apron.

"No, no. Thank you. I need to find someone," I said.

"The woman you were with yesterday?"

"You remember me?"

"She was pretty, but not your girlfriend, right?" She turned back to the oven, bringing a steaming pie out on a wooden paddle and sliding it into a cardboard box.

"Do you remember who I was with first, before she came in?"

"You mean the doctor?" She rang a bell, and a man in a red vest and matching hat appeared and scooped up the cardboard box.

My heart lurched at the sound of his name.

"Do you know him? Is he really a doctor?"

The woman with the earth-colored skin had moved away from the front of the counter. Her hands worked at stretching a circle of dough.

She pointed at the people behind me. "If you're not buying a slice, please move to the side."

"C'mon, buddy, order and get the hell out of the way." A large bearded man stood behind me; I hadn't even noticed his presence.

"I'm sorry, this is very important," I said.

"I'm on break for fifteen more minutes, and that's damn important. Get out of line if you're not ordering."

I looked over to the table where I'd first sat with the Doctor, and then afterward, Heather.

"I will have one," I said.

"One what?"

"With the meat."

"Pepperoni?"

I nodded. The woman stopped working her dough, moved to the glass case with the already made pizzas, and took one piece out and put it on her paddle. I went and sat down, not knowing what else to do. The people in line placed their orders. There were only four of them, but it was still an hour before the mid-day time called noon, when many from the City came to eat at these places. I needed to talk with this woman in the stained apron before that time. I breathed deeply, resting my hands at my side, seeking control, holding myself back from pushing past the others and forcing the woman to tell me all she knew of the Doctor.

She called me over to get my pizza.

"I need to ask you—"

"Wait. I'll talk with you after," she said.

I waited, thinking that every moment was wasted time. The Doctor may no longer be in the City. He could have found his way back to our home and left without me. How would he make this happen? He'd talked about killing a man.

Finally the four had their orders—two more had come for boxes stacked next to her. The bearded man left with two slices. The woman shouted something toward the back, and a younger woman came and took her place at the counter. The dark-haired woman moved toward me. She pointed toward another table farther away from the counter. I moved there and she joined me. Still wearing her apron, she'd brought a paper cup and a straw.

"I'm on a break for ten minutes," she said. She sipped from her drink. "Why do you want to be friends with this doctor?"

"He's not my friend."

Her face tightened as she put the straw in her mouth again. Her eyes held an intense light that glowed against her skin.

"That is good."

"Why do you say this?"

"When he comes, he is always alone. He's spoken with me, never in a friendly way. One time when his food took too long, he told me he was an important man, a doctor, and should not be kept waiting. Just like you said to me." She searched my face.

"So you're also important. You don't look like a doctor."

"I am not."

"I doubt a man like that would have any friends. I have known others like him back in my country." She tapped the side of her cup. "If you spend time with him, nothing good will happen."

"Where are you from?" I asked.

"I'm from Canada. Like you. Or that's what I tell people," she said.

"Before. Where were you before?"

"I could ask you the same."

Two young people walked in, a boy in ripped pants and a girl wearing bright colors with some sort of thick wrapping around her legs.

"Susan! Counter," she yelled back to the other worker. "It's good that you have lost this man. Let it stay that way."

"No, you don't understand. I need to find him. He has information."

It was difficult to keep my voice calm. I did not want to frighten her, yet I believed she was not a fearful person.

"This one is an angry man. I see it in his body, even when he doesn't say a word. I was surprised to see someone join him. That's why I remembered you."

"Do you know where he lives?"

"Why would I know that? He's just a customer."

"Does he come every day? At a certain time?"

"Not every day, and not at the same time." She eyed me. "If he's not your friend, are you in some sort of trouble with him? You don't look like police, you're too young."

"I need to talk with him."

"Right, because he has information. Maybe I was wrong and you are police."

Again, I felt her searching my face, trying to ascertain if I was truthful. Might she call the authorities? Then I would never find the Doctor.

"I'm sorry to take up your time. I will continue looking for him." I stood to leave.

She reached out and put her hand on my arm.

"He forgot a paper one day. At his table, it slipped out of a folder."

"What was on the paper?"

"Typed words. Names were on it, and addresses."

"Did you give him back his paper?"

"He was gone before I discovered it. I kept it, meaning to give it to him. But then I didn't."

I sat back down. "Why didn't you give the paper back when he came in another day?"

"I don't know. I thought I might need it someday. I know that sounds strange, but sometimes with a man like that—"

"Vera, break's over," the other worker called to her.

"I don't understand," I said.

"I have the paper at my home. Come there tonight and I'll show it to you. If you know this man, maybe it will make sense."

She pulled a pen from her apron and wrote down an address on a napkin.

"Why did you keep it?"

"Zimbabwe."

"I don't know that word."

"You asked where I was from. That is what they call my country now. It's a place ruled by a man not to be trusted. Living there, one learns to do certain things."

She held out the napkin to me, but didn't give it up when I grabbed it.

"You're someone to be trusted," she said.

"Are you asking me this?"

"This is something I see."

She released the napkin, and I folded it, careful to not smudge the ink.

"I will come to your home tonight."

"After nine. What's your name?"

"Gordo."

"That's a strange name. You don't look like a Gordo."

"Vera," the other worker called again. "Time's up."

I wanted to ask her what she meant about my name, if she saw something others did not, but she went to wait on a group of young people shouting orders.

Chapter Twenty-Nine

When the sun finally began to dip, I left my apartment and walked to an eatery in Chinatown. Unlike the Doctor's love for pizza, I still missed the food from my true home. I never found anything that was quite the same, but there were places that made a soup that reminded me of bowls I'd eaten in the market near the shōen. Slurping up the broth, the smell took me to that market, where amidst the steaming pots and butchered animals, I witnessed the murder of my brother. I now pursued his killer.

My deep desire to return to the shōen, and to the one I left behind, pushed me onward like a man trying to stay ahead of an avalanche of stones. I believed this man, this Doctor, could help me. In the pizza place, I had refused his invitation because of the force that spoke to my most inner self. He had killed a member of my family, and he planned to kill another man to go back. How could I ponder being in the presence of such a dangerous man?

I decided against a streetcar, and walked to the woman's

house instead, as there was still a restlessness in my legs. The woman was a stranger to me, and yet she had been placed into my life as yet another guide. People had come into my life this way, as guides in a City not my own. A sadness welled up when I recalled Harry, and then my heart was softened when Joshua's face appeared in my mind, and then Heather's. When I return to the shōen, I will miss these people.

I made out the woman's house number, lit only by a dim streetlight. She lived on a street a block from the main section of Chinatown, where rows of crammed houses with tiny green spaces were filled with families. I'd walked these streets before, noting how the young and very old occupied the same living quarters, once again reminding me of my true home.

I spoke with a person at the door, a Chinese woman with a deeply lined face.

"Downstairs."

I peered backward, searching for a path or an opening.

"Around back, a door at the bottom," she said.

I felt my way down a set of stairs to a door cast in deep darkness. What would it be like to live in such a place? Was this woman in hiding? I reminded myself that many people in the City lived in this type of quarters. Joshua told me of illegal apartments where people hid from the authorities. I imagined an underworld of citizens that held secret meetings, perhaps planning to overthrow those same authorities. The last part was only my imagination, a desire to have these people be something they were not.

After three separate knocks and pauses, there was still no answer. There was a small window in the door, but it was too dark to perceive anything inside. I ran my hand along the wall, searching in the blackness and then finding a small disk. I pushed it, and chimes sounded, followed by a rustle of movement.

"Oh. You came." The woman looked very different from her place behind the counter at the pizza eatery.

"You said I should."

"I didn't think you would."

"Can I see the paper?"

"This was a bad idea." She began to close the door. "I don't even know you."

I held up my hands to her. "Wait. Please. You said I was to be trusted."

Through the half-closed door, she studied me.

"Have you been out here long? I was in the bath." She pulled a robe tighter around her body.

"No."

She looked behind me, into the darkness, into the square of light formed on the ground from a lit pole in the house next door.

"Are you alone?"

"Of course, yes. Why would I bring someone?"

I heard music playing inside, singing in a language that was not the voice of the City.

She opened the door. "Okay, it's just you looked so sad before. Like you were lost."

"If you show me the paper, I will leave."

"Come in. Sit there. I need to get dressed."

She disappeared into a room off the side of a sitting area. Light came from another doorway, as well as a floral scent. I sat next to a lamp covered in a red shade. The music continued, flutes whistled, and sticks beat out a pattern. I had never heard this type of music, yet there was a familiarity.

"I enjoy this music," I called out.

"What? Oh, you can shut that off if you want. There's a tape deck in the kitchen."

She came out of the doorway, rubbing her hair with a towel. Her hair fell down past her shoulders, looking much different than in the pizza place. She had changed from the robe into a loose shirt the color of lemons. Under the light, the shirt shone next to her earthen skin.

"He came," she said.

"The Doctor? Here?"

She shook her head. "For pizza. An hour after you left."

"Did he say anything?"

"About what? Why would he?" she asked.

A tightness in her voice now. She went into the room with the floral scent, then came out again, sitting in a large chair opposite me.

"The paper. Could I see it?"

She narrowed her eyes, barely perceptible in the dim light. My teacher had trained me to watch an opponent's face. But was she an opponent?

"Why are you here?"

"You told me to come here, promising to show me a paper left by the Doctor."

"I think you are friends with him. Or working with him."

"This man is not my friend."

She moved her body to the edge of the chair. "He asked about you . . . in a way that says he knows you."

"He does know me. But he does not like me. I believe he wants to do me harm."

"You don't sound Canadian. The way you speak is like someone from my country who had to learn a language. Like me."

Hearing the distrust in her tone, I willed myself to quell the insistence in my voice.

"What did the Doctor want to know?"

"Maybe you should go," she said.

"Please. Does the paper have a message for me?"

She pulled a paper out of her pocket and unfolded it, staring at it. Then she folded it again.

"I don't understand. Are you playing a game with me?"

"I grew up in a country where it was hard to trust anyone, especially for women to trust anyone. I was lucky to leave when I did, as it's now run by an evil man. It's still home for me, and I will visit again. My mother is there, very old now and not well. I have three sisters, two have died since my leaving."

"Why are you telling me this?"

"I'm glad for my life here, though I miss my family. I see this same emotion in your eyes as well. I see your longing. My mother told me I had second sight. When I look at you, even with your white face, I see someone who's out of place. That is why I wanted to help you."

Her words enveloped me in a warm cloud. She did not speak like others I'd met in the City.

"But understand, you are a stranger to me. I need to be cautious."

"Yes."

Her face softened.

"This one we are calling the Doctor, I sense he is a violent man. He is capable of much evil. If he knew I was talking to you, and that I had a paper of his . . ." She trailed off, unfolding the paper again. "The day after I picked up the paper, he came asking for it. I lied and told him I hadn't found anything."

"I believe you are right about him. We both need to move carefully."

"Move where?" She raised her voice, and her eyes widened. "Are you with him? Yes, the two of you together. You are planning harm. You are planning an evil thing. The sense of danger I felt in the Doctor doubled when I saw you together. I never should have talked to you."

She shoved the paper back in her pocket and clenched her hands into fists.

I put my hands on my knees with my palms up, and leaned toward the light under which she shone.

"You are right about the Doctor. But I am unlike him. If you help me find him, or if something on that paper will lead me to him . . . then, I will make sure he won't trouble me anymore. Or you. Or anyone."

"Why would he trouble me? You mean kill me, don't you?"

"No." I paused. "I don't know."

I touched each of my fingertips, releasing a breath that I'd held for a long time.

"Who is this man? What are you hiding from me?"

"I don't think I can tell you. I—"

"Don't trust me?" She smiled. "Now, that is funny."

"Why?"

"In my country we are first given a name in our own language, Shona. My Shona name is Vimbo."

"Why is this funny?"

"It is a name that means trust."

"That's a very good name. I wonder if my name means something similar."

"You had a strange name, I don't recall it."

"Gordo."

"What does it mean?"

"I don't know. It was given to me."

"By who?"

"A person who is no longer in the City." I willed my muscles to relax, aware that my breath was still tight within my chest. "Should I call you Vera or Vimbo?"

"Only my family calls me by my Shona name. Here I am Vera."

"Vera, I see you are a good person. But if I tell you my story, I am quite certain you will think I'm not in my right mind. You will ask me to leave, and then I will be no further in my search."

"There is much in this world that we cannot understand."

Again, I became aware of the music, the rhythmic drums woven throughout the song.

"Is this music from your home?" I asked.

"Yes."

"I have heard similar rhythms in my home. My true home."

"Tell me about it."

There in Vera's underground dwelling, under the red light and the glowing yellow tones that emanated from her, I began to tell her my story. Since arriving in the City, I'd never been this open to another. Sitting in this woman's room, filled with music from her home, and a light from her that stretched into the past, I told her everything.

She listened intently. When I told her of who I'd left behind, and the pain I carried, tears rolled down her soft cheeks. When I felt there was nothing else to say, my head slumped to my chest. My muscles lost all their tension, as if I was made of liquid.

"You must be so lonely," she said in a whisper.

"How do you know?" My voice was like a child's.

She reached out to me, placing her hand on mine, and giving me the paper with the other.

"Because I know this feeling."

"How do you survive?"

"By living."

A warmth spread throughout my body.

"Will you tell me something in your language? Something from your home?" I asked.

"Wakadii."

"That is a nice sound. What does it mean?"

"It is a greeting for a friend. A good friend."

The music stopped abruptly, with a harsh click, and silence flooded the room.

"Do you believe me?" I asked.

"It doesn't matter. You believe it."

I looked at the paper. The letters were made by a machine, a numbered list, with hand-written notes in a red ink. Vera reached under the shade and clicked a switch two times, brightening the room.

"This is my name. And my address," I said.

"There are stars next to it."

"These other names have been crossed out. Except for this one at the bottom. It's circled."

"What are the symbols by that name?" she asked.

"It is kanbun."

"You can read it?"

"This one says 'center.' And then 'old man.'"

"Do you understand what it means?"

"Perhaps."

"There's an address written under the one that says old man. What is this word?"

"Riku."

Chapter Thirty

Once again the Doctor found them in the eatery. There were no patrons, only the owner, Riku, at the table writing in a book as the woman stirred a soup pot, steam forming a cloud above her. He had thought he would return with the young samurai, and then have him kill Riku. Then he would kill the young one, and this would make the door open the widest. With two samurai dead, he would easily cross over. But where?

Another concern buzzed at him like a gadfly. The young samurai named Gordon seemed strong and well-trained, much different than the one he'd killed in the market. He had no interest in finding out how much strength the young one possessed. He was certain he could defeat him anyway. But he had been in this stinkhole of a city far too long. He had decided against challenging the young samurai. There was a more direct and easier path to his goal.

The woman lifted her head quickly when he entered. He raised two fingers and pointed at her, as if aiming a bow.

Riku called over without looking up or stopping his writing.

"She is not a concern in this."

"Then she best put down the blade she has in her other hand."

The woman took a step toward the Doctor.

"Put it down, beibī. It will be fine," Riku said.

"I will not. You. Leave. Now," she said.

The Doctor lunged toward her, and she slashed his forearm. He twisted her wrist, but she didn't cry out. The knife fell to the floor, and he kicked it across the room. He spun her body, pulling her close, pressing down on the arm that had held the knife. She grasped his coat with her free hand.

He brought his own blade out of an inside pocket. He considered that he may need to kill her first.

"Release your hand or I'll slit your throat," he said.

Old Riku leaped up with surprising agility and stood in between the table and the counter. "Release her. This is between us."

He applied more pressure to her arm, eliciting a cry.

"Sit back down." He pointed his knife at Riku.

"You came back. Is the young samurai dead?"

"Change of plan. Tell me all you know, old man, or watch her bleed out on the floor."

"What else can I tell you?"

He drew the blade across her forehead; blood oozed from the swift cut. He placed the knife on her throat.

"Stop." Riku moved quickly, hands raised.

"No." The Doctor's eyes blazed. "It's you who will stop. This woman, is she your wife? Will you mourn her when she dies?"

"I know the place where it happens. You know this place as well."

"Of course you do." He brushed the blade across her skin. "And now you will tell it to me."

He released his grip on the woman, and pushed her away. As she went to her husband, she held her gaze boring into the Doctor's skin.

The Doctor knew the place, and he chastised himself for not realizing this earlier. Still, Riku added details that would prove useful.

"Is that all of it?" he asked.

"It is all I know."

He studied the line of blood that snaked down his arm from where the woman had cut him.

"Then you're no longer of any use."

A flurry of movement too fast to follow. The sound of clashing metal.

"Riku!"

—

The morning sun illuminated the buildings along Queen Street, outlining the edge of every brick. This clarity was not welcome, as there was nothing inside my thoughts to match it. I had spent the night with the woman from Zimbabwe. I felt a kinship with this woman from another country. She was also far away from home, and wasn't sure when, or if she would ever return. We were reflections in the same pond.

When Vera spoke of loneliness, it was as if she looked inside me. As she named for me this new emotion, the energy and blood that had coursed through my body in my search for the Doctor ebbed away.

"What is important to you?" she'd asked. "To seek revenge?"

"My brother has been dead a long time. Hundreds of years."

"Yes. But not for you."

She'd invited me to stay, and as we sat in her underground room, a wave of exhaustion came upon me. We drank tea and talked more of our homes. She never questioned my story as unbelievable or impossible.

"Do you believe the Doctor can help you get home?"

"I don't know."

"He is not to be trusted. He may want you to do something you're not prepared to do," she said.

"I know."

She made us some food, cabbage cooked in a peanut sauce with tomatoes. This was a dish from her home—her mother had taught her how to make it. The sweetness against the acid taste comforted me, reminding me of something I'd eaten years ago, centuries really.

We lay in bed next to each other, but we did not remove our clothes or become intimate with each other. Being close to another who knew our story was more important than pushing our flesh together. In this closeness, Vera told me of the poverty that she grew up in.

She told me her family was poor not only in food or goods, but carried a poverty of spirit. Her place of birth, what she called the village, lacked in hope. As a child she lived during a time of darkness and famine, and watched her young friends die.

"My mother was strong in spite of my father's long periods of absence. She's the one that held our family together . . . she held me together," she said. "My father was shot in the head by a white man whose land he had stepped on. My mother told me this on the same day she produced a small bag of money that allowed me to leave my country. I don't know how she came by this money, but I fear she gave part of herself so I could find another life here in Canada."

"And have you found it? The other life?"

"Of a kind."

"Will you return to your village?"

"I am not sure I can."

She pressed her face against me, softly sobbing into my chest. Her sadness enveloped me and intertwined with the river of emotion that spilled from my heart. I thought of my separation from home, from my father, the death of my brother, and of course, from the one I left behind. Did my dear one discover what happened to me? Was she told I was killed in the forest? Did she mourn my death after the birth of our child? Soon, I wept alongside Vera.

After Vera fell asleep, I lay awake thinking of the shōen, my father working the grounds, a sweat stain spreading across his back. The bright blue sky above him was empty of planes, buildings, wires, and all the clutter of the City. This image in my mind was like a painting whose color has faded. Would the lord let him stay, or was he living in some hovel, having relinquished our small house and farm when we moved onto the estate? Or had some other tragedy beyond the loss of his sons befallen him? When honor was lost, certain rituals must be undertaken. Would the lord force seppuku upon him?

One of my teacher's most repeated lessons was that of separation.

"You must detach from that which has too great a hold on your being," my teacher said.

How would my teacher instruct me in this time? Would he tell me how one separates from loneliness?

Now, as I looked into a sky as blue as the one I remembered above my father's head, I felt as if I were to be swallowed up by the City's skyscrapers, which jutted into the air like giant gray blades.

When Joshua had used the word "skyscrapers" to describe these buildings, I had wanted to ask if they actually scraped the sky. I held back my question in case Joshua would think there was something wrong with me. He already believed that I lacked intelligence, or perhaps that my mind was unwell, and I did nothing to dissuade him from these thoughts. If I told him the full story, like I did to Vera, or even the story I had begun to tell Heather, this would only have confirmed what he already believed—that there was something, indeed, wrong with me. Out of his concern for me, he would contact the authorities from one of the places that Harry had warned me about. That I did not want.

Still, my time with Vera had brought on an urging to tell Joshua the truth. Considering how I opened myself to her, someone I had only just met, it deeply saddened me to be so dishonest with Joshua, a friend that had done so much to help me survive. Joshua could be trusted to not turn me over to the authorities.

But what of the Doctor?

I needed to examine the name on the Doctor's paper that Vera had given me. This name would lead me to him, for in my heart I knew I'd meet the Doctor again. Like streams that flow in the same direction, eventually our lives would converge.

Chapter Thirty-One

When I stopped in front of The Pearl, it was as if my thoughts of him had made it so. There was my friend in his regular spot. He stood up from his seat when I entered.

"Gordo, where the heck have you been?" Joshua called over, adding a whooping noise.

"Settle down there, this ain't no rodeo," Stan said from his spot by the grill.

Joshua grabbed my shoulders and squeezed. My muscles tensed, but I relaxed them as I understood the gesture was one of friendship.

"You dropped off the planet, man. I was going to start checking the hospitals."

"Why?"

"Hey, something could have happened."

"Something did."

"See? Wait, what?"

"Please sit, I will explain."

Stan brought me a kettle full of hot water and tea.

"Hey, Stan, could we get an order of toast and jam for my buddy here?"

Stan looked at me and I nodded.

"I will pay," I said.

Stan waved me off as he returned to his cooking station.

"So, what the hell's been going on, Gordo?"

"I am okay—no harm has come to me. But the days have been strange."

"No shit, Sherlock. Last I saw you were heading off in a police car. You didn't pick up your phone, so I went by your place a bunch of times."

"Who is Sherlock? Someone else told me that once."

"Spill. Where you been? Did the cops hold you against your will? Dammit! I should have called my lawyer friend. But then I had this emergency, and my buddy Larry, remember him, his brother had this bad fall and he needed me to . . . sorry. I'm just glad to see you, Gordo. I worry about you."

Joshua's words came out fast, as they did when he was filled with excitement.

"Why?"

"That's what friends do, man."

I had planned to tell Joshua what I told Vera at her underground place, but I didn't want to do this in The Pearl. I couldn't be sure of how he'd react if I told him of my true home. Would it be the end of our friendship?

When my toast came, I uncovered the small square and spread the fruit across the bread, so thankful for the familiarity of tea, toast, and listening to Joshua.

"Gordo, are you all right? For real. You're so quiet. Are you in trouble?"

"The man we saw at the club with Rebecca and Sky. I met with him again."

"Oh yeah, I need to call her. Wait, the guy they threw out? That's the one the police asked you about?"

"Yes."

"Hang on, you said again. You'd met him before?"

Joshua tilted his head; the tone in his voice had flattened. I needed to proceed carefully.

"He is a doctor. Or pretends to be."

The door to The Pearl opened and my body tensed. I looked back to see a woman with white hair moving stiffly before taking a seat by the large front windows.

"Gordo, what's going on?" Joshua dropped his voice to a whisper.

"There's no need to speak that way."

"Who is this doctor guy? Where'd you meet him?"

"I knew him from before." I paused. "A long time ago. I only recognized him now."

I turned as another diner entered.

"Listen, I know a guy who Larry knows, and if you need some muscle, I can make some calls." Joshua looked over my shoulder. "Should we switch seats? Do you want to watch the door?"

"It's good to see you, Joshua," I said, but I heard the fear in my friend's voice, which made me afraid too.

"Damn, Gordo, it's good to see you, too. But tell me where you've been. I mean, if you don't want to tell me, I get it."

"I was with a woman."

Joshua's mouth hung open for a moment before he spoke.

"From the club? You got horizontal with Sky? Wait, what does she have to do with the doctor?"

"Not Sky. A different woman."

I told Joshua of my meeting with Vera at the pizza eatery, and how we'd become friends. I explained how she understood my story, ignoring Joshua's question about which story. As I spoke, I observed the range of emotions play across his face. At first he was saddened that I had trusted someone other than him—and then as he listened, he became softer, caring for me with his eyes. When I told him I was not intimate with Vera, his expression of doubt was clear. I was about to start telling him about the Doctor, and the paper that Vera gave me, when another person entered The Pearl and walked toward us. It was Heather.

"It seems I'm always interrupting you," she said.

"Hi there, I'm Josh." He extended his hand. "You a friend of Gordo's?"

Joshua gave me a slight nod and raised an eyebrow.

"It is very good to see you," I said.

"I won't stay, just wanted to say hi," Heather said.

"I'm sorry for how I left the park. My days have been strange."

"That's all right, Gordo. Well, I'll go now," she said.

Joshua moved to the empty booth behind our table. "C'mon, join us. Any friend of Gordo's and all that."

"Yes. Please sit with us," I said.

Heather sat down next to Joshua. Stan came over.

"You actually want to sit with these hooligans?"

"Ha ha, yes, it looks that way. I'll have a coffee, please," Heather said.

Joshua laughed. "I recommend the toast. Good price and usually not burnt."

Stan grunted and poured a cup for Heather before heading back to his station.

"I was worried something happened to you," she said.

"Yeah, me too." Joshua grinned too widely. "I mean, Gordo, you should tell your friends when you go out of town."

"I did not leave the City. I talked with someone who gave me information about the man, the Doctor. Heather, that was the man you saw at the pizza eatery."

"You saw him again?" Heather asked.

"Who is this Doctor? Gordo, what are you mixed up in? I don't like—"

I nodded my head at Heather then at Joshua. "I'm glad that the two of you met. Joshua, this is Heather. She is an artist."

"I thought she worked at a pizza joint?"

"That was a woman named Vera. Vera is from another

country. We talked and became friends last night when I stayed at her home."

Heather turned and shook Joshua's hand. "I'm actually an illustrator, which, yeah, is an artist."

"You're an illustrator? Cool! Like for comics and stuff? Do you do album covers?"

"Not yet. But I'd like to. Well, maybe not the comics. I'm not sure my style would fit that. But I'd love to do an album cover. I'm just starting out, got my first piece from a national mag this month."

"Wow, you're so talented. I just paint houses."

Heather laughed. They conversed so well with each other. Even though I fully understood their language, I felt apart from them. I wondered if I would ever forget the sound of my own language.

As I listened, though, something in Joshua's voice shifted. I'd heard him sound like this before, at the club, with the women Rebecca and Sky. Heather said something that made him laugh, and he put his hand on her shoulder.

"Joshua."

"Yeah, Gordo?"

"Nothing."

I looked away, pretending to search for Stan. Joshua still had his hand on Heather's shoulder. She did not ask him to remove it.

"I am going to pay Stan. I need to leave now."

"Gordo, what's wrong?" she asked.

The two of them exchanged furtive looks. I gave Stan a bill and quickly left The Pearl. I didn't look back.

Chapter Thirty-Two

Heather ran into her apartment and reached for the ringing phone. A dial tone and a click—she was too late. Dammit, whenever that happened she imagined an art director calling her and hanging up when an answering machine didn't answer. She needed to take some of the *Canadian Business* money and buy one.

Zach wouldn't be home for a few hours. She made a strong cup of tea and shoved a Talking Heads cassette into the player. The driving beat and the layered drums helped wash away the tensions of the morning. She'd dropped off the final illustration to the art director, who seemed to like it, and said he'd keep her in mind for a future one. She was elated walking back, and thought she'd peek into The Pearl on the off-chance she'd see Gordo in his usual spot.

She was sorry that Gordo left so abruptly. He was obviously hurt by something he'd seen, maybe between her and Joshua. She knew that Joshua was probably hitting on her, with the hand on her shoulder and the way he listened so intently.

After Gordo left, she moved to the other side of the table. She asked Joshua if he'd heard any of Gordo's story, the one about the samurai. When he said no, she moved away from the topic, not wanting to suggest there was anything wrong with Gordo. She also didn't want to try and analyze a mental condition, a skill for which she had no knowledge or training.

Still, on the streetcar ride back, she'd tried to consider, if only for a moment, that the story he told her was more than a story. Somehow, Gordo believed it was true. Her father's sister was a psychiatric nurse, and she recalled one of the few times she'd visited her father when they talked about her aunt's work with schizophrenics.

"I've read about people under hypnosis or deep trance who believed they were reincarnated. They could even bring up details from their past lives," Aunt Rita had said.

"Okay, so why do they all think they were someone famous . . . like Catherine the Great, or Genghis Khan? Why couldn't they just be some schmo who died on the battlefield of dysentery?" Dad said. He'd always thought his sister was a bit loopy, but he loved her.

"Well, that'd be pretty boring," Aunt Rita replied.

The memory of Rita's warm laugh filling their house made Heather smile. She'd been a teenager when she'd last seen her. She wished she had enough money to visit her out west. Rita told her once that there was so much in the world that remained unknown. Heather thought she got her artistic bent from her, if that sort of thing existed in the gene pool. She loved her dad, but her creativity sure wasn't from the guy that thought "art" was the guy who drove the Zamboni at the rink.

Thinking of the unknown and unexplained, she laughed at herself for believing in palmistry. The idea that a person's future was written in lines on the skin was absurd. But what if it wasn't? Heather still thought of the premonition, how she would come close to breaking, but if she could hang on, she'd make it. So why couldn't Gordo actually be who he thought he was? There was something truly strange about him. Mystical even. She wanted to see him again, if only to explain there was nothing between her and Joshua.

David Byrne's voice hopped along with its small exclamations, urging Heather across the kitchen to her drawing table. She could always count on Byrne to get her working.

She tore off a page from her sketchbook and taped it to the table. She grabbed a soft pencil and began to move it across the page. Dark lines took shape. Lines became fabric wrapping around a body, strong structure underneath, balance and weight and movement.

What if he was a samurai?

Why were people so boxed in by the reality they experienced? If Michael were here, he'd talk about how taking mushrooms gave him a view into the world we don't see. Why did her body feel lighter when she drew the warrior? Was it infatuation, or love, a romantic ideal? It sounded like a love story right out of a historical novel? Shit, was she falling for someone who didn't exist? That would be just like her.

She'd been infatuated with Michael when they first met. He was kind, thoughtful, great with Zach, and had the most honest eyes she'd ever seen. She really thought that. But that all changed, even more now, given the son-of-a-bitch was out there pawning her ring to pay off his gambling debts.

She stopped drawing, turned the music louder, sharpened the 2b Staedtler, and dove back in.

When she looked up from her desk, two hours had gone, her hand blackened by graphite. Was that how time disappears? When we are lost to something else? What was Gordo lost to? Where did his time go? What time was he from?

Zach burst in and headed for the fridge.

"I'm starving."

"There's some pasta from last night. Want me to heat it up?"

Zach came out of the fridge with an apple shoved in his mouth. "Ikinooit."

She laughed.

He crunched down and continued talking with his mouth full of apple chunks.

"Whottyedoink?" He came over to her desk and studied the drawings. "These are really cool, Mom. What are they for?"

"Just for me."

"You can do that?"

"Draw for myself? Yes, that's allowed."

"I thought you were trying to get some illustrations that paid money?"

She scrunched up her nose. The kid was lucky she loved him or she'd give him a blast on that comment.

"It's not all about money, Zach. But yes, these drawings could help me get some more."

"Cool."

He took another huge bite from the apple, then plunked himself in front of their small TV, flicking on Fraggle Rock.

She wanted to lecture him on what it meant to be an artist. Sure, she wanted to make money, but it was also about the act of creation. She tried to explain this to her friends before she left, but they only focused on the income thing.

"So you're leaving without a job? And going to a place that is tons more expensive than here?"

Her friend Liz couldn't believe Heather was leaving. Liz had just got married and was expecting her first child.

"I need to go," Heather told her.

"No offense, hon, but how do you expect to make rent? And you've got Zach. He's gonna need things."

"Michael will also work."

"Michael work? Right. Why not do some art around here? For sure we could use something in this town."

"Why did you say that about Michael?"

"Sorry."

Liz rubbed her stomach as they talked, like she was polishing a goddamn crystal ball.

"Maybe you need to do this, but at some point you have to settle down and take care of your family."

"What are you implying, Liz?"

"Hey, hon, I'm your friend. I want what's best for you."

But the judgement was plastered across her face.

Liz proceeded to lecture her about kids needing stability. She'd already taken Zach away from home when she went to art school in Calgary.

"Delay your trip for a year, or two. Get on some solid ground," Liz said.

"It's not a trip. I'm moving there."

She hadn't talked to Liz since leaving Garsen. She didn't listen to Liz's warnings about Michael.

"Are you sure this is what you want?" she'd asked Michael the night before they left.

"I want you, Heather." He'd leaned in and kissed her neck.

"I'm serious. This is a lot to take on. You've never been a father."

"How hard can it be? I've seen the movies."

She'd laughed. Back then she appreciated the light way he carried himself, never letting a hard situation pull him down. She never told him about her mantra that if things got tough, she would get tougher. She thought he'd be the same way.

All of those conversations came back to her as she watched Zach, still wearing his jacket, in front of the TV. Crumbs were airborne as he chomped on saltines.

"Hey, Zach, you wanna try and keep most of those crackers on the plate?"

"Serrr."

The phone rang.

"Can you turn that down a bit, Zach? Yes, hello. What? When did that happen, where is he, is he—"

Heather urged herself to not bawl into the phone.

"Mom, who is that? What's going on?"

Her son was at her side, tugging on her shirt like he did

when he was a toddler.

She looked down at him. "Grandpa. He's had a stroke."

"Is that like a heart attack?"

"Not quite. It's in the brain."

"Did he die? Mom, did Grandpa die?"

"They said the worst was over and he was very lucky. He's in the hospital."

"Can we see him? Can we go back home?"

"Yes."

Chapter Thirty-Three

"Only a pomegranate is he, who when he gapes his mouth, displays the contents of his heart."

Those were the words from my teacher that burned inside me as I returned from my meeting with Joshua and Heather. When I was first taught this, I did not understand, but now I know that it was about the ripe fruit that ruptures its skin and shows what is inside. I have been trained in self-control, but Joshua clearly has none. His movement and words toward Heather showed his intentions.

I was surprised by the flame of emotion that stirred within me, as Heather was a new friend. I enjoyed her company, and I trusted her. So why did Joshua's actions seem a betrayal?

"How far today in chase, I wonder, has gone my hunter of the dragonfly?" my teacher had recited to me.

"I do not understand."

"A mother grieves for her child," he replied.

"But what does this have to do with me?"

"You will experience much grief."

I did not feel grief, or even loss, when I thought of Heather and Joshua. The poem reminded me of the one I left behind, the one who carried our child. I had been gone so long now. How must they be? Thinking this way only increased my sadness. I should not have been thinking of Heather in any other way but friendship. I should have delighted in my two friends enjoying each other. But I did not.

Vera knew the truth of my loneliness, because it was her truth as well. Heather and Joshua lived in a city where they belonged. They did not experience the emptiness that Vera and I did. I saw Joshua's suspicion arise in his face when I talked about the Doctor. I now wondered if the two of them would conspire to send me to the place that Harry warned me about. The crazy house. They would do it thinking this would help me. And then they could be together without my interference.

"You will experience much grief."

Again those words filled my mind.

I now understood why the Doctor had come into my life, why he'd been searching for me. He also needed to go home, and he was willing to do things, grave things, so that he could cross over again. Like me, he was aware of the authorities and the crazy house.

The Doctor killed my brother in the market. And now, he wanted me to help him kill another. But how was death connected to the crossover? Giving into the burning desire to return home, joining with the Doctor, would certainly lead to a great violence. But if it meant I could return, then I needed to consider this alliance.

Violence was not foreign to me. I was trained to protect the shōen. My teacher said that though our shōen had been free of conflict for a number of years, that time was ending—I'd soon be called upon to do what was needed. Life could be snatched away with the pierce of an arrow.

Time is strange. Events from my past now flowed together with ones in the present. I had begun to give myself over to life in the City. The bluegrass musicians brought forth my longing, then Vera had named my emptiness, exposing it like a fresh cut on the battlefield. The music had drawn the streams of my life into one river. The bluegrass men with the beauty of their mournful voices, the music of the club where the Doctor tried to enter, and then Vera's music from her place of birth, all pulled on me. The musicians from the forest were the last ones I'd seen before leaving my true home. For this reason, I believe that musicians will be my doorway back to the shōen.

I will leave Joshua and Heather to their life together.

Once again I studied the address on the Doctor's paper. Like hunting a creature through thick foliage, I had to follow the path left behind. My only hope was that the man on the paper was still alive.

—

I was familiar with the street name, but needed to find it on the large map outside the subway station. I found it amongst the complex pattern of streets and avenues. My planned route would require an hour of travel.

Boarding the subway, I heard music emitting from another traveler who wore foam pieces over his ears. But in my mind, the sound of the forest musicians broke in and overtook the music from the traveler. The breath of a pan flute resonated alongside the plucking of a string and the stroke of a bow. The forest musicians acted as archers—their sounds entered my heart, matching the arrows that had pierced my back.

As I moved from the subway to the bus, and then onto the street, the sounds of the forest musicians came with me. My stride was fluid, passing small shops selling furniture, clothing that seemed worn, and windows full of tools for working with metal and wood. Barely half of the shops had numbers on their buildings. I counted up to what I believed was the number written on the Doctor's paper. It was an eatery, though all the tables were empty. A woman wiped a counter. Behind her, steam rose from a pot like a storm cloud forming.

I entered and the music from the forest abruptly stopped.

"I am looking for someone."

The woman didn't raise her head, continuing her spiral motion on the counter.

"A man. He is a doctor. Or he calls himself one."

When she looked up, I saw the cut on her forehead, not deep but recent. I observed a face full of pain and sadness.

"Do you know him? Was he here?"

She stopped her circular motion and flattened the cloth across the counter.

"Why?" she asked.

"Why am I looking for him?"

"Yes."

Her sad voice mirrored the sadness that enveloped the room.

"He has something I need."

"I doubt that."

A long silence was held between us. And then a recognition.

"Do you think you know me? We've never met," I said.

"I do know you."

"I have never been in this place."

"Yes, but you are known."

A gust of wind blew against my face. I looked to the door to see where it came from. There was no one, and the door remained closed.

"Who are you?" I asked.

She moved around the counter, past me to a door at the back.

"Come with me."

I followed her into a dark room. She turned on a small lamp, casting the tiny space in light the color of egg yolks. Stretched out on a table was a body covered in a red sheet. It was an old man, his face a spider's web of lines, white hair pulled into a top knot. A line of tears ran down the woman's face.

"This was your—" I stopped.

She brushed her hand across his face and stroked his hair.

"This is my husband. We met when I was very young. I knew this day would come. It comes to all of us. I seldom thought of it, focusing on the joy and love we had together."

I studied the man's face. He was like me, pale-skinned. His white hair had a glimmer of color, the shade of ginger, like mine.

"When he arrived at my place and ordered tea, I knew he was different. Only later, when our trust for each other had grown, did he tell me the reason behind the difference. Or I should say, the sameness," she said.

She spoke words in my own language to me. The woman's heritage was like mine, my true home.

"I understand. I am also different." I spoke back to her in the language of the shōen.

"I'm sorry, I know you're speaking Japanese, but I do not know that dialect," she said.

"You were not prepared for this day?" I asked in the language of the City.

"Who is?"

"Being younger, you knew that he would pass first."

"Not in this way."

"When did he die?"

"Earlier today."

An arrow of guilt pierced me.

"How?"

"The man you seek. He did it."

"The Doctor?"

"If that is what he is."

The light flickered in the room. A smell like something from the earth arose, and underneath a sweet fragrance, like oranges freshly picked.

"Where are you from?" she asked.

"From this City."

"You are not from this city, or you would call it by name. You are like my husband."

"How would you know this?"

Again, she stroked her dead husband's face.

"He was samurai. That is how I know. And you are as well."

"But he is white," I said.

"As are you."

A sensation brushed my face, a soft hand trailing a line across my cheek. Warmth spread over my body. It was as if I was in the middle of a vision, and yet there I stood in the backroom of an eatery, standing over the body of a man with whom I had much in common. The woman knew my story, she knew my home, she knew how I had come to the City. She knew because her husband had come the same way.

"How long has he lived in the City?" I asked.

"You mean in this time? Twenty-seven years have passed. Twenty-six of them with me."

"I am sorry for your pain."

"I held him as he died. The man you call the Doctor struck me, but was in too much of a hurry to do more. I was able to share words with my husband at the end."

"He must have been a great man."

"He still is. I believe he has traveled back to his home, his time, his family. He is there, sitting under a tree with those he loved, sharing stories. I would hope that he tells his family about me, about us."

"That is a beautiful vision. May it be true, and comfort you in your loneliness."

She closed her eyes and gave me a small nod.

"Why do you search for him? The Doctor."

"I believe he might be able to help me."

"He helps no one."

I turned to exit the small room. "I am sorry to intrude on your grief."

"How did you find this place?"

She turned out the flickering light and followed me into the other room. Steam continued to rise from the boiling pot.

"A friend gave me a note that the Doctor left by accident. I will leave you now."

The warmth I felt turned into a weight. I moved to leave.

"Please stay. Have something to eat," she said.

"It smells very good."

She pointed at a table. A moment later she set before me a bowl of broth, noodles and cut vegetables. It was the best thing I had eaten since I arrived in the City. She joined me at the table.

"This Doctor had come here before. He told my husband he was looking for a young samurai. I believe he planned to harm you."

"He planned to kill me."

"He was brash, demanding food and sake, treating me like a dog that would fetch whatever he asked. My husband told me not to worry. He said the man was full of bluster, but could be controlled."

I observed a large, dark stain under the table.

"Did you call the authorities?"

"There is little point."

"But his body—"

"It will be taken care of."

She was right about the uselessness of the authorities. The Doctor would not be found. He would cross over. It may have already happened.

"Can you help me?" I asked.

She slurped her soup, not saying anything for a long time. I took in her sadness and mingled it with my own.

"My husband told me of the place where he first arrived in Toronto. I don't know how it all works . . . or really any of it." She paused. "Now the Doctor also knows this place. He went there to wait."

"Wait for what?"

"I'm not sure. The death of my husband will cause something to happen."

Her shoulders dropped.

"What is your name?"

"I've used Phoebe for so long it has become my name. It was not the name my parents gave me. I am Yui."

"Yui, did your husband want to return to his home?"

"At first, yes. As the years passed, less so, and more recently he'd given himself to living the rest of his life here. With me." She covered her face as the tears came.

"There's no shame in this. You gave him a beautiful life. He was not lonely."

"He gave me the same." She wiped her eyes, then returned energy to her posture. "Listen, Samurai."

"My friends here call me Gordo."

"The Doctor killed my husband so that a door would open. If he is there, he will be able to step through."

"A door?"

"It's how my husband explained it. Not an actual door, but something opens, and someone is brought across to the City."

"This happens when another dies?"

"When another samurai dies, yes." She tilted her face, a line of light from the ceiling cutting across her forehead. "Three years ago, a close friend of my husband's died. I believe he was distantly related to my husband. Not here in Toronto, but in the other place they were family."

"Did this friend die naturally?"

"He was very old." The light on her face disappeared, and I wondered if I'd imagined it. "My husband went to the place his friend had told him about. It's a forest. He told me he watched someone emerge through the door. That person was you."

"Your husband was in the ravine? Why didn't I see him?"

"He didn't talk much about it. I believe he worried it would make me sad—the idea that he would want to travel back. He only told me that someone else had crossed over."

I closed my eyes, trying to redraw the scene of when I came into the ravine. The old man was not one of the people that helped me.

"Is the door always in the ravine?" I stood up from the table, already planning where I needed to go next.

"My husband thought so, yes. But it's a large area. The door is not always in the same exact spot."

I reached across and touched her hand.

"You've been a great help to me. What was your husband's name? I will bring him to my memory during my meditation."

"He was called Allan."

"But what was his real name?"

"His name was Riku."

"I will leave now, but I will bring both you and your husband to my mind during my meditations."

She stood. "I'd like to give you something. Wait here."

She went into the room where Riku lay and came back carrying a black rectangular box. Setting it before me, she lifted the lid.

"Riku told me this was forged in the Hirazukuri style."

I studied the tantō, flat without ridgelines, and with a soft curve to the blade. My teacher had trained me with a similar blade.

"This should go with your husband—it is part of him."

"I would rather you bury it in the chest of his killer," she said, her voice firm, with no hint of a quaver.

She closed the box and handed it to me. I nodded deeply to her and left.

Back on the street, I broke into a run. I knew what I had to do.

Chapter Thirty-Four

It had been years since the Doctor had visited the ravine. He berated himself for not thinking of it earlier. Still, it all depended on whether the old Riku had told the truth. After he'd threatened to kill the woman, he was certain the old man spoke his truth. He had no interest in killing the woman. She meant nothing to him. She could help him in no way. Her screams rang in his ears as he left, but faded to nothing immediately.

Searching the ravine, he rethought the decision to let her live. What does a man tell his wife? Perhaps she did know more. Still, the old man thought his information would prevent her death, and truth surely arises in that situation.

The plan with the young samurai had changed. The door might not open as wide as if he killed the one called Gordo. But it was no matter. He should have chosen the more direct route to begin with. What was that saying he had heard in the City? Keep it simple, stupid. Ha! Truths spoken by stupid people.

The place Riku mentioned was different from where he had emerged a decade ago. He had entered on the other side of the ravine. He recalled the brightness of the green. Traveling from the gray mud and hard rain of the battlefield, his dark blood draining out of him, out into the bright sun and too-rich colors, had made him lose consciousness only seconds after he awoke.

A couple whispered to each other on a bench, the woman pointed a finger in his direction, the man placing his hand over hers to hide it. Not that it mattered. He didn't care if he was being watched—he had washed the dried blood off his hands at the fountain near the entrance.

A young man in shorts came toward him. What did this little shit want? He moved on the boots with wheels, rollerblades they called them. Ridiculous, as they weren't blades at all. He wore the plastic pieces that filled his head with inane noise. He would escape all these idiots. The young man rushed past him, stopped and talked with the people on the bench. Did they conspire to stop him? Did he need to kill someone else today?

His plan was simple. When the door opened, he would rush through. If another appeared, he'd shove a knife in them. On his return he would go back to the landowner, who would see his invincibility. He had survived a battle where so many lives ended. The landowner would fear him.

Nothing would stand in the way of his return.

He had studied much in the City. In the past year, he'd made drawings of machines, their inner workings, including the engines that ran them. He spent many hours at libraries absorbing the words contained in bound pages, books written in a language he now understood at the highest level. The Doctor went to one of their schools, sitting in with the others, learning of the workings of the human body and the medicine of the City. When it was discovered he was not a student, they'd expelled him.

The library's books contained not only writings but drawings, and the capturing of pictures called photographs. All showed different cities, different people, different times. On one visit he saw drawings of a place that resembled his home. The

Doctor studied the places and the people that came after. He was shocked at what had transpired through time—wherever man had settled, a trail of blood followed. Then again, that was always the way.

The Doctor was especially interested in the writings about weapons, and the power behind electricity. He'd kept detailed notes in a series of small books. Those books were now tied together and buried into his jacket pocket. They would travel back with him, as would a few other pieces of science from this city. He even brought a music player with the plastic pieces like the rollerblader had worn in his ears.

With this knowledge, he would become the landowner's top retainer, receive his own land, and then gather his own force. They'd worship him like a god.

Police of some kind came up the path toward him.

"Excuse me, sir. Are you waiting for someone?"

He had been observing a section of thick leaves, which he thought was moving in a strange fashion, possibly signaling a doorway.

"Why does what I'm doing matter to you?"

Both men were broad at the shoulders. "There's been a complaint," one said.

The other policeman had his hands placed on the hips of his uniform.

"Of what nature?"

"People say that you've been here for hours, not moving from this spot, except to pace back and forth under that tree." He pointed to the place the Doctor had been watching closely.

"You got a home you can go to, buddy?"

"I am not your buddee." Such a ridiculous language. "Of course I have a home. What business is this of yours?"

"We were told you were bothering the children."

"What children?" He had a vague memory of yelling at a couple of urchins who ran toward him, chasing a flying disc.

"Look. Just move along and everybody will be fine." The

policeman placed a hand on the stick he carried around his waist.

The Doctor clenched and unclenched his hand. If he fought these two, even if he bested them, as he knew he could, he might lose the window of opportunity. The opening could come at any time.

"I needed rest. This City wears on me," he said.

"We understand, sir. But there are strict loitering laws, and—"

"Loitering? That's what you think? I am a doctor. I heal people."

The policeman stepped forward and put his hand on the Doctor's chest. He could break the man's thumb with one movement.

"You're a doctor like I'm a circus performer."

"I think you better come with us," the other one said.

It took everything inside him to stifle the urge to destroy these two. He could snap them in two.

"Okay, okay. I'll move along. That's what you call it, correct? Moving along?"

"You just wait a second." The angry one pulled at his jacket, bringing him close. A sweet chemical smell emanated from the officer. "We'll tell you when to move along."

"Clarence," the other one said.

The angry one snorted like a wild animal, released the jacket, and stepped back. The Doctor straightened his clothes and forced himself not to glare at these weak authorities. He made his way down the winding path, not looking back to see if they followed.

He walked a long loop around the streets that circled the ravine. Walking past the squat brick houses, he realized the folly of his plan. Riku had told him where to go for the crossover, but he had not given enough detail, and the area was too vast to search. How much time did he have? Riku had been dead for hours. The Doctor cursed himself for not forcing the young samurai to come with him. He could have killed the samurai in the ravine, and if something opened, he would be ready. Still, the time between a death and the crossing over might be longer. When he killed the boy in the market, nothing had happened until weeks later.

He panned around. He needed to refine his plan, be more strategic in his searching, divide the area into sections, study the grouping of foliage for a break in the tree line. Would there be a flash of light, or some sound? The couple on the bench were gone now, and the young man on rollerblades was nowhere to be seen.

Under a pair of arching trees, he noted a lighter green shade in strong contrast to the darker plants and bushes behind it. As he got closer, the green pulsated, and yellow beams emerged from the edges of the tree. On the far west of the ravine, the sun had begun its final descent, but the light he observed emanated from somewhere else. Then, the ground under him trembled lightly, and there was a sweet smell, which tugged at a very distant memory.

Then he heard music.

Chapter Thirty-Five

I ran all the way to the subway station, my mind on the dear one I had left behind. Had she experienced, like Yui, a depth of sadness after I left? How did she explain my disappearance to our child? Was she told that the archers hit their mark?

I studied the map above the train doors, though I'd seen and read it a hundred times, and observing it did not make the train go faster. I felt another's eyes on me, and turned to face a man who immediately averted his gaze. Though I traveled in a dark tunnel, I knew the sun was dropping. As the train climbed to the Davisville station, I saw that twilight approached. If the Doctor had slipped through the door, would he have left a remnant, some sort of trail?

The train squealed to a stop. The man who had been studying me tried to push past, but I held him back and sprinted out onto the platform into the crowd that flowed like a muddy stream. I fought my way around them toward the rising stairs.

Outside, the color of the sky had moved from faded gray-blue to a purple glow. What was left of the sun glinted off the four skyscrapers standing sentinel-like on the street corners. As I ran toward the setting sun, I realized my mistake—the ravine was too far.

Minutes were disappearing. No bus was in sight. A yellow car pulled alongside me, the driver observing my frantic movements.

"Need a cab, buddy? You look like you're in a hurry."

"Yes. Drive me to the ravine."

I got into the back seat and slammed the door.

"You mean Cedarvale?"

I recalled the name. "Yes, yes. Quickly, please."

The driver whipped his vehicle back into traffic. A wave of horns erupted around us as he sped down the street.

"Gonna be a nice night. If it weren't for these buildings, we'd see a pretty sunset. Look at the light on the clouds."

"Yes. It is beautiful. Could you drive faster?"

My forehead was wet, and sweat crawled underneath my clothes.

"You late for something? Funny place to have a meeting. Not that I'm nosy."

A cacophony of horns blared as the driver sped around another car and through a light as it turned red. I slowed my breathing, aware that the driver watched me in his mirror.

"I am meeting a friend. I don't like to be late."

"Hey, good friends understand. Y'know what I mean?"

"Yes."

"Good ones are hard to find."

"Yes."

Minutes flew until the driver veered off the main street and began a series of serpentine moves through the neighborhood.

"This is the absolutely craziest part of town. These one-ways make me nuts—y'know, they did that so people wouldn't drive through."

"Are we soon there?"

"Almost. I had a house here for about five years. Good

thing, or I'd never find my way. You know, they were gonna put a roadway through and bulldoze all these nice little houses. Stupid politicians."

The tires squealed when he took a hard turn and drove over a raised part of pavement, slamming the car down on the road.

"There ya go, Cedarvale. Good enough?"

"Yes." I jammed my hand into my pocket and pulled out a bill.

"Just a sec, I'll get you some change."

I bolted out the back of the car toward a path. A broken branch lay at the opening to the ravine—the bark was stripped, the limb pale and gray, as if it had been there for weeks or years. It pointed to an area south of the winding path. The air warmed around me, and a soft buzzing grew in my ears. As I dipped down the path, I scanned the trees in full foliage, wind rippling through them like a cascade of voices all calling to me. The arrow of the broken branch etched in my mind, I stepped off the path, moving onto a small decline that sloped toward a line of bushes.

Dark leaves shimmered in the dying sun. Bright shades of green overlapped the darker ones, and yellow beams shot out like lines in an ancient painting. I reached the edge of the bushes and stopped. I ran my hand along the top of the glowing plants, and I slowly rotated, absorbing the light. Then, the buzzing in my ear became a long musical tone, notes weaving together. It was the sound of the forest musicians. The beams wrapped around me, pulling me into the dark bushes. I looked one last time to the ravine. It was empty except for a faraway figure moving down the path in a fluid way that suggested he was on those wheels I had seen on people's feet in the park.

A force pulled me into the thicket. Leaves like soft hands caressed my body, and an aura of white appeared on the edge of my vision. I rotated my body again, taking steps down a path, blades of grass bent under my feet, cushioning my movements as I descended further. The foliage closed behind me as if a sea filled in my wake.

A cry. Ahead or off to the side, it was impossible to tell. Someone in sharp pain. And then again a cry.

The path reached a plateau where smooth stones formed a circle. I stood on them. The stones dissolved and I fell. Lights passed outside me and flashed in my mind.

A third cry, and then all sound stopped. A breath, barely a whisper, escaped in the air. All around me went black.

Someone had died.

Chapter Thirty-Six

I awoke in a meadow of brown grass. A body lay next to me. By his head lay a sharp gray rock stained in blood. I watched for a moment but observed no rising and falling of the man's chest.

I got to my knees and my body ached, as if it resisted the movement. The meadow stretched in all directions. Far off, a line of hills, and then farther yet the point of a snowcapped mountain. Ishizuchi.

Tendrils had fallen out of the dead man's topknot and stuck to his bloodied forehead, so I brushed the hair back from his face. It was difficult to ascertain his age, as his face had been beaten so badly, but from the lines on his skin, I observed he was much older than me. He wore the dress I knew well—a hitatare. I had worn one when I'd fled the estate. I rolled him onto his side, observing no other marks or patches of stained blood, except on his swollen face and skull. His assailant had struck him repeatedly.

I gently brought him back to his original position, straightening the leg so it was more natural. His body was still pliable—he had died recently. It was his cry I'd heard when I was pulled into the thicket. He had the skin color of my true form. I looked at my own hands and forearms and saw that my color had returned.

I began to walk toward Ishizuchi, but my legs tensed. I must have been injured from my long fall. I pushed forward through the long grass. My muscles continued to protest, not an aching but an unwillingness to move. I ignored them. A soft wind blew across my face, and the distant mountain's sharp edges rose out of the horizon like a weapon against the sky. I didn't know where I was going, or what I walked toward, only that I had to keep moving.

The sun warmed the meadow, and I was glad for the breeze cooling the line of sweat that trickled down my neck. I was, of course, no longer in the ravine. In this place it was earlier. By the position of the sun, I guessed mid-day. The season was different as well, perhaps early summer.

I walked for miles. At times my legs felt as if they were moving through thick mud, and then they would release. It was a curious feeling. Over a hill, I came upon a vista that showed where the meadow ended in a harsh line of trees, a forest much thicker than the City's ravine. I saw no path into the forest—the trees appeared as a solid mass.

Where had the dead samurai come from?

From my vantage, I searched for an entry point as the breeze shifted and swirled around my head. The wind grew in intensity, and I was forced to take a step back, and then another. The gusts became like snakes' bodies wrapping around me, attempting to lift me off the ground, pushing me back to where I'd come from.

A figure rolled out of the forest, as if the trees had parted and forced him into the open. Was there an animal that moved in such an unusual way? I saw that it was a man being pushed by the same wind that tried to remove me from the hill. The figure stopped rolling, grasped onto a large boulder, and righted himself.

The man twisted his body and raised his arm. His finger pointed to me like an arrow.

"Leave! Leave now."

It was the Doctor's voice shouting against the wind.

I fell back, slamming my head into the solid earth. A distant teaching attempted to form in my mind, but I could not bring it forward as the ground began to roll like a wave. I struggled to my feet, and strengthened my stance, as if standing on a ship and riding the sea. Looking down on me was the same mountain that stood over the estate where I had trained. As a child, my father taught me its name, Ishizuchi.

I pivoted my body to focus on the Doctor. He was still there, but now he was airborne, his body gliding in the sky, coming toward me. He flew over me, and then dipped sharply, plummeting to the ground. Then he lay flat against the undulating earth. The impact had killed him.

But then he screamed. "Stop!" And the earth stopped its movement and the wind slowed to a faint breeze.

The Doctor stood, brushing off his hitatare, and wiping the dirt from his face. His hair was whiter than before. His eyes held the same intensity, yet now they were an ebony color. His skin was no longer the pale color of the City—like me, he had regained his tone. His robe was tied with a sash the color of blood. He was the man who ended my brother's life.

"What the fuck are you doing here?"

"You don't belong," I said. "You killed an old man to open the door. And you killed another who had tried to cross."

"Ha. You found Riku. I shouldn't be surprised—our bodies are pushed together on both sides of the door. Look around, samurai. This is no longer your home. You and that City deserve each other. Go back to your so-called friends, those mindless fucks that scamper around their metal buildings."

"This is my home. I belong here."

I moved my hands into my own hitatare, searching for the tantō. It was not within the folds of fabric.

"What do you search for?"

"Nothing," I lied.

"You will discover that certain objects from the City will not cross over. Lucky for me, I quickly acquired another."

He reached into the folds of fabric, pulled a long blade from a sheath, and came at me with it. I jumped back, my feet quick and light.

He rushed past me, stopped, and spun around. His arm was a blur, reaching again into his robe and coming up fast. A glint of silver flew at me. I shifted my weight, my body bending only a couple of inches. The spinning blade nicked my shirt and cut a line on my chest.

Scanning the ground, I tumbled and grabbed two stones as I rolled. I came up and threw the stones while still in motion. One clipped his elbow, the other slammed into his shoulder and caromed off his face. Blood poured from a cut on his cheek.

He yelled and came at me again. I shifted back and forth, trying to gauge his angle of attack. The Doctor changed his direction, and I observed the shift in his weight. I stepped a few inches to the side. It was enough. His blade came down on my arm, but I already had a firm grasp on his outer garment and used his momentum to throw him over me. He landed hard, a breath away from a boulder that would have knocked him out, or maybe killed him. His knife lay between us.

"So the City didn't knock all the training out of you," he said.

Blood seeped from the wound on my forearm. Under my feet the ground rippled and undulated.

"Even the land rejects you," I said.

"Ha. I control the land. Soon, I'll control everything."

The ripple grew into a low wave, lifting my feet out from under me. When he lunged for the knife, I launched myself at him. He reached to grasp the blade as my foot struck his forehead. He flew back and slammed the ground hard. The wave of earth reached him, lifting him upward.

"Stop!"

This time the ground didn't listen, and another wave followed. The wind pushed hard behind me. I tried to grab the knife, but it was useless. In a moment, I was also airborne. The Doctor yelled again, but the wind and earth drove on. The wind held us above the field. We both attempted to hold our position, but we were kites let loose without owners.

The Doctor cursed the wind and was answered with pelting rain. We traveled in this strange flight-dance over the meadow. Below, I made out the figure of the samurai with the smashed-in face.

"In this place we are dead," I yelled over the rain and wind. "We no longer live here. We are being forced back."

"Only because of you. One can stay, two cannot. Go back to the City and leave me."

"If you stay here, you will do much harm."

"Go back to the ravine." The Doctor's tone shifted. "I give you my promise—I'll harm no one you know."

As if a string was cut, we fell from the sky and toppled to the ground. The air grew still, and the pelting rain slowed, then stopped.

"Why would I believe you?" I asked.

He grabbed my hitatare and brought me close to his face. His features twisted as he screamed in guttural sounds. I shifted my hands under his arms, searching for points, and applying pressure. He screamed again, but did not let go of me. His face reddened, his mouth opening wide, as if he would swallow me. I struck blows to his body. He flinched, then he took his hands quickly from my robe and grabbed my throat.

"I have trained samurai just like you. Did you know that?"

I struck blows on the inside of his wrists. It was no use.

"And always the teacher holds something back from the student," he said.

He applied more pressure to my throat. My air cut off and flashes of light appeared.

"You will die now, like the other samurai. I didn't waste my blade on him. It felt good to crush his skull. When I lay your body next to his, this place will accept me."

I could form no words, struggling to break free. I would die here, as I did before. Would I cross again?

Then an explosion of light and a roaring wind lifted my body again and spun me faster and faster. Was I imagining this? Was this how I would enter death? This time there would be no ravine, no crossover. I would travel to the true afterplace.

The sound of the wind was like a rushing train.

I was swallowed by the darkness.

Chapter Thirty-Seven

When Heather saw her father lying on the hospital bed with all the tubes and layers of cloth and plastic, and smelled the chemical stench of the cleaning products, she could only think of one thing. Why did she leave home?

She called Shauna from the hospital, in tears, just needing to talk with someone.

"He could have died, here alone. And I'm where? Chasing some fucking magazine job in Toronto."

"But he didn't die, hon," Shauna said. "And you're there now. It's a good thing. How's Zach holding up?"

"He's not saying much. Which is good because I don't know what to say to him anyway."

"Lots of hugs. That's what he needs. You too."

"Thanks, Shauna. You okay with looking in at my place? Alice has a key."

"Of course."

He was going to be okay. Okay. Heather kept saying it in her mind, and then in a whisper, as if something auditory would make it more real. "Okay." The doctors said he came out of the stroke fairly well, no paralysis, and a therapist would work with him on the slurred speech.

Her dad was in and out of sleep. He was on a lot of meds, so in his waking state he wasn't thinking straight. She wasn't sure he knew that she was there, or if he thought she was a figment of his addled brain. Zach sat quietly in the hospital room with her, and never complained. He'd brought a couple of books to read and some homework. After visiting hours, they stayed at her dad's place, ordered pizza, and watched TV.

The next morning her father woke and called out for Anna.

She inhaled sharply at the sound of her mother's name.

"It's okay, Dad, I'm here. It's Heather."

"Heathher? Where's Sachh?"

"He went to the cafeteria to get something to eat."

Hearing her father say her name, the "th" heavy in his mouth, and the slur of her son's name, sent a jolt of sadness through her. They told her to expect he would talk like this, but it was hard to take in.

The next few days were back and forth from the hospital to her father's place. She cleaned the small house, getting ready for his return. Heather spoke with the doctor, the nurses, the speech therapist, and the social worker who would be arranging the home care visits. Small towns like Garsen might not have all the cutting-edge equipment, but they did believe in community support.

"What do you think of being back here?"

"It's okay," Zach said. A line of ketchup and gravy ran down his chin. She and he had been having fries and gravy every afternoon at the diner in the basement of the Co-op department store. "Kinda dumpy, but in a nice way. Good fries, too," he added.

She laughed for the first time since they'd got there.

"No, I don't mean here in the Co-op. I mean Garsen."

"Oh. It's okay."

"You like Toronto better?"

"I dunno, maybe."

"What about your friends?"

"They're back in Calgary."

She looked away. If she continued the conversation in this way, Zach would get awkward and clam up. She wanted to give Zach a stable place where he could make long-term friends. Early on in art school, she'd known Toronto was the goal, and after that maybe New York. But now, back at the place she'd always called home, she reconsidered what was important.

"We're gonna stay a bit longer, is that okay with you?"

"Is Grandpa getting better?"

"Yes."

And, slurring or not, her father demanded to get the hell out of the hospital, so they released him. His doctor hadn't been fooled by his gruff manner. Everyone in town knew her father's kindness.

She had paid the rent a couple of days before leaving Toronto, and Shauna and Alice were looking after her place, watering the dying plants, and making sure no one broke in. So now she phoned the school, telling them that Zach would be missing for a week, maybe more. The teacher expressed condolences, to which Heather blurted out that her father was not dead, and that she and Zach would be returning to Toronto. She couldn't help but notice she'd said Toronto, not home.

She phoned again a week later, saying they would be staying a bit longer. The teacher suggested some things for Zach to work on, saying he'd have a lot of catching up to do.

"You should go back," her father told her. "Ssach will fall behind in school. And whath about your work?"

"Don't worry about it, Dad. This is more important."

Each meeting with a doctor or occupational therapist made it more difficult for her to leave. It wasn't how they explained her father's condition—they were really positive about his healing from the stroke. It was hard for her to admit that the drive to become an illustrator had superseded her relationships, including the one with her father.

One night, as she sketched her father asleep in his recliner, and Zach with his nose in a book on the couch, she thought, why couldn't she just be happy doing art here? Sure, there was no place in Garsen to publish it, no magazines or advertising agencies, and the local newspaper had the editor's nephew drawing horrid editorial cartoons, even for a teenager. But she could still do art here, couldn't she?

The thought reminded her of the inane conversations at art school, all the "what is art" debates. She'd chimed in like the other students. In her last year, the talk shifted to what people were willing to do for money—and how if art ever became just a job, then it was time to quit. What was wrong with making money? Especially if you had someone besides yourself to support. None of her art school friends had kids, after all—they had no basis in reality.

So if she stayed, what was she supposed to do? Paint pictures of the wheat fields and hang them in the little gallery by the public library? Was being in a national magazine more important than helping someone she loved?

A couple of days later, she sat with her father in his small living room drinking tea. She was flipping through the local paper, and her dad was watching baseball.

"At ssome point you're going to be wishout me." He turned the sound down. "I don't want you to give up what you worked so hard to accomplissh. There's no thense moping around here waiting for me to die."

She crossed her arms, holding onto her shoulders. "Dad."

"Oh relax. I'm gonna be around for a good stretch yet. As long as I can lose this loopy Thessame Ssstreet way of talking."

He was drawing out the esses for her benefit, and she laughed through her tears.

"It's good to be home, Dad."

"Whell you can alwaysh come back. I'll be here."

After that she stayed one last week. He'd made good progress in therapy. She gave him a big hug and had her last cry before the taxi picked them up for the airport. She promised him they'd be back for Christmas.

With the green-and-yellow checkerboard of fields gliding under the plane, she folded and unfolded the tiny napkin the attendant had given her with her soda water. Zach was asleep next to her, his face drooped in that way that showed how deep kids sleep, until he sat up with a start.

"Where are we?"

She stroked his hair. "Somewhere over Ontario now. Won't be much longer."

"Can we call Grandpa when we get home?"

"Of course."

—

It had been a whirlwind month since she'd got back. There were lots of late nights with Zach, helping him catch up with school, lying in bed with him while he fell asleep, and lots and lots of tears from both of them. Garth, her manager at Grafite, was surprisingly empathetic, for the first week anyway. Then he went right into guilting her about taking more shifts, as she'd taken a whack of sick days. She didn't bother reminding him that she flew home to see her father who had almost died. She knew that Garth wouldn't care or even pretend to.

She needed the extra hours anyway. She'd got another small job from one of the little indie magazines, but they only paid sixty bucks each for three black-and-white drawings. Still, it was printed work that she could use in the portfolio. She was frustrated by the Catch-22 art directors presented to her—if she didn't have printed work in her portfolio, they weren't confident in giving her work. And how the hell was she supposed to get printed work anyway? Portfolio showings? Yeah, right. They just told her to send printed samples when she had some.

And then there was the greatest mystery of all: What do

A.D.s want? She was going to figure that out if it killed her.

She left Zach with Alice one night and went for drinks with Vince to pick his brain.

"You gotta give them something they've never seen before, but at the same time, stuff they've totally seen," Vince said.

"That makes no sense."

"Don't make art that's focused on the market, Robsen. It'll stifle you."

"I'm calling bullshit, Vince." Three gin and tonics in, she got straight to it. Vince was being cagey as fuck. "You're telling me that you don't think about the market? Your promo got you work at *Report on Business,* the *Financial Times,* and that Air Canada magazine."

"*En Route.* Yeah, they pay decent, you should send them something."

"What? Send them what?"

He stirred his scotch and soda. "Business guys."

"Vince."

"Little business guys walking on a tightrope over some deep crevice or some metaphorical shit like that. Those money types love that. Makes them feel all profound and mystical."

Heather stared at him, trying to figure out if he was serious. "For real?"

"They eat it up, Robsen."

It was the clearest advice he'd ever given her.

That night after Zach went to bed, Heather ripped some pages from a couple of business mags she'd picked up at the Sally Ann and taped them to her board. For the next two hours she drew businessmen in different scenarios, free associating with whatever popped into her head. She drew them on tightropes, on giant chairs, at the top of mountains or rowing long skinny boats. She played with size, having the tiny men dance across the giant head of another man. She drew giants that walked Godzilla-like down Bay Street. She knew Vince took heavy influence from New York illustrators like Brad Holland, but put his own spin on it. What was her spin?

Heather studied the drawings taped to the table, pleased with their energy. Her figure drawing skills had always been strong. Vince had noticed those skills when they first met, and he admired them. She knew it was one of the reasons he liked hanging with her. Vince respected her work. Now she planned to get A.D.s to feel the same way.

The phone broke her concentration.

"Hey, sorry for calling so late, you still up?"

"What do you want, Michael?"

"I didn't wake you up?"

"I'm working. What do you want?"

A long pause. She contemplated hanging up.

"I came by while you were gone. I ran into Shauna at the Beverly."

"Uh-huh." She didn't hide her impatience.

"Jesus, Heather, I'm calling to say I was sorry to hear about your dad. How is he doing?"

"He's fine. What do you want, Michael? You already pawned my ring. So if you're calling to—"

"I just wanted to see how you are. How's Zach holding up? He was close to his grandpa, right?"

"My dad's not dead. I gotta go."

"Okay, okay, wait."

Another long pause. She heard Zach cough.

"It's late. I'm going to bed," she said.

"Can I come by tomorrow? In the morning? I'll bring you a coffee and something good."

"Not a good idea."

"I won't stay long. I'll get there before Zach goes to school. I'll help get him ready."

"He doesn't need any help."

"Please, Heather?"

She heard Zach cry out.

"Fine, whatever. I have to go."

Heather went to Zach's room, ran her hand across the back of his head, pulled the covers up tighter, and sang quietly. Zach's breathing slowed and deepened. She watched him sleep for a while, then went to take one last look at her drawings.

Her gaze stopped at one in particular, a businessman with a familiar face, someone she hadn't thought about for weeks. Even in a suit with a briefcase in his hand, he still looked like an ancient warrior. That morning in The Pearl felt like a hundred years ago. She wondered if she'd ever see The Warrior again.

Chapter Thirty-Eight

I awoke, no longer in the time before with the Doctor. I had left the ravine, having no recollection of how I'd made it back to my apartment. Had I died again? This time by the Doctor's hands? How many times could I cross over to the City? Was I destined for that form of immortality?

I sat in my dark kitchen, staring out at the night, the stars obscured by clouds. Red and yellow lights from the signs below lit the wet sidewalks. When had it rained? My body was dry, and without any sign of injury. Riku's blade had reappeared on this side of the crossover. I placed it on a soft fabric and slid it underneath my bed.

The emotion I carried was similar to the time three years ago when I first awoke in the ravine. Though, this time I knew where I was. A sadness washed over me as I recalled my first guide, Harry. I longed to see him again, to thank him for his kindness. Where had he crossed over? Was there an afterplace for the City's inhabitants? Is there one for any of us?

I went down my fire escape. I needed to be alone, and I did

not want anyone even to see me exit. I had no destination in mind, only that I needed to leave my apartment.

The colors that bled from the lit signs and so many tall buildings made it hard to see the constellations. Back on the shōen, there was an old man whose prophecies were based on the position of the stars. As I walked, I felt the air on my cheeks; only then did I realize I was weeping.

The Doctor had his hands on my throat, he had stopped my airflow, and I knew I was about to die. Once again, for whatever reason, the gods, or force, or whatever spirit moves the chess pieces of our lives, had decided that it was not my time. Instead of the afterplace, once again I was in the City. Toronto was its name.

My tears dried and I increased my pace. Unsure of where I was going, I pushed on, blind to all those around me, hearing nothing but my feet on the hard gray surfaces. Small eating establishments, brightly lit signs for closed stores, the grid of white-and-yellow squares in the skyscrapers, all created a barrage of unwelcome light—even the beams from car lights cut into me. I took a train, riding until the voice coming from a speaker said, "End of the Line."

Outside the station I stopped a yellow car with lights and told him to take me out of the City. He explained that he didn't go outside the city limits unless a price was negotiated.

"I need to leave," I told him.

"You want me to drive to a bus station?"

"Will that take me away from the City?"

"Last time I checked, yeah."

—

On the bus, exhaustion overtook me and I slept for a number of hours. I watched the sun rise on fields more vast than anything I'd seen in the City. The bus had taken me away from the towering skyscrapers and hordes of people. Still, I longed for the bus to drive where it couldn't go.

Time passed without anything to mark it. Day became night.

My mind continued to jump through the night. After the first long sleep, I slept little on the trip, only for short periods. I had no plan for how long I would travel. At certain times the bus stopped, and we filed into low buildings that smelled of smoke and sweat. I ate small meals with my limited money.

I counted the bills in my pocket, knowing that a decision on my return would be needed soon. The bus pulled over to a shelter on the side of the road.

"Need to make some calls and check in here with another driver. You folks can get off and stretch your legs. I'll give a honk when we're ready to go."

I had no idea how far we'd traveled. The vast fields had disappeared, and the road was now crowded by long bands of trees. I observed a small break in the forest. A tall man, a giant, bent over in the wind, his many arms shaped as if made with thick paint strokes. The arms waved in the wind, matching the fury of water that boiled below. As I moved closer, I discovered it was not a man, but a large tree. This gnarled tree was alone, growing out of bald rocks, anchored to them. If not for the boulders, the tree would be flung into the water and carried away by the crashing waves.

"He looks lonely."

I turned with a start. A small boy, another rider on the bus, had followed me to the vista.

"Do you mean the tree?" I asked.

"He's out here by himself. No one to keep him company."

The boy wore a bright blue coat with a covering that reflected the sun.

"He is keeping watch for the others," I said.

"Watch for what?"

"For whatever bad things might come to the other trees. He protects them, standing bravely against the wind."

"Hmm. Maybe."

A hawk screeched above and we both looked up, following

its path across the clouds.

"I saw some paintings in school that looked like that tree," the boy said.

"Like that one?" I asked.

"Yes. I wonder if the artist knew they are brave."

"Artists sense things that we cannot."

"I want to be an artist," the boy said.

"That is an important desire."

The bus horn honked, but neither of us moved.

"The woman on the bus with you, is she your mother? She will be worried for you."

"I told her where I was going." The boy's young face carried its own light. "How about you?"

"Where am I going?"

"Yes."

"I'm not sure."

The bus honked again, this time two quick sounds.

"We should go back," I said.

I followed the boy and his blue jacket back to the bus. The mother stood outside waiting for the young artist. She did not look worried, possibly used to her son's wandering.

A sign said the next city was fifty kilometers away. My journey would need to stop there. I didn't have enough money to stay at a lodging, so I would attempt to sleep on the bus. I was neither joyful nor saddened on having to return to the City. I did not think I could talk to Heather and Joshua.

"In the face of a disappointment, even one of grief or disaster, you must learn to say that it is ultimately good that this happened."

Such were the words of my teacher. And yet, I saw nothing good of any kind. Perhaps I would speak with Vera. She too had abandoned her place of birth.

The Doctor was no longer in the City, this I was sure of. His presence had ignited my longing, giving me hope that I might cross over. Like the old man, Riku, the longer I lived in the City, the more I had to surrender to it. I pondered if I'd helped the Doctor and killed Riku, would the land have let us stay in our true home?

My body was heavy, and I slid into a deep sleep. The tree sprouting from the rocks, where I'd talked to the boy, appeared in my dreams. In the dream, I was the tree.

The harsh lights of the station fell on me, and I awoke as we pulled into a stall. Once off the bus, I turned back, wanting to say something to the boy, but he didn't exit. He may have gotten off while I slept. Or did the boy in the blue jacket actually exist?

"Pay attention to all dreams, whether sleeping or while awake. They express what is inside." This was another of my teacher's lessons.

Perhaps I did dream the boy. But the City to which I returned was real. Too real.

—

"Mom, Michael's here."

Heather came out of the bedroom and checked the kitchen clock.

"Zach, where's your backpack? I made you a sandwich, and there's an apple and a cheese slice in the fridge for you—hustle it up or you'll be late."

"She's a bit of a drill sergeant, hey, Zach?"

"A what?"

"He thinks he's funny. Now c'mon, get going," she said.

Michael's hair was longer than she'd seen before, and greasier. He also had a two-day stubble, and a redness around his eyes. He had one hand jammed in the pocket of his black jeans that looked two sizes too big on him. He looked like hell.

"Hey there. Sorry I forgot the coffee and—"

"I don't have much time, Michael. I have drawings I need to drop off, and then a portfolio showing before I work my shift at Grafite."

"Look at you kicking ass and taking names."

"Mom, have you seen my reading book?"

"Check the floor on the other side of the bed." She turned to Michael, lowering her voice. "If you're here about money, forget it."

"Sounds like things are taking off for you."

"Seriously, if that's why you're here, you need to leave right now."

"Relax, relax, Heath'."

"Why is Michael telling you to relax? What's going on?" Zach asked.

Heather saw the worried look on her son's face. She'd sat up with him many nights after they got back from their time away, soothing his tears and assuring him about his grandfather.

"It's okay, Zach. He's just dropping off something. You find your book? Good. I'll see you after school. I'll make something good tonight, and we can watch *Knight Rider* together."

"It's not on tonight."

"Then we'll watch something else."

She hugged her son. Michael held up a hand for a high-five, and Zach weakly slapped hands.

"Be nice. Don't fight."

"Got it." Michael gave Zach a thumbs up.

Zach left and Heather listened to her son's sneakers clump down the stairs.

"Okay, spill it. I've gotta go in fifteen minutes."

"I can walk you to the streetcar," Michael said.

"For fuck's sake. What do you want?"

"Jesus, Heather. How's your dad? Shauna told me he had a stroke—does he have someone taking care of him, or a nursing home or something?"

"Getting better. He's still at home, working with an occupational therapist, and another therapist helps with his speech. Homecare visits a couple of times a week."

"He can't talk?"

"I really don't have time for this, Michael."

"Sorry, sorry. I was just worried about you. And I always liked your dad."

"I already told you on the phone he's not dead."

"Can I have a cup of coffee or something? Lukewarm glass of water?"

He gave the smile that used to melt her. Now it just pissed her off. She grabbed a cup out of the cupboard and poured the last of the coffee into it. Michael sat down at the kitchen table, and she looked up at the clock again.

"I know, I know, fifteen minutes."

"Ten."

"Heath', it's hard for me to come to you. But I'm in trouble."

"This is about money. Fuck. Why is your hand still in your pocket? What are you hiding?"

"No, no, listen. I mean, yes it is . . . but listen, this is really bad."

His hand shook as he gingerly took it out of his pocket, revealing a splint and gauze wrapped around his pinky and ring fingers.

"What the hell did you do?"

"They broke them, Heath'. And they said they'd do worse if I didn't come up with the money." He broke down, gulping huge breaths between the tears. "I have nowhere else to go. It's going really bad. I think they might . . ."

"Might what?"

"Cut me. Beat me up. I don't know, kill me." More sobs, and he reached out for her with his unbandaged hand. She took it.

"Michael, I'm really sorry, but I can't help you. Can you call the police or something?"

"And report what? That I gambled money with an illegal source, who now wants it back and is threatening to kill me?"

"Can you get a bank loan?"

"Who's going to give me a loan? That's why I went to this guy in the first place."

"I wish I could help. But I can't."

"Didn't they give you the right? You know . . . to the account?"

"What?"

"To your father's account. When my mom got real sick, they gave my sister control over her account."

"My God."

"Power of attorney, that's what it's called. If you have that, you could take some money from there, just a loan. I'd pay it back as soon as I could."

Heather shook. She wanted to rip or punch something. Michael. She wanted to punch him right in the face.

"You piece of shit. Get out of my apartment."

He started to cry again. She grabbed his jacket and pushed him toward the door.

"Don't call me again. Ever. Or come by. I fucking mean it, Michael. Get out."

He sputtered a bit more before she slammed the door on him. She grabbed the counter, stifled a yell, and sat down at the table.

"I will not cry for that son-of-a-bitch."

Heather listened to herself breathe for another minute. Dammit, she was going to be late. She grabbed her portfolio, tucked the envelope of mounted drawings into the inside pocket, and zipped it up. She'd placed a number of the businessmen drawings on the last few pages. She'd say they were works in progress, not the usual thing she'd put in a portfolio, but maybe they'd hold some interest for the A.D.

She scanned the street outside her apartment, but he was gone.

Return

Chapter Thirty-Nine

I wanted only solitude. Although, I needed to earn wages, as the bus trip had exhausted all my currency. So, I returned to my work with the painters—they took me back; no one desired an explanation for my absence. They'd acquired a project repainting all the rooms in a large school and needed extra painters.

I didn't answer my phone, even on the days it went off many times. One day, I pulled the cord that attached my phone out of the wall and threw it away. If someone buzzed to be let in my apartment building, I ignored the sound. It was not my concern if Joshua was worried about me. Heather didn't know where I lived. They could have each other. I needed no friends.

I now left the building only by way of the fire escape, and only after being sure that no one would observe my descent. I painted all day without speaking, though that didn't stop the other workers from their loud storytelling or singing along with the music machines they carried into every room.

One of the nicer men, an older man named John, put his hand on my shoulder at the end of the day. "Whatever you're going through, Gordo, she isn't worth it."

I didn't tell John the depth of my despair. How would someone, anyone, understand that I'd failed to return to the one person who was still a part of me? I cradled my humiliation like a hurt animal that I alone could care for. It pained me to bring her face into my mind, so I pushed it away. But it swept in, along with the one she carried within her. I had been forced from the shōen before casting my eyes on new birth. The child, our child, would be almost three years old now. Ignoring my teacher's lessons on self-control of my emotions, I let the tears cascade down my cheeks.

In my apartment, I continued my training. The discipline was rooted deep within. It was not to prepare myself for battle. I had already been defeated. The training brought solace, shifting my focus to the controlled movements of my body. I retrieved Riku's tantō from under my bedside and added exercises with the blade to my regimen.

After the training, I meditated, then read from a book Joshua had given me, then undressed and went to bed. I had no visions in my meditation time. I believed they would not come again. Nightly, I examined and honed the edge of the tantō. Increasingly, I considered the path of the ritual that would allow me to escape the City. I knew of samurai who performed seppuku, though I'd never witnessed it. Yet, I had no second to slice off my head the moment I slid the blade across my stomach and spilled my bowels.

I was not sure how long I could hold back the desire to end my life. Even if I did, would I simply cross over and cross back again?

Today, I was to be at the school and painting by eight o'clock. I'd been awake since six o'clock, which gave me time to sit in front of my kitchen window. A cloud moved in two directions, as if someone was drawing open a curtain, and morning sun cut through the gray mass. Rays of sunlight streamed across my kitchen floor and stretched into the living room.

I followed the rays to my spot of meditation. As I closed my eyes, sitting in lotus, a feeling of warmth spread across my legs. I began to sink into the floor and slowed my breathing. Air moved below me. I bent my neck, opened my eyes a slit, and observed a vision of clouds underneath my folded legs. The clouds parted, revealing a vast field.

In the vision, a battle raged below. Many bodies were strewn across the field. Arms and legs were separated from the figures—men with arrows in their back, neck, and chest lay in the unnatural way of the dead. I witnessed the carnage. The vision was vivid, but without sound. I saw a group of men chasing a lone man. Suddenly my body dropped lower in the sky. I feared the men below would see me and fire arrows at the floating demon, which is how I must appear.

The silence in the vision ended as wind rushed in, along with cries of the pursuers. The man ran in a long arc, dipping down and swerving his body, as arrows flew past him. He launched himself from a large rock that jutted from the ground. I thought he'd taken flight until he landed again, stumbled, and continued his sprint. He headed to a line of trees, trying to reach them before one of his pursuers found their target. I believed he would make it until a horse and rider appeared. As the rider drew back his bow, the man took a bad step and fought to regain his balance. The arrow struck the man through the neck. He fell a few yards from the tree line.

On the ground, his body twisted and he raised an arm, pointing to the sky where I hung in mid-air. His eyes widened, and he mouthed the phrase I'd heard him say that day in the market.

"Too late," the Doctor said.

All went black in the vision. Echoes of music rang in my mind, stringed instruments being plucked. Orange tones from the underside of my eyelids drifted in, as the room grew into focus. I felt stiffness in my knees, unaware of how long I had sat.

The clock read 7:30. If I moved quickly, I could arrive at the school on time and begin painting. But I knew I would not.

—

The morning had already lost its coolness, the air thick with humidity. A pair of men, followed by three women, ran on the path. A dog barked, the owner pulling the animal away from the runners. I'd grown accustomed to this sight of people running, not away or toward anything, but just running. Joshua told me they did it for their health.

I once again stood at the place where I'd followed the Doctor's path and rode a spiral of yellow beams to the time before. How many days had passed since that crossover? I had lost count. I now waited in the ravine without knowing what, or who, I waited for.

I refocused on the patch of green, studying the dark leaves, looking, waiting for the yellow beams to appear. My ears were attentive should the sound of the forest musicians waft into the air. Was there only one spot where the door opened to let in the dead, or to receive the living? I couldn't be sure. My vision this morning had shown the Doctor dying on the battleground, blood trailing from the arrow in his neck. The vision went black before I saw life escape his body. But why else would I be shown this vision? The Doctor said our bodies are pushed together on both sides. We are to meet again. He was coming back. I only had to wait.

On the train to the ravine, I fashioned a theory on the crossovers. The number three was paramount. On the side of the City, three samurai from the time before existed at all times. When one of them died, another samurai was called forth. The Doctor had killed the one meant to cross, and since he had crossed before, he was forced to leave the time before. The land and people rejected him, pushing him back to the City. In this way the balance of three was maintained.

However, that left only two of us when the Doctor came back. Would there be another crossover to replace the one the

Doctor killed? Perhaps this had already happened. If so, where was this other samurai?

I couldn't fully explain this arrangement of three, or who controlled the forest musicians. Where was the Creator in all this? My teacher told me to look only to the beauty of the lotus to know that hands much greater than ours were at work.

"Why must there be a Creator?" I had asked. "Water meets earth, seeds blown in by the wind are heated by the sun. Life is created by the elements."

"Your arrogance is matched only by your stupidity," my teacher said.

If I'd listened to his teachings, and his warnings, I would still be at the shōen. Now when I returned, I would be an outlaw, forbidden to see the woman who carried my child. Wait! My child, if he were a son, would grow and train as a samurai. Was I not both excited and frightened by the thought of him crossing over to the City? I had surmised that the samurai who crossed over were somehow connected. Perhaps they were members of the same clan or family. My son and I could be united in the City. How long would I have to wait? And his crossing would mean his death on that side.

I had lost focus thinking of these things, so again I stilled myself by the door of leaves, waiting for the beams of light. I had no plan of action beyond confronting and battling the Doctor when he came through the door. It crossed my mind to run past him into the wake of beams he left behind. But would the land reject and spit me back as it did before? Was it different for me because of my family or because of my training as a samurai?

As the sun climbed into a still, cloudless sky, the heat and the humidity rose with it. There were no more runners, only a few people with dogs and some small children, a mother pushing a cart with wheels with another child inside. I paced the area, keeping watch over where I believed the door would open. Hours went past, and yet still I waited. I fought back hunger, but the heat demanded I find drink or I'd become ill.

I signaled a young man on a board with wheels.

"If I give you money, will you go and buy me something to drink?"

"Can't buy no alcohol. I'm only fifteen." He began to push off.

"No. I only need water. Can you bring me a bottle?"

"Why can't you get it yourself?"

"I need to wait for someone."

He pointed his thumb over his shoulder. "There's a store a couple of blocks over."

"Yes, I know." I handed him currency.

"You just want water?"

"Yes, please. I will wait here."

"All right."

He rolled off down the path. After a long period, I decided I wouldn't see him again. I scanned the ravine for a more trustworthy person to call over. Then I saw the young man coming down the path toward me.

"Here, I got you a couple." He pulled two bottles out of his backpack. "And I got you this."

He handed over a bar of chocolate.

"I didn't ask for this."

"Whatever. You looked like you needed something to eat, and you gave me a ten." He watched me take a long drink. "I suppose you want your change? I bought myself a Snickers."

"You may keep the remainder. Thank you for your honesty."

"Whatever."

The young man rode off, a boy really, and I felt lightened by the transaction.

Later in the day, an older woman stopped to stare at me. Fearing she might call an authority, I called over to her.

"It's a beautiful day. I'm waiting for a friend of mine."

She moved away briskly.

The afternoon disappeared, and as if time slipped into a hole, the evening approached. Perhaps the Doctor had entered somewhere else in the ravine. Would I feel a sensation as he crossed over, or hear the musicians? Throughout the day, I believed the Doctor could appear at any moment. But as the light bled out of the sky, despair flowed back into my mind. Had I only imagined the vision? Had the Doctor really died on the battlefield?

When the first star came out, my heart sank. I was overtaken by grief. I left the ravine, walking the long way back to the subway, ignoring the bus that passed me. The train was full of people, and yet I felt as alone as I'd ever been. All these passengers pushed together, none of them knew me, or where I'd come from.

Needing someone to talk to, anyone, I turned to a woman next to me.

"My name is Gordo."

She looked straight ahead, pretending not to hear.

"I don't belong here," I told her.

Her neck twitched. She stood and moved around several passengers deeper into the train car. A man with black drawings across his arms and neck took her place.

I rode the rest of the way in silence, alone.

Chapter Forty

It felt as if he were being squeezed through a tunnel of mud and grime and human excrement. He barely recalled the last time he'd crossed. It was long ago, but it wasn't like this. This time the land vomited him out into the City. He emerged from a hole in the street, his body soaked not in blood but human waste. He looked into a black sky and squinted as the hard rain battered his face. Lightning flashed and the darkness rumbled like a volcano erupting. The hot rain formed steaming puddles, the air was dank, and his mouth tasted of sulfur.

The road and walkway ahead was empty, boards across metal horses sectioned off the street. Another flash exposed the signs in lurid colors telling him the area had NO EXIT. Next to the signs a huge machine loomed, clad in metal the color of rotten lemons, black wheels with square knobs bigger than his fist, and a long arm connected to a wedge of metal teeth. In the daylight he had seen such a machine belch smoke as it tore the ground. He pictured the teeth ripping through his enemies.

Lighted squares in a geometrical pattern towered above

him. Walking away from the barricaded street, round lights on long poles appeared, and hordes of people walked amongst them. Some moved under domed sheaths, others with papers or cloth over their heads, and yet others defiantly walking, as he did, with no covering. He knew what these objects that blocked the rain were called, but he resisted the memory of the word. The people chattered, some laughing, others cursing, all in a language he wanted to forget he ever knew. But he heard and understood every utterance.

"If we bolt, we can make it to Paupers, or the Trinity."

"Brunswick is closer."

"The beer is shit."

"I'm soaked."

"Who cares, let's run for it."

He reached into his coat, running his fingers over the handle of the knife. Why had all his clothes changed, and yet he still carried his possessions? Yet, when he crossed back to the time before, objects did not travel with him. This surely came as a surprise to the young samurai who had followed him through the door. He'd probably wondered what happened to his weapon.

Grasping the hilt of the knife, he was comforted by its shape. How many could he kill? On the battlefield in the time before, he'd put down countless men with a sword, and then a broken sword, and then an arrow tied to another shaft, and then this very knife. Men took their last breath as he slid it into their ribs, or jammed it hard into their chest with strong enough blows to break bone. The blade would do just as well on this side of the crossover.

Two women in reflective clothing ran past laughing, their boots kicking up water and splashing him. He hated the patterned light in buildings that reached higher than buildings should rise. Even greater was his hatred for those that inhabited this place. How many could he kill? Would he be caught by the authorities and thrown into a prison? Or did they execute people here? He hoped they did. He would rather perish a hundred times on that bloody field than return to this cesspool of civilization.

"Are you okay, sir? Are you lost?"

A tall man in a long coat with too-clear skin held out his hand. He growled at him, and the man moved quickly away.

Why couldn't he stay in the time before? It was where he was born. After he had crossed back, he was hired as a retainer by a lord.

"I will put you in command of all who guard this shōen," the lord had told him.

"Why put so much trust in me?" he'd asked.

"I sense your power."

He held back from sharing his knowledge with the lord, not wanting to reveal anything too soon. The books he'd tried to carry through the door had vanished. From memory, he remade his drawings and notes. His understanding of chemistry would lead to the development of explosives that when unleashed would shatter the earth. After those weak and ignorant people of that time experienced his power, he would ascend and command all. Even the lord would have to recognize and bow to his greatness.

But other unknown forces, the land, or perhaps time itself would not allow this to happen.

When news spread of another shōen from the west starting to advance their forces, swallowing other lands, he was called to lead the lord's forces into a battle that couldn't be won. He killed many, but the group of men he commanded were badly trained idiots. He did not have the time needed to show his knowledge gained from the City, and to work on the experiments that would release tremendous power.

The estate was surrounded and the fighting began, spilling over the grounds and onto the surrounding fields. The other retainers fell around him, and he found himself the last man standing. The only thing certain was his death and those he would take with him. But then a window of escape presented itself—a forest to disappear into. He bolted across the field, hoping to lose his pursuers in the forest.

When the arrow pierced his neck, his only thought was of his journey to the afterplace. If that was what awaited, so be it. As the life force drained from him, he felt the presence of another, as if being watched from the sky. Then he heard that damn music. He was too late to run from it. In that half-second, he understood that he would return to the place he despised— the City. He was sucked up by the beams, and his screams were swallowed by a tunnel of shit.

Denizens of the City sprinted past.

"Sharon, I'm totally soaked. Let's go home."

"Come on, you wimp. The Brunswick is less than a block."

How could it be? His hands had been on the samurai's throat. He had killed him, hadn't he? But it was the samurai's eyes he felt upon him on the battlefield.

That fucker was still alive.

Fingering his blade, he wondered how many he could kill on this side. It didn't matter. To return, he only had to kill one.

Chapter Forty-One

In the darkness it was hard to see light. My longing and desire had only resulted in failure. My solitude had brought me nothing but more sadness.

"The end for all samurai is either ronin or seppuku," my teacher had said.

"So I drift like the wave-man, or end my life in the ritual? Surely there is a third way."

"When you are sick, in trouble, or disaster strikes, true colleagues will not disappear. But know that every person you grow close to will become another responsibility," he'd said.

The teaching came back to me as I woke this morning. My friends have each other. They do not need me. If I reach out to them in my pain, will they stand with me?

I have had guides in this City. Without Harry, I would never have survived. Though my time with Vera had been brief, she knew what it meant to be displaced—and in her own way, she guided me. But there was one who stood above those other two. I meditated on this for a long time before I finally left my apartment.

It was mid-morning, and I stood outside The Pearl observing my friend through the window for a few minutes before I entered.

"Holy shit."

Joshua stood up at the table and knocked over his coffee rising to greet me.

"Shit, I mean holy shit, Gordo. I thought you were dead."

"Why did you think that?"

"Where have you been, man? I phoned you for days. I went to your place and buzzed. Some raggedy-ass guy outside your building told me he thought you moved. I was gonna call the cops, but I stopped on account of I didn't know if you wanted to be found. And I guessed if you were dead, then someone would have smelled something . . . or I don't know. I even called some hospitals."

"It's very good to see you, Joshua."

Joshua shook his head like he had just awoken. "Well, yeah. It's great to see you, too. I thought you were, uh . . ."

"Dead."

"Shit's sake, tell me what's been going on."

I pointed at the pool of coffee on the table, and he mopped it up with a napkin, saying, "Stan, can I get another cup? Look who came back."

"Good to see you, Gordo. I'll bring some tea," Stan called over.

"Okay, spill it," Joshua said.

"Again?"

"No, no, not the coffee. The story. Dammit, Gordo, if you don't want to tell me where you've been, okay . . . but you gotta tell me. I was worried, man. Especially after that morning we talked in here. And so was she."

"You've seen Heather again?" I closed my fist and then willed the muscles to relax.

"Oh geez, yeah. In fact . . ." Joshua checked his timepiece.

"She should be here any minute. We were going to have a late breakfast together."

"She is joining you? I will leave you two, then."

"What? No. Stay, Gordo. She will love to see you. We talked about you. We've both been really worried."

A tightness grew in my stomach. I nodded to my friend.

"Has she been well?"

"Heather? Yeah, sort of. I mean, she had to go back home 'cause her dad was really sick, a heart attack. But she's back now."

"Did her father die?"

"No, he's okay now. Gordo, did you go on a trip, or did you go to a hospital? I mean, some of the stuff you were saying."

"A hospital for those not in their right mind. A crazy house?"

"No, not like that."

My friend paused. I saw compassion on his face. I understood that Joshua would always protect me.

"Well, maybe a hospital like that, yeah," he said.

My skin felt warm, and the tightness in my belly began to relax.

"I am fine, Joshua. I needed to be alone for a while."

Stan brought tea and refilled Joshua's coffee. He laid down fresh napkins.

"Stan, could I please have some toast with honey? I can't stay long, so if I could get it right away."

"Sure thing, Gordo," Stan said.

"That's it? You needed to be alone? And now you're fine?" Joshua's eyes grew wider with each question.

"I am not really fine, but I know that's what people say." I poured tea into my cup, thankful to be sitting in The Pearl again.

"Why can't you stay long?"

"I need to see someone. But I wanted to see you first. Joshua, I need to trust you with some things."

"Anything, buddy. Lay it on me."

"Someone is coming to the City to look for me."

"Who? And coming from where? You in some kind of trouble?" Joshua smacked his hand on the table. "Dammit, see, I knew not to call the cops."

"Yes, I am in a form of trouble. But I did not cause it. And you were right not to call the authorities. The person searching for me is disturbed and angry. And violent."

"Whoa. Some sort of gangster? Do you owe money . . . ? I can get you some money, Gordo. I'll talk to a guy on my crew."

Stan brought my toast just as the chimes above The Pearl's doors rang. I glanced over my shoulder. I was still uncertain if the Doctor had crossed over to the City.

"I don't owe any money. You have seen this man before," I said.

"Where?"

"He professes to be a Doctor, but this is untrue."

"The guy the cops asked you about? The one who tried to bust into Sneaky Dees?"

"Yes."

"I don't really remember what he looked like."

I described the Doctor's appearance to Joshua. He nodded, looking very serious.

"I can ask some people I know to have a look. Maybe you should call the cops. I mean, if this thing isn't your fault."

"I don't want to involve the authorities. Please don't tell anyone of this."

"Uh, okay. What about Heather?"

"Yes. You may tell her."

"Gordo, I gotta tell you, she likes you. I think she likes *you* a lot."

The warmth in my stomach spread into my chest and then my neck. I felt my face flush. I looked down and then away, toward Stan, toward the front door.

"Awful quiet, buddy, whattya thinking?"

"Joshua, I do need to leave now. I want to meet with you and Heather, but not right now. Perhaps we could all meet in the park. Do you go to your work today?"

"I do. But why don't you call her? I mean, are you sure you want me to come?"

"I no longer have a phone. Heather has a son. She may need to make arrangements. When is your work complete?"

"Late one today—right until seven tonight. An outside job."

"Ask her to meet us at eight o'clock tonight," I said, using the word for time the people in the City were so obsessed with. "You remember the park location, do you not?"

"Of course." He leaned close to me and spoke in a whisper. "Are you gonna tell me where you've been?"

"I went on a trip. I saw a beautiful tree and I met a boy."

I finished my tea and stood to leave. Joshua reached out and grabbed my hand.

"I'm really glad you're all right, Gordo."

"Thank you for being my friend."

—

I left The Pearl and moved fast along Queen Street, feeling both the joy and the weight of Joshua's friendship. I might be exposing my friends to an enemy unknown to them. Now, I had to consider not only my safety but my friend's protection. I needed to push away my desire. Like the tree on the edge of the great sea, I would stand sentinel-like to protect others from the coming storm. Yet, even in my pushing away, I saw her face.

If the Doctor had crossed over, he would seek me out. He had not found me as of yet because of my hiding. As much as it pained me to believe it, I no longer saw him as a doorway back to the shōen.

I crossed the lights at University Avenue. A group of men were huddled against the iron fence surrounding a gray stone likeness of a man on a horse. They wore stained and ripped clothing. Their faces were misaligned: sunken cheeks, one higher than the other, and drooping eyes over off-center noses. They sat on a dirty blanket, a cup full of coins in front of them and a hat with a few bills inside. The sun lit the face of the stone man staring into the glass and steel buildings. I put currency into the hat as I passed.

"Hey, God bless you, buddy," one of them said.

"Buddy" was what Joshua called me. It was a name I never understood, but it always warmed me to hear it. Now, I needed to talk to my most recent friend, the one who understood my loneliness. To Vera.

Chapter Forty-Two

Riding the streetcar, Heather sunk into the din of noise around her. The small indie magazine had loved the drawings. They told her they'd process her invoice right away. Vince had said that when he used to work for small magazines, they used to give him another job whenever he finished one for them. The art director, who was also the editor, asked if she could do another set of drawings for their next issue.

"Love to."

Her portfolio meeting at *Report on Business* was only a couple of blocks away, but because of the extra time with the indie magazine, she had to sprint up Front Street to make it. The A.D. there was old school and probably had seen every illustrator in Toronto. Still, he did say "Nice" when he saw the two sheets of drawings.

"How would you put some color in these?" he'd asked.

"Watercolor. Like my other work."

She'd kept the sarcasm out of her voice, but what the fuck did he think she'd use, purple crayon?

"Uh-huh. Send me one when you do that."

"A print, you mean? Or a postcard?"

"Yeah, something."

And that was it. Heather realized art directors had a steady stream of illustrators looking for work, and it was getting harder to get actual appointments with them instead of portfolio drop-offs. Still, she'd hoped for more, especially with the inclusion of business guy drawings. *R.O.B.* was a glossy financial mag that always won a lot of awards, both for design and illustration. She knew it paid well, because Vince had done a half page for them and he got six-fifty. Heather thought about name-dropping Vince, but knew it didn't matter a wick who she knew. It was one of the things she loved about illustration: it was the work that counted, not who you golfed with.

She got off the streetcar a couple of blocks before her stop. She still had an hour to kill before her shift at Grafite, and wanted to see if Pages Books had anything new in stock. Lately, she'd been thumbing through the graphic novels, what she still called comic books even after Vince corrected her. The novels were a lot thicker and beautifully bound, different than the stack of Marvel and D.C. comics Heather had in her room growing up. It's where she first learned about figure drawing.

As a kid, and then as a teenager, Heather copied Green Arrow and Green Lantern comics. She brought a stack with her to Toronto because she still loved looking at the figure drawings. She had showed them to Zach.

"Are those guys superheroes? Do grown-ups read stuff like that?"

"I used to. But more, I love the drawing. Look at this ink. That's done by a guy named Steve Ditko. And this one is Neal Adams."

"The ink is the black lines, right?"

"Yep."

Shauna told her about a new series with turtles that were some kind of ninja warriors. Turtles with swords and arrows

. . . okay, that's what people were into now? Last time she was in Pages, she found the turtle book, and saw that the drawing was tight and the color palette was rich. She was going to pick it up, thinking Zach would like it, until she saw the twenty-dollar cover price.

A man stepped in front of her as she turned to go inside. She held out her hands, trying to stop from slamming into him.

"Hey. Excuse me."

He ignored her comment, grunted something, and went into Pages ahead of her. In the graphic novel section, Heather thumbed through the shelf, though her attention was on the man browsing the bargain table. He periodically looked up. She knew he was watching her. She decided to leave. The man turned and walked quickly after her. Out on the street, she spun to face him.

"You need something, or should I call a cop?"

"I recognize you. You are his friend."

"Who are you talking about?" She took a step back, firming her stance on the sidewalk, fists clenched at her sides.

It took her a few seconds, but then she realized she recognized him. "You were in the pizza place. You were really rude. Now you're being an asshole again."

"I need to find him. He no longer answers at his home." His voice was clipped, talking too fast.

He dipped his hand into his pocket.

"Stop!"

He moved his hand slowly out of his pocket. She wanted to scan the street for any kind of cop or person that she could call over, but didn't want to take her eyes off him.

"Where is he?"

"I haven't seen him since that day in the pizza place. Now, if you don't mind—"

"Has he moved? Do you know where?"

Her stomach tightened.

"I'm late, and need to pick up my son."

The man that Gordo had called the Doctor slid his hand back into his pocket. She stepped around him, pushing his shoulder as she moved, and started up Queen Street, listening for footfalls behind her. What was he about to pull on her, a gun? A pleasing image of violence flashed in her mind's eye—her knee into his crotch—like the night Gordo stopped the punks. Dammit, why did she feel the need to mention her son?

She took deep breaths. Her walk was a jog by the time she crossed Peter Street; a band of sweat ran across her forehead and down her neck. It took her a minute to realize that Joshua was coming toward her.

"Oh damn. We were supposed to meet at The Pearl. I totally forgot."

"Gordo's back."

"What?"

"Hey, are you okay? Why were you running?"

"I'm fine. Where is Gordo?"

"Here in the city. I was just at The Pearl with him. I wanted him to wait until you got there, but he had to go do something. You didn't show up, so I figured you just forgot."

"Where has he been? You told me you thought something happened to him."

"Something might have. I'm not sure, he's acting kinda strange."

"Strange how?"

"He really wants to see you. Us, I mean. Listen, can you meet us at eight tonight, in that park he likes? You know the one?"

"Off Beverly?"

"Yeah." Joshua pinched the skin at his throat. "Heather, I think he's in some kind of trouble."

"Is he sick? Do you think he went to a hospital?" She didn't want to say institution, but it was there in her mind.

"I worried about that, too—if that was why he's been away. But he said someone was looking for him. A guy who pretended to be a doctor."

"What?"

"I've never seen Gordo's face look scared like that," Joshua said.

"Shit. I just saw him."

"Wait. You saw Gordo?"

"No. The one looking for him. I met him once before. There's something between the two of them. Gordo never said, but I think he's pressuring him. Or worse."

"Where did you see him? You gotta be careful—Gordo said the guy was nuts. And violent."

"He followed me into Pages."

"You think it's a money thing, or drugs? That's why the pressure?"

"I really doubt Gordo does drugs. The Doctor asked me where he was."

"Did you tell him?"

"Joshua, I don't know where he is." She checked her watch. "Damn, sorry, I need to get to work."

"Can you come tonight?"

"I'll have to see if my neighbor can watch Zach. But yes, I can come. What does Gordo want us to do?"

"I dunno. Maybe he'll explain more in the park."

"Okay, I'm really late. I'll see you at the park tonight."

As she ran to Grafite, she realized how much she wanted to see Gordo again. Oh yeah, get involved with another guy with mental health problems. Did a gambling addiction even count as a mental health problem? Not that it mattered. Michael was an asshole, plain and simple.

But Gordo. Gordo was a whole different situation entirely.

Chapter Forty-Three

I walked along Yonge Street waiting for time to pass. The eatery where Vera worked did not open until 11:00. I passed a set of pillars that bordered a large wall covered with photographs of almost-nude women.

I knew the doors behind the pillars led to staircases that descended into darkness. I was led down those stairs once. At the bottom, I entered into a room where a fully nude woman gyrated onstage, her legs grasping a pole that came down from the ceiling. I had seen drawings of women in only their flesh, and under cover of night I had seen my lover. This was different than those times; it was more animal-like. When I quickly left the room, I heard laughter, which only deepened my shame.

Passing by the place in the bright sun, I recalled this shame. It was one of the many things that made me long for the shōen. I'd never told Joshua about visiting that dark place, and I never again entered it.

I looked into a store full of timepieces on glass shelves, square black boxes, and other electronic devices whose purposes were unknown to me.

As the morning stretched on, more and more citizens appeared on the sidewalk. Yonge Street was a long river that flowed in a north–south current through the City. The people had lined faces, their mouths in a permanent frown, studying the gray sidewalk ahead of them and never looking up. This day the City seemed cast in a different light. I wanted to tell those citizens to look up and observe the sun.

I stopped at a place selling hot beverages and drank a cup of strong tea before taking the long walk back to Vera's eatery. When I arrived, they had just opened and already two patrons were lined up waiting for pizza. Vera was not there, but I recognized the other female worker from my last visit.

"She hasn't come in today, but she should be here."

"Is she often late?" I asked the woman.

"Vera is never late. It's super weird."

I moved to the side as she served another man, and then continued our conversation.

"Can you call her? I'd like to know if she is coming in today."

"You a friend of hers? Don't recognize you."

"I'm a new friend. I've been in here before, and I remember you."

"Well, I don't remember you, sugar. And yeah, I did call her, but she didn't pick up. She better get her butt in here, because it's gonna be a busy one."

"When did you see her last?"

"We did a shift yesterday. She had to leave early. Someone came to get her."

"She left with someone?"

The woman's eyes narrowed.

"You a cop or something?"

"No. Only a friend. I told Vera that I would meet her at work today."

Before arriving in the City, I'd rarely lied. It saddened me how easily it came to me now.

"She never said anything to me. But sometimes Vera gets quiet. Anyway, that guy rushed her out of here yesterday. And she gave me a funny look when she said goodbye."

"What kind of look?"

"I dunno. Funny."

"What did this man look like?"

"He was a regular, but hadn't been around for a while. Oh yeah, now I remember, Vera told me he was a doctor. Tall guy, kinda intense-looking—his eyes, y'know?"

—

A streetcar arrived at the exact time I reached College Street; otherwise, I would have run the entire distance to Chinatown. I grew impatient with the many stops, jumped off, and began to run. The Doctor had returned. Our paths merged like two archer's arrows aimed at the same target. The Doctor must have discovered that Vera possessed the paper that led me to Riku's eatery. He failed in his search for me, so he sought another solution. My stomach burned.

I raced to Vera's basement apartment. I banged on the door, but there was no answer. Peering through the window in the door, I made out dark shapes in the room. I thought I saw a stream of smoke, but I couldn't be sure, and there was no smell of fire. I went upstairs, around the front of the house, and knocked on the door of the woman I'd met before. No answer.

Back down Vera's stairs, I slammed my fist harder on her door. I pushed my foot into the crack of the door, applying pressure until the wood split. I drew back my foot, concentrated all my power in my leg, and kicked hard. The door burst open and stopped, held by a chain. I kicked again and I was in. Steam escaped from a boiling kettle, filling her kitchen. Someone had made tea and not shut off the stove.

"Vera?" I said, shutting off the stove.

Blankets and pillows were strewn on the floor of her living quarters. The door to the bedroom was ajar, and a dim light shone from within. The door wouldn't budge when I forced it open. I slid in and froze.

Her legs were splayed out in front of her, and her head was propped against the bed, neck bent at an unnatural angle. Blood had flowed from her stomach across her legs, pooling in a small, dark lake on the floor.

As a boy, I'd seen men and women come back from battle— but Vera was not a warrior. She listened to me, understood my plight, and was now laid out in an unfair death. Was death ever fair? The belief that honor was present even in death was a facade.

I sank down beside her body, yet in my mind I saw Vera crossing over, back home, back to her country. The vision softened the ache coursing through my body.

I ran my hand across her cheek, wanting to soothe her even in death. "My friend."

My attention was drawn away by a torn piece of paper stuck against the reflection glass. I observed myself for a moment before removing the paper that was adhered to the glass. A message was written using both the language of the City and in kanbun. The dark ink was not ink alone. My heart ached knowing that the Doctor had used Vera's lifeforce to make the symbols. This message was a threat, a taunt for my benefit.

Samurai. One by one I will kill your friends. I will flush you out of hiding like a boar in the weeds.

I peeled the note off the surface, then cleaned the glass with a wet fabric from Vera's kitchen, being sure to leave no trace of my presence. I did not want the authorities to find this message. I looked one last time at her slain body.

"I am sorry, Vimbo. May the crossover to your afterplace bring you peace."

I stepped carefully out of the room, closed the broken door, and ascended the stairs. A breeze had risen, cool on my tear-stained cheeks. If I'd never asked her about the Doctor, Vera would be alive. Her death was by his hand, but it was my burden now.

At a street phone, I called the number that Joshua had taught me. I told them a person had been killed and gave the address. I placed the phone on its cradle as they asked me questions.

It was still a number of hours before I would meet Heather and Joshua in the park. Joshua said she would be glad to see me. That thought had drained me of any jealousy I had toward Joshua. But now, with Vera's broken body emblazoned on my mind, how could I even—

Oh no. The Doctor had met Heather. He surely knew of Joshua as well, seeing me with him. Could he know of Heather's young son? I needed to protect my friends. They were more important than any lord.

Masterless, I had become the wave man, a ronin. I was now the retainer for my friends. Their protection was my utmost purpose.

But where to go now? I did not know where Joshua would be working. I could not recall Heather's place of employment, and I did not know where she and her son resided. I could not simply roam the streets looking for the Doctor.

The hopelessness of it all washed over me. I walked the blocks back to my apartment, only climbing the fire escape when I was certain of no observers. I went to my bed. I lay awake and wept.

Chapter Forty-Four

Heather hated the late afternoon–evening slog shift when Grafite stayed open until 7:30. Customers slowed to a trickle, and for whatever reason it was the time all the senior hobbyists came in. It's not that she didn't like older people, one guy even reminded her of her dad—but their questions and complaints ground her down.

"This canvas was floppy. I need to return it," one of them said, waving a painting of a fuzzy line of purple mountains Heather guessed were meant to be trees, or maybe rocks. The woman was dressed in a series of scarfs and possibly a cape, which must have been hot as hell in the Toronto summer.

"Sorry, ma'am, but you've already painted on it. I can't really take this back. It's looking pretty good. You should keep working on it."

"I only discovered the floppiness when I was painting this morning. This is an inferior product."

"You've bought these before, though."

"They've changed them. The quality has gone downhill, like

most things."

The older woman's name was Beatrix, like the storybooks, she told Heather, and she was a regular. Heather had sold her a stack of six pre-stretched canvases a week ago, the same order she'd placed many times. This was the first time she'd seen Beatrix's work, although she had wondered what her paintings looked like. She seemed to be churning them out.

Heather relented and gave her another canvas for free.

"Should I throw out this faulty one?" Heather asked.

"God no. I don't want people having my unfinished work."

Heather followed Beatrix to the oil paint aisle, listening to her talk about how there were never any sales, and asking why the Winsor Newtons kept going up in price.

"It takes a lot to make Cobalt," Heather said.

"Well, I don't need it. There are lots of blues in the world."

At six o'clock, she called Alice at home and asked if she could stay with Zach into the evening.

"I've got an appointment after work."

"Sure, no problem. But did you know if Zach was going somewhere after school?"

"He's not home? No, he didn't say anything. I'll call the school."

When she phoned the school, the receptionist said, "He left with the other kids. Had you arranged a pick-up?"

"No. Zach just walks home."

"Sorry, Ms. Robsen, we're not responsible for the children once they leave the schoolyard."

Heather called Alice back.

"Any sign of him, Alice? Has he called? The school was no help."

"He's probably just at a friend's," Alice said. "Kids are like that."

"Right. But he always tells me. Or I ask him to call home or your place if he can't get me at work. Call me at the store if he comes in or calls, okay?"

"Will do."

There was no way she was going to make it to the end of the shift. That son-of-a-bitch Michael had picked up Zach and taken him somewhere. Michael would pressure her for money again. Shit, they broke his fingers. There was no way in hell she'd tell him she actually had access to her dad's accounts—but only in emergencies. Was keeping her ex from getting killed by a loan shark an emergency?

"Heather, you got a call. Keep it short," Garth called.

She went to the back and took the phone from her manager. It was Alice.

"A neighbor just called, that older Portuguese woman a couple of places over?"

"Mrs. Diniz, yes."

"She said she saw Zach walking past her place with a man she didn't recognize. She wondered if you knew about it."

"Not sure she'd recognize Michael," Heather said.

"She said he was tall, wearing one of those men's scarves. Michael doesn't wear those, does he? In this heat?"

"Listen, I'm going to get off early and head home."

"Heather, do you want me to call someone?"

"Mrs. Diniz?"

"No. Like the police."

Heather swallowed.

"It's fine, Alice. Michael is being an asshole lately, and Mrs. Diniz probably didn't recognize him. His hair is longer, and he looks different."

"How different?"

"I'll see you at home."

Heather hung up and went to talk to Garth. She first went to the bathroom, splashed some water on her face, and messed up her hair before talking to him.

"I just barfed, like a lot. I'm gonna have to go home."

Her manager took a step back like he expected her to do it again.

"You don't have any sick time left," Garth said.

"You want me to puke on the customers?" She stepped toward him.

He waved her back. "Go, go."

Heather left quickly, holding her stomach as she exited the store. Where would Michael take him, and why wouldn't he phone her at work, or talk to Alice? This was low even for him.

Heather shoved herself onto the streetcar as the doors were closing.

"Sorry, you're gonna have to wait."

"Dammit, let me on, there's room."

She pushed her way up the stairs and found a gap between two Asian women, each laden with plastic bags.

Toronto the Good, she repeated in her head. She had told her dad the city was the safest in Canada. That's why she let Zach walk to school on his own. Another parent told her she did it all the time, Bellwoods was a good neighborhood.

It had to be Michael. Zach wouldn't go with anyone else. She pushed a dark thought from her mind. Michael must really look like shit for Mrs. Diniz to not recognize him. And he never wore a scarf—maybe he was hiding from someone. Mrs. Diniz was a nice older lady, a bit nosy at times, but a good neighborhood watchdog.

She bolted into her apartment, expecting to see her son and Michael.

"Alice?"

"Your phone was ringing a lot, so I used your key to get in."

"What's going on? Was it Michael calling?"

"I think you should call the police."

Chapter Forty-Five

I lay in my bed thinking of both my friends in this City and those on the shōen. All those in the time before were dead, their bones long since transformed into earth. The ones here in the City I could protect. I would meet them at the park tonight and let them know they did not need to fear.

I arose and went to my small kitchen. Reaching for my tea, I saw the herb that Joshua had given me as a gift along with a crudely made pipe. I had never tried it before. I packed the leaves into the hole, lit the contents, and inhaled the smoke. The smell and taste of the herb sharpened the memory of my teacher.

One day my teacher burned leaves in a bowl with a similar scent.

"What is this?" I asked.

"Breathe. It will relax you."

I did as he asked.

"I know you will leave today," I said to him. "I saw the pack on your horse in the stables."

As I breathed in more of the sweet-smelling smoke, a strange sensation moved into my legs, as if my body rose above the floor.

"The burning plants you are breathing were given to me by my teacher. I have been cultivating a small number of plants in the forest. I use them sparingly, when I need to see."

"To see what?"

"To observe what awaits, or perhaps the possibilities."

"You have seen into the time ahead?" I asked.

"Don't speak. Breathe and listen." My teacher put his hand on my head. "Because of what has transpired, you will be banished from the shōen. But you will travel much farther."

I held my silence as long as I could.

"Where will I go?"

"The place is also foreign to me," he had said.

Drawing in the smoke from Joshua's herb, I finally understood my teacher's lesson from that day. He had seen the City. This was the last time I saw him, and only days before I escaped into the forest pursued by the archers. I refilled the pipe and lit it again.

My eyes grew heavy as I finished the last of the smoke.

A face hovered over me.

"Am I dreaming?"

"In a manner, yes."

"Are you with me in the City?"

"I am in-between."

It was my teacher.

"Why are you visiting me?" I asked.

"Your life edges close to a precipice."

This was something more than a vision.

"Why have I come to the City?" I asked.

"Many years ago, my teacher crossed over to where you now exist," he said.

"Your teacher is here in the City?"

"Riku is no longer there. His life was ended by the one who ended mine."

"Riku was your teacher?"

"Yes."

"Are you alive in the time before? Is that where you are speaking to me from?"

"The musicians called me to take Riku's place. But the one who killed me found me at the doorway. He prevented my crossing over."

"Oh no. I saw you. Your face was bloodied, and I didn't know."

Only now did I understand the dead samurai who I had found when I passed through the ravine was my teacher.

"I failed you," I said.

"My end was swift. I have been in a waiting place for some time. There may be another crossing."

"But why come to me now?"

"To remind you what you have forgotten."

"Tell me."

"You must prepare. You possess tools that will help you in the battle," he said.

"The elements."

"Good, you have not completely forgotten."

When I battled the Doctor and the land rejected me, I thought nothing of my teacher's many lessons about the tools of earth, water, wind, and fire.

"When the door opens again, he must not enter."

"I'm not sure I can stop him."

"You must restore the balance."

"The three," I said.

"Yes."

"Is there another in the City? Did another samurai cross after your death?"

"Yes. But they are not of use to you."

I finally asked the question that burned deep inside me.

"Will I return?"

"That is unseen."

The corners of the room pulled themselves up around my teacher, squeezing the entire space into a misshapen ball. The ball containing the room rolled away, and I sat alone in a field of black grass. A large black bird swept down and landed in front of me. If not for his bright red beak, he would have disappeared against the background.

"I'm waiting for you," the bird said.

"Where?"

"Ha! The green place, of course."

I reached out for the bird and it skipped back, letting out a loud caw.

"This is our battle. There is no need to bring in others," I said to the bird.

"Don't talk of need. I'll kill who I want to kill."

"Leave them. I will come willingly and you can strike me down."

"Oh I plan to strike you down, samurai. And then your friends will die, and all who know them, their parents, their children. I will cut them down like weeds and erase any memory of you in this City."

The bird let out another caw, and then a shriek as it flew into the wide expanse.

The scene, myself included, was swallowed up into another ball.

My eyes opened and I stared into the ceiling above my bed. I knew who the black bird was in the vision. How he came to me in this way, I could not understand. I needed to restore the balance. Destroy this evil being, before he could kill again. Kill innocents. Kill a child.

—

The Doctor had gone to the samurai's apartment, but as he'd guessed, he was no longer there. Somehow the samurai survived the battle. And now he was in hiding. Cowardice was well-known amongst the bushi—their code was bullshit. The only part of the

City's language he liked were the curses. Telling someone to fuck off had a harshness similar to a thrusted blade.

He decided to track the woman from the pizza place. He'd suspected that she'd found a note of his. He applied pressure and learned she'd befriended the samurai. She held little information, but her dead body sent a message as clear as the one he had written in her spilled blood.

He remembered seeing the samurai with another woman. Walking the street where he knew the samurai traveled, he spied her in a merchant's window, employed in one of the City's many useless shops. He waited several hours until she came out.

He followed the woman for two days, thinking she would lead him to the samurai. His patience waned, and he decided to take her. Then he discovered another opportunity.

He followed the boy to his house before sliding up behind him. The child struggled and kicked at him, and was about to cry out, until he told him what would happen to his mother if he didn't go with him.

The Doctor took the boy to the room he'd rented for the last five years. It had remained empty since the time he crossed over. He seethed with anger when he returned to it. The boy sat in front of the television that came with the room, his face red from tears. He told him to stop crying or he would hurt his mother. It made no difference.

"Here."

He put a box of biscuits on the table and a carbonated beverage. The boy ignored it.

"Fine. It matters not if you starve."

He was undecided on whether he would need to get rid of the boy and his mother as he did with the pizza woman. He felt nothing for any of them. If it caused the samurai more pain, all the better. He went to the phone and dialed the number the boy gave him. This was the fifth time. This time someone answered, a woman.

"Are you the mother?" he asked.

"No, I'm a neighbor. Who is this? Are you calling for Heather?"

"Where is she?"

"Is this Michael? It can't be because you would have said her name. Who are you? I'm calling the cops, you bastard. If you've harmed that little boy—"

"Have the mother call me at this number."

He gave the number only once and hung up the phone, the woman yelling at him as he slammed it down.

He waited fifteen minutes, considered dialing one more time, and then the phone rang.

"Who is this? Do you have my son? Are you the one after Michael? Listen, he has no money, I can pay his debt. Just let Zach go. I'll do anything."

He listened to her voice dissolve into sobs.

"Where is your friend?" he asked.

"What friend?"

"The one called Gordo. I've seen you with him."

A long silence on the phone.

"Who is this?"

"It doesn't matter who I am. Where is Gordo?"

"Are you the one from the bookstore?"

"Where is he?"

"I don't know. What does this have to do with Michael?"

Her voice came out in gulping breaths.

"I don't know this Michael. When are you next meeting Gordo?"

Another long silence.

"How old is your son?"

"You leave him alone, you fucker!"

"I never had children. They were always a bother to me."

"Stop. Okay. I'm meeting Gordo at a park. It's in between Beverly and . . ." More silence.

Her fast breathing annoyed him.

"Dammit. And McCaul. Do you know that place?"

"Yes."

"Bring Zach there, you son-of-a-bitch."

"If you call the authorities, there will be no reason to go to the park."

"What? No. No, I won't. Just leave my son alone." Another sob. "Have you, have you done anything to him?"

"The boy is unharmed. What time are you to meet?"

"Joshua said eight o'clock."

"The shaggy-haired one, I've seen him. Is he a bodyguard? Ha, a ronin of this City."

"A what? He's just a friend of Gordo's. He won't do anything. Just come."

"I will come. And the authorities?"

"I'll tell no one." The woman gasped. "Can I talk to my son?"

"No."

"Why do you want Gordo?" she asked.

"He has something I need."

He hung up the phone. He called to the boy.

"I will take you to your mother now. Stop that crying."

He had crossed over seven days ago—a week, in how they counted time in the City. Each hour he remained here, his rage increased. The citizens were empty-headed fools in an overcrowded landscape of steel, glass, and fumes. The smell of the air was the worst assault, though the people's stench was almost as bad. They emitted fake floral scents and chemicals that made his chest ache and his nose burn. He preferred sweat or blood to these falsehoods.

He would kill the samurai first. And then all those who knew him.

Chapter Forty-Six

The hour before I went to the park was near. I needed to recall everything my teacher had told me. It was inside me. I only needed to bring it forth. I was like water, both in mind and flesh. My mind was an eddy, turning a slow, steady current. I would sense the Doctor's every thought. Like fire, I was a cauldron of power and energy. I burned in a single line of flame, or was engulfed in a wall of heat. Wind would push me toward my destination. I would ride it like a strong horse.

If I could control the elements, I would defeat the Doctor.

I carried Riku's blade, the simple yet strong tantō, adorned only with three thin stripes on the hilt. Yui gifted me the blade knowing the enemy I would face.

The Doctor would be in the park; I knew this from the vision where he appeared as a bird. He would carry a blade similar to the one he used to slit my brother's throat. Sharper than his blade was the Doctor's cunning. My training would be tested more than it had been during any time on the estate.

The Doctor and I were pieces on a shoji board.

I wondered. Did the musicians watch us from their place in the forest?

In minutes I would leave to meet my friends. After I killed the Doctor, I would go back to the ravine and await the appearance of the door. Unlike the Doctor, I would be able to stay because it is in my lineage. My clan were amongst the ones destined to cross over.

I was saddened that my friends could not travel with me, for then they would finally understand the truth.

I am samurai.

Chapter Forty-Seven

Heather burst out of the streetcar, almost knocking over an old woman pushing a cart full of groceries, then swerved to miss another pair of slow walkers, slamming into a suited businessman who swung his briefcase to the side as if he was a matador. She refused to think about what the Doctor had done to Zach. He was evil personified, like something she'd heard a preacher say when she was a teen. She pictured taking a rod like Gordo did that night and smashing it against the Doctor's skull.

Why did he want Gordo? Who takes a kid so he can force someone's hand? Scanning the park, she jolted with recognition, seeing Joshua on a bench next to the playground equipment. He jumped up and came to her.

"Why are you running?"

"Is he here yet? Did I miss him?" Her chest ached.

"Gordo? No, but it's not quite eight."

"Not him. The other one. The man."

"Slow down. You're not making any sense. It was Gordo who wanted us to come here."

"The one Gordo calls the Doctor. That man. He's coming too."

"He's coming here? Oh shit. Gordo said he was bad news, violent even. Why are you crying?"

"He . . . he has . . . Zach."

She collapsed into Joshua's arms.

"Your kid? How did that happen? How did he even know where you live?"

"I don't know. He came up to me at the bookstore. Maybe he followed me." The pain in her chest threatened to rip her insides apart. She thought she might be sick.

Joshua rubbed her back. "It's okay, it's okay. Gordo will get here. He'll know what to do."

Some children entered the park laughing, running ahead of their mother, a black woman wearing a bright orange dress. Heather pulled away from Joshua, turning to the sound of children's voices. Behind them stood the man, holding her son's hand. Even from this distance, she saw the fear in Zach's eyes. She ran toward them.

"Heather, wait! Let's wait for Gordo."

She kept running. To her surprise, the man let go of Zach's hand, and he sprinted to her.

"Mom! Mom!"

She gathered Zach in her arms and pulled him tight. He was crying hard. She ran her hand through his hair.

"You're safe, Zach. I'm here. It's going to be okay." She kneeled down and looked into his face. "Zach, did he . . . The man. Did he . . ."

"He just kept me in a room. He said I had to keep quiet, or he would hurt you. Who is he, Mom?"

She stood and faced the Doctor.

"I've not harmed the boy. He cries like an infant."

She pushed Zach behind her and took a step forward. Joshua ran up next to her.

"Mom!"

"It's all right, Zach. Joshua is a friend."

The Doctor scanned the park, looking to the playground where the woman in orange sat on a bench reading a magazine, her children climbing the equipment.

"Where is he?" he asked.

"He's not coming," Joshua blurted.

The Doctor moved his hand in a blur and pulled out something that flashed like metal.

"The woman said he'd be here. I don't give a shit about either of you. But if you're lying . . ." He rotated the long blade and pointed it at them. "I'll do what needs to be done."

Joshua held up his hands. "Whoa, whoa, whoa."

"Mom. What's happening?"

"He will come," she said.

The woman at the playground looked up from her magazine. The Doctor slid the knife back in its scabbard. He wore a scarf that looked like a long rough tongue.

"That table over there, by the large tree. We'll wait together."

"Mom, can we go home?"

"Soon, Zach."

They walked ahead of the Doctor. The picnic table sat under the shade of a huge oak. Initials were carved across the top and down the legs. Heather was drenched in sweat from running in the heat, but under the shade of the oak, she shivered. Joshua pulled a bottle of water from his backpack.

"Put the bag down," the Doctor said.

"It's just water. Geez, relax, man."

The Doctor grunted. "You people speak like idiots. You call everyone *man* no matter their gender. Or 'buddee.' This language I'm forced to speak is like dry leaves in my mouth."

"What do you mean forced to speak?" she asked.

The Doctor continued to scan the park.

"You hungry? I got a couple of granola bars," Joshua said.

Zach shook his head. She put her arm around him and drew him closer. The woman at the playground had gathered up her children and was now exiting the park. A figure appeared at the entrance. The small boys running ahead of their mother blocked half the view, but Heather saw who it was.

"Wait. Stay there," she yelled out.

The Doctor flashed a look and then leapt up. Heather tried to grab his scarf to slow him down. He yanked it from her grasp, and in a few steps was running with a ferocious energy. The woman exiting the park called to her boys to watch out. The Doctor ran past the children's mother and clipped her shoulder, sending her spinning to the ground, as she yelled obscenities.

For a second, Heather thought Gordo had disappeared—and then a long shadow was cast in the evening sun. He was in flight.

—

I entered the park. My eyes, muscles, tendons, organs, and skin were focused like an archer's arrow. I scanned the landscape, seeking anything that gave me an advantage. How might I get higher ground on this flat field? A metal box stood four feet from the ground. I'd seen workers from the City open the box, exposing wires within. The walls were of metal construction, thick and strong. With three quick steps, from a bench to a fence, I leaped onto the metal box. I launched myself, hanging in the air, defying the force that pulled me down.

The Doctor sprang toward me, but I fell upon him like water off a cliff. Cords of fire wrapped around my legs, torso, and arms. My entire body was a weapon.

I suppressed my anger—rage would diminish my control. I moved with the elements, earth, water, wind, and fire. I accepted and channeled their power, delivering fast blows to the Doctor's head, shoulders, and neck.

Sound swirled around me, a woman's voice exploding from a yell to a scream. I pushed back the noise and listened to my heart pound, and then the Doctor's, sensing the beats in his chest. He rolled away and was upright again. He lunged forward and I sprang back. I realized my mistake in an instant. The

Doctor had hidden his true movement.

The Doctor shifted his weight, coming at me with a wide swing. His blade flashed in the sun. My body was fluid enough to flow under the strike. The blade ripped through my shirt and traced a line across my chest like a stick running across a pond. Blood rose through my skin.

The burn from the cut added to my inner fire. The Doctor swung again, and then thrust the blade, trying to drive it into my organs. I slid away from both strikes. Again, I heard his heart beat, his lungs filling with air, his muscles tightening, ready for release. I saw his next move before he made it. I leaped onto the metal box again. Another leap and I sailed over the wooden slatted bench. I ran past the screaming woman who still screamed. Vera's face flashed in my mind. For the woman's safety, I needed to move the fight away from her. I ran in an arc, leaping over a line of bush, the Doctor at my heels.

"Gordo!"

The sound of my name stopped me. The voice was male. It was joined by another voice, a woman's, I immediately recognized. My friends were off to the right—from their tones, I gauged the distance. In the second it took to listen, my focus dropped, and he was on me. Blows struck the side of my head. My skull rang, and then another flurry of strikes to my side. Air escaped me with each hit. I fell to the ground, taking his weight, moving with my body's current, and pulled him over me.

With my free hand, I grasped the hidden tantō. The Doctor slashed with his blade, and I met his with mine. Our edges hit together, shrieking and sparking. I turned the ridge of my blade until the point hovered on his abdomen. With enormous energy, he flipped me over his body, struck my blade with the edge of his, and sent Riku's blade flying. My lungs fought for air as I smashed into the ground.

I righted myself, spun, gathering energy, and flew at him with my leg extended. My heel caught his chin with a satisfying crack. Another ringing began, though this time from the outside.

It was a repeating pattern. Sirens. Authorities were coming. Blood ran from the Doctor's lip. His eyes were black circles. A flash of movement, his hand fast out in front of him. The sting of his thrown blade pierced my shoulder . . . no, it was closer to my heart. My flesh was split.

The pain released the rage coiled inside me. *Crimson foliage.* Take the opponent's blade as your own. I pulled the blade out in a smooth stroke; circles of white appeared in my vision. I drew it back to throw, but like candle smoke, he'd vanished. Did I complete the strike?

My sense of time was askew. Where had the Doctor gone? Was I falling? The ground reached up to meet me. The wind fought to hold me up. I commanded my body to stay fluid, but the fire energy had been extinguished. Had I released the blade?

Voices. Movement. The tearing of fabric.

Flat on my back, the circles of white turned to black. Something was placed over my mouth, a rush of fresh cold air, like I'd felt when climbing the mountain behind the shōen. Its name was Ishizuchi.

"He was defending himself."

"Hold it there. Let's get him stable."

"The other man attacked."

"My children were there. They could have been hurt or worse."

Too many voices now, a cacophony. They rose like waves, and then were taken out to sea. A pinch in my neck.

Then blackness as I sank to the bottom of the ocean.

Chapter Forty-Eight

The Doctor stumbled, and a bolt of pain erupted from deep in his bowels, signaling his inner organs were torn. From the bile in his throat, he guessed his liver had been pierced. He bounced off a large metal bin full of rotting black bags. The stink made him retch, his vomit mixed with blood.

He slammed against a tree, caroming off the hard bark and across the black street made of unknown substance. What chemical made these roads? He needed to find out this formula, memorize it, and take it back after he crossed over. Men shouted, horns assaulted his ears as he traversed the road. He clutched his stomach, staggering, urging and propelling his body forward. It had taken everything within him to escape the battle.

How? How? How?

He was the better warrior. He had more cunning, more speed, more strength. He had more will. How did this happen?

His throw was perfect. It was right at the samurai's heart—or close enough it should have taken him down. Did he miss?

Impossible. This young shit, barely a man, was not remotely close to his match. But who'd trained him? The samurai's movements were much more fluid and powerful than when they first battled in the time before. Never underestimate the opponent. This was the reason his organs were about to spill out of him. The samurai's dying effort threw his own blade back at him. It had pierced his stomach. Another wave of pain surged. He cursed his mistake.

Sirens sounded in the distance. Ha. The authorities would be too late. His throw had killed the samurai. He was certain of it.

Footfalls in the distance. Wait. Were they after him? If he could make it to the train, he would head for the ravine. Gordo. What a stupid name. With Gordo dead, he would re-enter the spiral. If another samurai attempted to cross over, he would kill them too. Nothing would push him from his home this time. Not being of the right lineage meant nothing. He was the true samurai. Gordo's death had given him power. He would return and command many men and rule over many more.

Children kicked a ball down the alley ahead of him. One had a cloth tied to his head. He'd seen this before on a warrior.

"You. How far to the train?"

"What train?"

"He means the subway, dumbass. Mister, what's wrong with your stomach? And your face, is that blood?"

"Holy crap."

He pushed past them.

"Hey, you should see a doctor. Sammy, go get your mom."

"She's a receptionist for a doctor."

"Get her to call 911, asswipe."

The Doctor steadied himself on the flat plane of another metal bin. He knew he was close to the stairs that led to the train. He only had to reach the end of the alley and turn. His legs softened, and he went to a knee. A large bird with a white head swooped at him. He beat it away with his weakening hands. It swooped again, blood on its yellow beak.

"What's he swinging at?"

What language were these children speaking? Why was it so cold? He reached for a wooden pole that stretched to the sky. Wires were wrapped around it like snakes. He took solace in the fact that he would finally leave this place of strange and vile objects.

The Doctor spoke aloud in the language of his home. He thought of the many machines he'd studied. What part did this pole with the wires play in their functioning? The lines in his mind were washed away by an unseen rain. His body pressed against and then slid down a brick wall. The edges of the City curled inward. Swashes of red and brown flowed in, filling the impossible geometric skyline. Trying to block out the City, fingers splayed over his pale face. Too exhausted to feel rage, he waited to exit this white shell of skin.

He sank deeper until his body became a part of the black road. He realized there would be no crossover this time. It didn't matter. He had finally escaped the City.

—

The forest musicians were playing. Sweet tones from their plucked strings floated in the wind that weaved through the foliage. I sat in the middle of a grove, my eyes closed, and listened to the melody. The fragrance of lotus flowers mixed with the notes, birdsong joined in tandem. It was as if the wind itself made this music. A voice sang out—this was different, and the musicians in the forest did not sing.

I opened my eyes and she came into focus. Her pale skin radiated light. But it wasn't her voice, for though my lover's voice lilted, she did not sing. I knew this. Her lips turned into a gentle smile. Behind her, Ishizuchi rose, its sharp angles softened by clouds that hung like fabric draped across the horn of the great mountain.

"You are not singing," I said.

"No."

I closed my eyes and listened again.

"Then who? The forest musicians do not sing."

"It is another," she said.

"I don't understand." The scent of lotus faded. "Have I returned to you?"

"Not yet."

"But I am seeing you. I hear you. I've returned."

"Desire clouds your mind."

"Don't tell me this," I said.

She sat with her legs tucked under her, with no roundness to her stomach.

"Where is our child?"

"She calls you back," she said.

A river of pain began in my shoulder and spread across my chest like a tsunami. The strings grew quiet, the birds were still, the wind stopped. A voice singing one high note remained.

I opened my eyes to a figure perched over me.

"Hesback. Getsomeonenursenursenurse."

The grove had been replaced by a room of shiny surfaces. I was tied by a tube to a pole, where a translucent bag hung. The lights were harsh. There was no birdsong at all.

"Gordo?"

It was as if she sang it. I'd never liked the name given to me in the City. But her voice made it sound like a melody. Someone I didn't know leaned over me. She smelled of ammonia.

"He's stable. BP's good."

"Gordo, my man. Nothing can put you down. I knew it. Holy crap, I'd never seen anything like it."

My tongue felt thick. I wanted to speak, but could not form words. The one who smelled like ammonia was gently touching me.

"All his vitals are good, strong even. He needs to rest."

"We'll come back, Gordo. You rest. I have to go and relieve Alice."

Heather put her hand on my forehead. Her touch was soft. She smelled of lemons. I heard music. It was not the forest musicians, but it was pleasant.

"You want me to shut that music off, buddy? I thought maybe it would soothe you. But I can turn it off."

"It's okay. I like it," I said.

My voice brought a smile to Heather's face. Joshua turned to leave.

"Please wait."

"What is it, Gordo? They say you're gonna be okay. You lost a lot of blood. But they stitched you up."

"The Doctor."

"He will be back to check on you shortly," the ammonia-smelling one said.

"No. The Doctor."

"They're looking for him," Heather said. "The police. I don't think he'll go far."

"Why?"

"Oh man, Gordo. I guess you didn't see it. We watched the whole thing. You hit him with something, he doubled over. I don't know how he got out of the park before the cops got there. I started after him, but—"

"I stopped him," Heather said. "The police will take care of it."

"They want to talk to you, Gordo. They've been here in the hospital waiting for you to wake up. There was a guy outside the door until about a half hour ago. He must have gone out for a doughnut or something."

"Okay."

"And Gordo . . ." Joshua's voice dropped to a whisper. "I picked up your knife before the cops got there. It's back at my place."

The woman with the ammonia smell hovered around me. She picked up the tube with her fingers, turned it in her hand.

"I'm going to give him a bit more morphine. He'll likely go

out again. You two go home now . . . You can see him later."

The grove came back into focus. The clouds on Ishizuchi were gone, as was she. The birdsong returned.

Not yet, she'd whispered.

Not yet.

Chapter Forty-Nine

"Is it a good one, Mom?"

"Yep, it's a feature," Heather said.

"That sounds really big."

"Big enough. Between that one and all the work I got last week from the educational publisher, I can quit Grafite."

"Do you think that's a good idea?"

"Who's the mother here?"

"Huh?"

"I didn't come to Toronto to work at an art supply store, Zach." She hugged and kissed his forehead.

"C'mon, Mom. Ugh."

"C'mon, Zach." She kissed him again. "Let's hold off the teenager years for a bit longer."

"What do you mean?"

"When you can't stand to be around me."

He hugged her back. "That'll never happen."

"Okay, I've got a lot of work to do, and you need to get to school."

Heather went to the fridge and took out the sandwich, cheese, and fruit she'd put together for him.

"I bought salami from that Italian place on Bathurst."

"Whoa, awesome. Are we rich now?"

"Ha. Far from it. Get your coat."

Zach was halfway out the door when he stopped.

"Mom. Is it okay if I don't see Brian today?"

"Why? Is there something wrong? You told me he was helping you."

"He is. I just don't feel like talking about everything all the time."

She opened the door and kneeled down to face him. "You don't have to talk about it if you don't want to. But you experienced a lot of bad things. Stuff that shouldn't happen to a great kid like you."

"Is he okay?"

"The man who took you? I don't—"

"No, I mean Gordo. Is he okay, now?"

Heather smiled.

"Yes, he is. I saw him and Joshua yesterday. He's out of the hospital now." She paused. "Zach, would it be okay if Gordo came over and visited us?"

"Is he going to be your boyfriend now?"

"No. No, he isn't. He's feeling a lot better, and said he wanted to meet you."

"What about Michael?"

"What do you mean?"

"Are you going to see him again? He didn't come by after, well, after I got home, and . . ."

"I'm sorry, Zach. Did you want to see him? I'm not sure if that's possible."

"No. I liked him. But I don't really want to see him. I was just wondering." He gave her a fast peck on the cheek. "You're the coolest, Mom."

She went down the stairs with him until he waved her off.

Even though she knew the Doctor would never threaten them again, until two days ago she'd walked Zach to school every day. But she wasn't going to live in fear, or push that anxiety onto her son.

One of the officers that questioned her and Joshua suggested she look into counseling for Zach and gave her a card. That was how she found Brian, who worked for the province for low-income families. Brian told her she should talk to someone also, as his field was in child psychology. Heather assured him she would be fine.

Heather never told her father what happened with Zach. He'd worry too much. When they flew out at Christmas, Zach would tell him anyway. Still, she'd rather talk to her dad in person about it. And she never told Zach they found the Doctor dead in an alley a few blocks from the park.

Heather had read the manuscript for the feature article in bed last night, making notes and circling words to help her come up with some visuals. The piece was the lead in the *Financial Post* magazine, a full spread, with some spot illustrations that would flow through the story. It was the most she'd ever made for an illustration project. The article talked about the competitiveness in the market, calling it a battlefield, and compared Bay Street bankers to different types of warriors. The metaphors were a stretch, the article a testosterone-fueled guy-fest, but it gave her a chance to draw what she really wanted: guys in suits with swords swinging at each other.

On the way to her drawing table, she glanced at the calendar in the kitchen. She'd circled yesterday's date in red, but couldn't remember why. She popped in a cassette of Tangerine Dream to set her mood for drawing. An hour went by, and then another, until the phone knocked her out of the flow.

"Heath', it's me."

"Jesus, Michael. Why are you calling me? I told you—"

"Listen, wait. I'm not in Toronto anymore. I left. I'm not calling to bug you, or ask you for money or anything."

"Where are you?"

"I'm back home."

"Saskatchewan?"

"No. My parents' place in High River."

She'd already forgotten that Michael grew up in Alberta.

"What do you want?"

"I don't want anything, Heather. I fucked up. I'm calling to say I fucked up."

"Is that supposed to be an apology?"

"God, yes. I'm sorry. Things got really dark. I had to leave Toronto in a hurry."

"Did you settle with the people you owe?"

"Yes. Sort of. No." He sniffed. "It doesn't matter. I'm not there anymore. And my parents are helping me a lot."

"You told me they hardly spoke to you."

"I'm trying to change that. My dad had a heart attack, so it's good that I'm here. Wait, how is your dad?"

"He's better. Therapy helped a lot. He still slurs his words, but he's almost back to normal."

"Are you going to go see him?"

"I might. I got some work that could pay for Zach and I to go out there at Christmas." She told him about the new project, but then cringed right after for having said so much. He didn't deserve to know anything more about her.

"That's great, Heather. I really want you to make it out there. You're one of the most talented people I know. I'm sorry I couldn't have supported you more."

"I didn't need your support, Michael."

After a long pause, he coughed and cleared his throat. "Zach doing all right?"

"Yes, he's fine. Listen, Michael, I've got some deadlines and I need to work."

"Of course. For sure. Heather, do you think if I came to Toronto I could see you guys? I mean, just to see how Zach is doing?"

"No."

"Right. Sorry for asking."

Neither of them said anything for a while.

"I'm gonna go," they said in unison.

"Michael, stay with your parents. Take care of your dad. Don't come to Toronto."

She almost felt empathy for him. He needed to get his shit together or he'd end up in a lake with cement shoes—if loan sharks really did that sort of stuff.

Heather had berated herself for thinking Michael was the one that took Zach, even after Mrs. Diniz told Alice it wasn't him. She still didn't understand who the Doctor was—obviously some criminal-type like the one threatening Michael, but much worse.

Heather switched the cassette to Miles Davis's *Birth of the Cool*. There were a lot of sleepless nights for both her and Zach. Disappearing into her work was one way to forget, or at least to move on from what happened in the park.

Back at her table, the trumpet lines flowed along with her pencil on the paper. She loved the feeling of a figure moving across the page, as if in battle, but at the same time a dance. She lost herself to it, becoming the observer to what formed in front of her. Lines on a page became figures, and those figures became humans with lives, struggles, expressions of passion and determination on their face. She knew it was only drawings for a business magazine, a very well-paying one, but she couldn't help thinking about these people she'd created. One figure boldly stood in a warrior stance in front of all the others.

Who was he protecting?

Chapter Fifty

"And do you want to learn to paint and draw like your mother?"

"Yeah, she's cool. But we draw different stuff."

Heather made pancakes for Gordo and Zach, watching them together at the table, each with a glass of orange juice.

"It is a good way to observe the world. If you really want to learn about something, then draw it. You will see things in a deeper way."

"Like if I want to know how a car works?" Zach asked.

"Perhaps, yes. Or a building, animal, a tree or a flower. A person."

"My mom has drawings that look like you."

"This is true?"

Heather delivered the plates with pancakes, a container of maple syrup, and fresh blueberries. She refilled their glasses.

"Wow, Mom, thanks."

She sat down with them and sipped at her coffee. "He means I've drawn figures of men fighting."

"Like in the park," Zach said. "How did you do that stuff?"

"Zach, I don't think Gordo wants to talk about that."

"Curiosity is a good thing. It leads to wonder."

Gordo began to tell a story as if they were around a campfire. He talked of a place with mountains, fields of bright flowers, and a red sun. An enraptured Zach asked a few questions but mostly sat quiet, taking in every word, never asking if the story was true. She wasn't sure if Zach heard the sadness in the story, the longing underlying the tale.

Gordo brought the story to the point where he went to the park to meet the Doctor. He said it was unfortunate, but there was no other way.

"You had to fight him?" Zach asked.

"Yes. To do battle."

"Well, Zach, there's always another way," she said, although she didn't want to lecture. Gordo had told the story with such gentleness and compassion; she didn't want to ruin that impact.

"What happened to that man? He was the one that took me."

"Yes, I know. And I'm very sorry that happened. He is no longer in the City."

"Did he move?" Zach asked.

"He died," Gordo said.

"Oh."

Again she held back.

"He has traveled to a place where he can do no harm. There is no need for any more worry. Your mother takes good care of you."

Zach seemed satisfied with that. He finished his breakfast without asking any more questions.

"Mom, Richard asked me to go to his house and read comics together. Can I go?"

"Sure. Be back before supper. You've got some reading to do for school."

"I liked talking with you, Gordo. Can you come over again?" Zach asked.

"Perhaps."

After Zach left, Heather showed Gordo the drawings she was working on.

"These are well done. You have captured not only movement but passion in these figures."

"That story you told Zach . . . it's like the story you told me of the boy that day in the park." Heather paused to study his expression. "I'm not sure it's a good idea to tell fantastical things in a way where a ten-year-old might think they are real."

"Have I offended you?"

"No, no. It's okay. I just know I'll be answering a lot of questions about what is real and what is not."

"Those questions do not have easy answers. But your love for each other is very evident."

"Thank you," she said. "I hadn't told Zach that the doctor had died."

"It is good for young ones to learn of death."

"I know, you're right. It's just hard."

Gordo placed his hand on her shoulder. Heather looked at the drawings of warriors spread across the page. She had taken some of the movement from the fight she watched between Gordo and the Doctor.

"Where did you learn to fight like that?"

"I had a teacher, my master, who taught me about movement, the elements, and much else."

"Where are you from, Gordo? I mean, where are you really from?"

He removed his hand from her shoulder, and traced his fingers along one of her drawings, a figure that leapt across a wide chasm.

"I told Joshua I would meet him at The Pearl. He's not working today. Thank you for the cakes, and for the conversation."

"You're a really interesting guy, Gordo."

"And you are very kind," he said.

She didn't know what else to say to her new friend, most

likely not her boyfriend. She'd heard the longing for another in Gordo's story. Who was she?

After Gordo left, she taped a new sheet of paper to her drawing table. Instead of figures, she sketched in the top edge of a mountain, and then a field below. She grabbed a red colored pencil and made marks in the field amidst the gray strokes, hints of flowers poking through the grass. In the foreground she drew a tree, and then a small figure sitting cross-legged under it. It was a woman, her legs tucked under her, head tilted up, face expectant, eyes catching the light that bounced off the mountain.

—

"Cool, cool. You had breakfast with Zach and Heather. She's really nice—you should call on her more often."

"It's very good to see you, Joshua."

"Hey, my man. It's always good to see you, Gordo. You all healed up?"

"There is some stiffness in the wound, but mostly yes."

"I can talk to those guys on the painting crew, get you back on."

"Thank you."

A different man came and took our order.

"Is Stan ill?"

"Went to Cuba for a week with his daughter. What can I get you?" The man, younger than The Pearl's owner, spat out the sentences.

We gave this new man our order of coffee and tea. The man appeared sour. I surmised he expected we would purchase food. Joshua leaned toward me.

"I still have your knife. I can bring it over to your place. I didn't want to carry it around, not sure how legal something like that is."

"I no longer need it."

"No. I'll bring it to you."

"I'd like you to have the blade."

"Really, are you sure?"

I nodded, and was warmed by my friend's smile.

After more conversation, we left The Pearl and went for a long walk along Queen Street. We came upon a park that I had previously passed but never entered.

"I love how these little parks just pop up. You're walking past some ugly gray buildings and then all of a sudden there's these trees and a little fountain. You gotta love this city."

There was a lightness in my chest as I listened to Joshua.

"I need to go now, Joshua. I enjoy spending time with you."

"What? Oh, okay. I had the day off, thought we'd just hang."

"There's something I need to see."

"You okay, Gordo?"

"Yes."

I extended my hand for Joshua to slap it in his usual manner. He looked like he was going to ask another question, then he smiled and wrapped his arms around me. The long embrace was a surprise, but not an unwelcome one.

I took the Queen Streetcar to a street called Roncesvalles. I'd walked in this neighborhood before, delighting in the rich smells and the people and dogs that called it home. A bus took me to the station, and then two trains took me east, north, and then another bus west. Last night I had dreamed of these lines of travel.

As I recovered from my wound, I learned of the Doctor's death, and I knew my opportunity had passed. I had believed that the crossover had already happened. The door would not stay open long: another samurai would cross over.

After my time in the hospital, I began to resign myself to my life in the City, as Riku had done. But then yesterday outside my apartment building, I was met by a young man.

He was dressed in the denim fabric that was common in the City. His slender, pale face was covered in marks, which were called freckles, like a dusting of seed on a field.

"I know you," he had spoken as he stepped in front of me.

"You must be mistaken."

"No. I dreamed of you." He stared at me intensely.

We both had blue eyes, but there was something else.

"You are like me," I said.

"Yes."

"How long have you been here?"

"A number of months," he said.

A flash of knowledge and emotion entered my body with such force that I stumbled.

"So you didn't cross over when the Doctor died?"

"I do not know any doctor. I only saw your face in the dream. And this building was in my dream. I live close by."

He was a samurai, at least a decade younger than me. He must have crossed over when the Doctor killed my teacher in the time before.

"What else did your dream tell you?" I asked.

"The musicians will play tomorrow. The door will open to allow another."

I touched the young samurai's shoulder.

"You must be careful with who you share your story," I said.

"I will share it with no one."

"Some will understand. Seek them out."

He wished me luck and walked away. I should have warned him of the mental institutions, now that I knew their true name. But he would learn.

As I traveled to the ravine, I heard the plucking of springs. There was something different in the melody. Then I understood. This was what the old man and his mandolin played. The men in white suits who played bluegrass against the black walls wove their sound with the forest musicians. I had never considered the color of the grass. Blue grass. Last night's dream was full of that color—a blue dream.

The ravine glowed in the warm sunlight. There was no mountain to be seen, but I would see one soon. The first leaves had begun to turn: yellows, oranges, and rich crimsons dotted the landscape. I ran my hand along the rough bark of one of the trees, a layer of vibrant color nestled at its base.

My blue dream had told me that the door would be in another place this time. I stared into the dark foliage above me. An unheard and unfelt wind moved through the leaves, lifting them up and setting them down in waves. The leaves created a spiral within the tree. I reached out, standing on the balls of my feet. My body lifted from the ground. The leaves were warm and soft, lifting me higher and higher into the tree. I broke through the canopy and soared above the ravine, the City below, and all of the surrounding lands.

I traveled in a blur of color and light, finally setting down in a patch of green where another young man stood. He was not dissimilar to the one outside my building yesterday; the features of his face suggested a familial connection.

"Where have you come from? Is this the afterplace? Moments ago I was in the midst of battle, my body pierced with many arrows."

There was a tremor in his voice. This one was, finally, the Doctor's replacement. His eyes widened. I turned and saw the spiral pulsing behind me.

"Are you a ghost?" he asked.

"You will be okay. When you cross over, there will be people who will help you. You will find friends."

He took a step toward the spiral. I didn't watch him leave, as my eyes were focused on how beautiful Ishizuchi looked this day. The sun had broken through a mist and cast long rays down to a tree below, under which a figure sat with her legs tucked under her.

There under the sakura was the object of my longing. She was the one that both created the need to escape the shōen, and the deep desire to return. The musicians' notes floated in the air above the mountain. I thought of my father, most likely gone now, as they would not have allowed him on the estate after my shameful act. I thought also of my brother, and the years we lost not being together. Wherever he was now, did he know that I had defeated the one who took his life?

Behind me, I felt the first pull of a distant spiral. Down below, a small child ran across to meet his mother. She embraced him as the sun caught both their faces, reflecting back to me a beauty deeper than what could be seen with the eye.

I took a step backward. A decision needed to be made before another young samurai was called forth, for there must always be three on the side of the City. That is the balance. The musicians' song echoed in the air. In the melody there was sadness, and yet the song held out a hope, perhaps a freedom. In a few scant seconds, my mind filled with a vision. I could not bear the hardship visited upon the one I longed for, and upon our son. The lord would not allow me to follow my desires. More pain would be created. Not only my pain, but of those I loved.

Seeing my lover and my son under the shade of the sakura, I came upon my decision. I could not stay. I let the spiral embrace me.

"You will experience much grief."

This was what I had prepared for. This was what my teacher meant. It was death that I had to leave behind. The future awaits.

I am Gordo.

Acknowledgments

Writing a novel is a marathon—but there are many along the track who are there to help, to support, to hand you a cup of Gatorade, or kick your butt down the road. I'm full of gratitude for these butt-kickers and beverage givers. Thanks to early readers Sally Ito, Steve Griffiths and Phil Krymusa, who gave me invaluable notes. Theresa Therrien and Martine Proctor, your encouragement, killer editing, story instincts, and friendship mean the world to me. Thanks to Larry for conversations that matter.

I read a stack of books and listened to a wagon-load of podcasts about Japanese history, too many to reference here. But one notable shout out is to the Samurai Archives podcast, where I learned about the history of the samurai, and how to distinguish the truth from the myth. The hosts also answered some nerdy history questions, and pointed me in the direction of other scholars who helped with questions like, "Just when did they start using the word, Daimyo?"

Mandy Miller besides being an expert butt-kicker, is one

helluva editor. She fine-tuned my vision for this novel, and her notes made it approximately one million times better. A big huzzah and group hug to all the fine folks at Literary Wanderlust who believed in this odd tale. And finally, and most importantly, to my family and friends who support me in ways that they might not even realize. Above all, I am indebted to the lovely, who is forever in my corner.

About the Author

After graduating from the Alberta College of Art and Design, Craig Terlson moved to Toronto and began a 26-year career of illustration, working for magazines and newspapers across North America. His work has appeared in and won awards for The Boston Globe, Philadelphia Enquirer, Psychology Today, and Graphics World London. In the 90's, Craig took his studio to Winnipeg, where he continued his illustration career, pursued a comic syndication contract, and began writing fiction. His fiction has been published in literary journals in Canada, U.S., U.K., and South Africa; as well as writing two short story collections, and four novels. He was a finalist in the Glimmer Train contest for new writers, and his story, Night Birds, was named one of the top fifty online short fictions of 2008. He has written essays on the craft for Write magazine and Lit Hub.

His 2017 novel Fall in One Day gained him a McNally Bestseller status, and a nomination from the Manitoba Book Awards. In 2021, he received his second Manitoba Book award nomination for his novel, Manistique, the second book in his crime fiction series featuring Luke Fischer. His prose possesses a cinematic quality and an eye for detail stemming from his years as a professional illustrator.

Find Craig Terlson on social media:
Twitter: cterlson
Instagram: cterlson
Facebook: craig.terlson
Linkedin: Craig Terlson
substack: Craig Terlson Talks Story
Tiktok: craigterlsonwrites

CPSIA information can be obtained
at www.ICGtesting.com
Printed in the USA
BVHW042314050623
665421BV00002B/62